PASSIONS OF THE DEAD

Books by L.J. Sellers

The Detective Jackson Series
The Sex Club
Secrets to Die For
Thrilled to Death
Passions of the Dead
Dying for Justice
Liars, Cheaters & Thieves
Rules of Crime

~~

The Lethal Effect
(Previously published as *The Suicide Effect*)
The Baby Thief
The Gauntlet Assassin

PASSIONS OF
THE
DEAD

A DETECTIVE JACKSON MYSTERY

L.J. SELLERS

Printed in the United States of America.

Published by Thomas & Mercer
P.O. Box 400818
Las Vegas, NV 89140

ISBN-13: 9781612186191
ISBN-10: 161218619X
Library of Congress Control Number: 2012943267

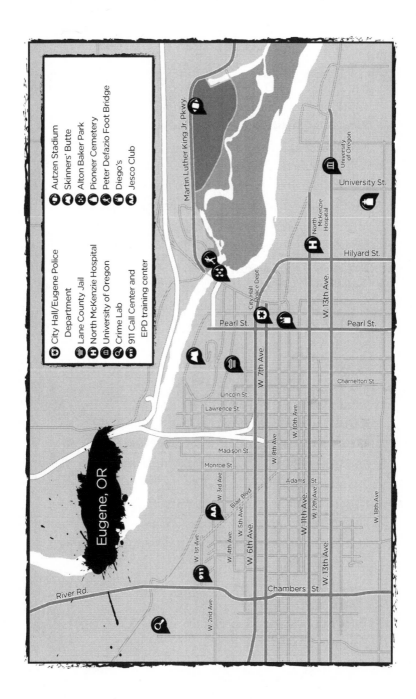

Eugene, OR

Legend:

- City Hall/Eugene Police Department
- Lane County Jail
- North McKenzie Hospital
- University of Oregon
- Crime Lab
- 911 Call Center and EPD training center

- Autzen Stadium
- Skinners' Butte
- Alton Baker Park
- Pioneer Cemetery
- Peter Defazio Foot Bridge
- Diego's
- Jesco Club

Martin Luther King Jr. Pkwy.

University of Oregon
University St.
North McKenzie Hospital
Hilyard St.
W. 13th Ave.
City Hall Police Dept.
Pearl St.
Pearl St.
W. 7th Ave.
Charnelton St.
Lincoln St.
Lawrence St.
W. 10th Ave.
W. 8th Ave.
Madison St.
Monroe St.
Adams St.
W. 3rd Ave.
Blair Blvd.
W. 11th Ave.
W. 12th Ave.
W. 18th Ave.
W. 5th Ave.
W. 4th Ave.
W. 6th Ave.
W. 1st Ave.
W. 13th Ave.
River Rd.
W. 2nd Ave.
Chambers St.

Cast of Characters

Wade Jackson: veteran detective/violent crimes unit
Kera Kollmorgan: Jackson's girlfriend/nurse
Katie Jackson: Jackson's daughter
Rob Schakowski (Schak): detective/task force member
Ed McCray: detective/task force member
Lara Evans: detective/task force member
Michael Quince: detective/task force member
Denise Lammers: Jackson's supervisor/sergeant
Sophie Speranza: newspaper reporter
Rich Gunderson: medical examiner/attends crime scenes
Jasmine Parker: evidence technician
Joe Berloni: evidence technician
Rudolph Konrad: pathologist/performs autopsies
Victor Slonecker: district attorney
Jim Trang: assistant district attorney
Jared Walker: homicide victim/father
Carla Walker: homicide victim/mother
Nick Walker: homicide victim/teenage son
Lori Walker: homicide-attempt survivor/teenage daughter
Tracy Compton: Jared's stepsister
Kevin Compton: Tracy's husband/Jared's brother in law
Shane Compton: Kevin & Tracey's son/Nick & Lori's cousin
Lisa Compton: Kevin & Tracey's daughter/Shane's sister
Rita Altman: Carla's sister
Roy Engall: Jared's ex-boss/painting company owner
Noni Engall: Roy's wife
Tyler Gorlock: Noni Engall's son
Zor: drug dealer

PASSIONS OF THE DEAD

CHAPTER 1

Monday, June 1, 8:15 a.m.

"Final decisions about layoffs will be announced Friday." Sergeant Lammers panned the room, stopping to make eye contact with Wade Jackson. He and fifteen other detectives were crammed into an overheated conference closet. They shifted in their seats and tried not to glance at each other.

"Two detectives will be cut, one from vice and one from violent crimes." Lammers' voice was deadpan, and for the first time in his twenty-year career, Jackson worried he might lose his job. He'd been written up and suspended recently, and now he had a health issue the department might consider a liability. What would he do if he lost his job? He was still a month away from his twenty-year pension.

The door flew open and a desk officer rushed in. "Excuse me, sergeant, but there's been a mass homicide. Four people dead in a house at 1252 Randall Street. No reports of the assailant. A relative found the bodies and called it in."

A mass of men in dark jackets jumped to their feet, and the air hummed with adrenaline. Lammers shouted over the din. "I want Jackson, Schakowski, McCray, Quince, and Evans at the scene. Everyone else is on standby for assignments as needed." She strode toward the desk officer. "Get the mobile crime unit out there. I'll call the DA and the ME."

Jackson hustled toward the door, thinking that for the moment he still had a job.

As he raced over Ferry Street Bridge with the rushing water of the Willamette River below, Jackson worried about what was happening to his hometown. For most of his life, Eugene, Oregon, had been a safe midsize college town—a tree-loving, friendly place to grow up in, with the mountains and the ocean only an hour's drive away. A perfect place to raise his child. Now Eugene was a small city with a growing crime rate, a meth scourge, high unemployment, and a dying downtown—and no money to fix anything. They'd never had a mass homicide though. He'd worked several murder-suicides in which a man had shot his wife or girlfriend then himself, but never a crime scene with four people killed. What if some of the victims were children?

The home was in the Coburg Road area, in one of the older neighborhoods where the real estate had less square footage but bigger yards. A modest house that needed paint but otherwise looked cared for. The front lawn had been recently mowed and someone had planted petunias along the walkway—signs of an unusually warm month of May. A red F-150 pickup and an old green Subaru sat side-by-side in the driveway. The Subaru sported a bumper sticker bragging about a student of the month and another that read *I Love Al Gore.*

Two patrol units sat out front in the curve of the long cul-de-sac. One of the officers was on the sidewalk next to a weeping woman with a cell phone to her ear. An older couple huddled together at the edge of their adjoining yard, and across the street a woman in sweatpants stood on her front step, watching the activity. Another blue Impala screeched to a stop behind him.

Jackson climbed out of his car, wishing he'd taken some naproxen before leaving headquarters. The pain his ten-inch abdominal scar still produced surprised him. His kidneys, which had been compromised by the fibrosis, also bothered him if he moved too fast. As he approached the people on the sidewalk, the uniformed officer said, "This is Rita Altman. Her sister is one of the victims inside. She came by this morning to pick her up and found them."

The woman, late thirties and heavyset with hair to her waist, glanced at Jackson, then continued weeping into the phone as she described her ordeal to a listener.

"Don't let her leave. I need to talk with her in a minute," Jackson said and hurried past. He needed to get inside the home and see the scene before it was swamped with people doing their jobs. Behind him, the scream of an ambulance raced up Harlow Road. *Why the siren?* Jackson wondered. They wouldn't need its paramedic services, just its cargo space to transport bodies.

Ed McCray, an older detective fond of brown corduroy, joined him on the sidewalk. They looked at each other without speaking, then started for the house. Jackson visually searched the driveway as they walked past the cars. He had a small hope of finding something the killer might have dropped.

At the threshold, Jackson grabbed paper booties and latex gloves out of his shoulder bag. McCray did the same. Jackson suspected that today he would need nearly everything the bag held: flashlight, crime-scene tape, an assortment of prelabeled paper bags and clear plastic bags, a box of latex gloves, tweezers, and three cameras: film, digital, and video.

He braced himself, nodded at McCray, then pushed though the door. A sour metallic smell soaked the air, overpowering even the odor of meat scraps in the garbage. The front door opened into a narrow hallway with vinyl flooring, bordered by a step down into a carpeted, crowded living room. With a sweeping glance, Jackson took it all in: two well-worn couches huddled around a big TV, a cluttered desk in the corner with an older computer, a bookshelf with more sports trophies than books, and a wall covered with family photos.

Then he saw the wide archway into the kitchen. And beyond it, the bodies.

A patrol officer squatted near the bloody mess. He jumped at the sound of their footsteps. "This girl is alive," the officer said in an excited rush. "After we cleared the house, I went back to the kitchen to stand guard. I was taking pictures and realized she was still breathing, so I called for an ambulance."

A survivor! *Thank god.* Someone would be able to tell them what the hell had happened here. Jackson started toward the kitchen, then froze. He looked down at the floor and spotted bloody footprints leading away from the bodies toward the front door. Critical evidence and they were walking on it. He turned to McCray. "We need samples of the blood on these footprints right now." Jackson wondered about another way into the house, maybe through the garage. He let the idea go. The paramedics would charge through the front door no matter what he requested. Their objective was different from his.

Jackson took five quick photos of the footprints while McCray scraped and bagged some dried blood. They hurried over to the bodies. Jackson forced himself to shut out everything but the girl who was still breathing. She looked about seventeen and her head rested on the stomach of another woman. Based on their matching reddish-blonde hair and freckles, he assumed the body underneath was her mother.

Knowing the paramedics were a heartbeat away and would alter the crime scene when they carried the girl out, Jackson knelt and snapped another round of photos. He took one of her face, one of the congealed bloody gash cut through the belly of her blood-soaked shirt, and one close-up of each hand to document the defense wounds. For a moment, her eyes fluttered open, pale green and distant, then closed again. Jackson stepped back and took two pictures of her position, relative to the other bodies, before the paramedics rushed in.

"Stop there," he said. "You're not wearing booties, and we have to do this carefully. McCray and I will carry her to the gurney."

"No, *we* have to do this." The taller paramedic rolled the gurney into the kitchen and pushed past. He shifted to the other side of the bodies and squatted near the young woman's head and shoulders. The other paramedic grabbed the girl under her knees, and they gently loaded her on the gurney. As they tended to her wound and gave her oxygen, Jackson hung back and let them work. The foot-traffic patterns in the crime-scene area had just been obliterated. As the paramedics rolled the girl out, Jackson said a little prayer, asking God to keep her alive.

In the distance, cars raced up the street, followed by the rumble of the mobile crime unit's diesel engine. The white, truck-style RV would serve as their base today while they processed the house and questioned the neighbors. Jackson looked over at the patrol officer. "Please stand by the door and don't let anyone in yet, except the medical examiner and my team of detectives. We need a few minutes alone in here."

"Yes, sir."

Jackson panned the room, finally taking in the whole scene. Adrenaline rushed through his veins, and he felt a little light-headed. The kitchen, once a yellow-and-white invitation to domesticity, was now a scene so gruesome it almost looked staged. A teenage boy was facedown near the door to the garage, his T-shirt soaked in blood. The forty-something woman, who looked like the girl they'd just carried out, lay near the center of the once-white vinyl. She was on her back in a pool of blackish-red blood. Jackson's eyes were drawn to her right wrist, stuck in the congealed mess. Someone had hacked off her hand. Chipped pink polish topped the appendage, which lay nearby, and blood pooled around it, thickening. The offending kitchen knife lay on the floor two feet away. Jackson scrutinized the woman's amiable face and wondered what she could have possibly done to inspire such violence. Blood had run down one side of her cheek from a trauma to her forehead.

What had she been struck with? Jackson's stomach curdled. He wished he had some mint gum to keep the sour-rust taste out of his nose and mouth.

Near the sink McCray squatted next to a male body partially propped against the lower cabinets. Even from eight feet away, Jackson could see the father had also been bashed in the head. Yet his life had poured out through the stab wounds in his chest. Typically, in a scenario like this, Jackson would suspect the man of the house to be the perpetrator of a murder-suicide, but this poor guy had not gouged open his own chest.

"Check his pulse, just to be sure," he called to McCray. Jackson knelt down next to the boy and touched his arm. Even through gloves the boy's flesh was cool.

The chirp of a cell phone broke into the quiet. Jackson pivoted toward the sound. The beep came from the pocket of the dead man by the sink. Jackson and McCray looked at each other, uncertain of the correct response. "We'll let it ring, then see who called," Jackson said. "Maybe they'll leave a message and tell us something important."

The chirp stopped after six rings, and Jackson retrieved the phone with gloved hands. He flipped open the cheap Motorola and the screen said *Missed call. Check messages?* Jackson pressed *Yes* and put the phone to his ear. "Jared, it's Noni. Have you seen Roy?" The caller sounded worried and maybe a little pissed off. "He didn't come home last night. If you know where he is, please call me."

Jackson chose option #4, *Save message.* While he clicked through, looking for the name or number of the last call, McCray asked, "Who was it?"

"Someone named Noni, looking for Roy. She says Roy didn't come home last night." Jackson found the data he wanted. "The call is labeled Roy Engall in the directory. Probably a married couple. I *also* would like to know why Roy didn't come home last night."

"Holy mother of god." Lara Evans stood in the archway, mouth open, her heart-shaped face registering horror. She was the youngest detective in the unit, and at the moment, the most unprepared for this assignment.

Michael Quince, a step behind, opened his mouth, closed it, then finally said, "What the hell?" Jackson had never heard Quince curse before. Behind his movie-star looks, Quince was a quiet, respectful man. No one in the unit had ever seen anything like this.

"We saw the ambulance go tearing out of here," Evans said. "Is someone alive?"

"The daughter still had a pulse, but barely. We have three dead that I know of." Jackson needed more time to visually process the scene before the house filled with detectives, technicians, and prosecutors. "Time is critical. The perpetrator is likely on the run. We need to canvass the neighborhood and find out if anybody saw a vehicle. Evans, start by talking to the sister outside. Get the names of everyone who lived here. Then both of you talk to the neighbors. From the looks of the congealing blood, I think they were killed last night."

Evans said, "I'm on it."

Quince nodded, and the detectives turned and headed out.

McCray rose from his position near the dead man. "I think this victim was hit in the head with that baseball bat, then stabbed after he was down." He rubbed his wrinkled face as if to wash the scene out of his eyes. "Thirty years as a cop, and I've never seen anything like this."

"Me neither." Jackson turned to the wooden bat leaning against a lower cabinet near the refrigerator. It had surprisingly little blood on it compared to the rest of the kitchen. "Will you check all the victims for ID?" Jackson reached in his bag for his video camera. He didn't use it often, but for this scene it could prove critical.

It was a relief to put a lens between himself and the carnage. The distorted view allowed his brain to start working more objectively. He filmed the kitchen slowly, recording the positions of the bodies, then moved to the baseball bat.

He hit pause, backed up to the archway, then zoomed in on the teenage boy. From what little he could see of his face, Jackson guessed his age at fifteen or so. Five-seven and about 140 pounds. The boy had sandy-brown hair and eyes, but his skin had the same coloring as that of the females. Blue, baggy basketball shorts, white T-shirt, and white basketball shoes—a typical teenage boy. Only this young man's life had been cut short by a large knife in the back. Jackson wanted to roll him over and fully see the victim's face, but the medical examiner would not appreciate it.

He panned the camera over to the woman. She looked about five-five and muscular, like someone who exercised but still couldn't lose the last fifteen pounds. Her white T-shirt with colored beading had been stained even before the blood spurting from her severed hand sprayed the bottom half. With her reddish-blonde hair and pink sunburn, she reminded Jackson of his sister-in-law Jan, who often looked after his daughter when he worked difficult cases.

Jackson forced himself to focus. From the position of the woman's body, he guessed she'd taken a blow to her head first, then was knocked to the ground and slashed. The pathologist would likely report she had died of blood loss.

"Jared Walker, age thirty-seven." McCray read from the driver's license in his hand. "His wallet was in his back pocket and there's still seven dollars in it."

Jackson made an involuntary noise in his throat. Jared Walker hadn't been killed for quick cash. He swung the video camera over to the cabinets and aimed it at the body on the floor. Jared Walker was about Jackson's size, six feet tall and two hundred pounds. That was the only resemblance. Walker's blond hair curled at the back of his neck, his face was long and thin, and his Adam's apple bulged in an almost freakish way. Faded jeans and a navy-blue T-shirt topped bare feet. The slashed and blood-soaked shirt had once said *Hawaii*. Jackson recognized the white floral pattern above the letters. Based on the house and the vehicles in the driveway, Jackson guessed Jared had never been to the islands and had picked up the shirt at a garage sale.

While Jackson filmed the bloody bat, McCray rummaged through a purse on the kitchen counter. "Carla Walker," McCray announced, "age thirty-six."

Time seemed to have nearly stopped. They'd been in the house for ten minutes, yet it felt like an hour. Jackson heard footsteps and paused the camera as the medical examiner entered the kitchen.

"Isn't this some crazy shit?" Rich Gunderson, dressed in his usual black, was in his fifties and had seen more dead bodies than anyone ever should.

"It looks like a lot of rage," Jackson said, stepping to the side, uncertain of where Gunderson would start.

"Or the work of a cold-blooded psycho." Detective Rob Schakowski stood in the archway, looking paler than usual. He'd lost a little roundness since his heart attack, but his buzz cut and square face still made him look mean, which he was not. Unless you were an uncooperative lowlife criminal.

"Hey, Schak. Glad you're here. Let's start a room-by-room search." Jackson slid the video camera back into his bag. "We're looking for anything that doesn't belong and any form of communication either from the killer or the family. Round up cell phones and open e-mails if you can."

Schak headed to the desk in the corner and McCray started down the hall. Two evidence technicians entered the house and Jackson told them to start with the front door, then move to the bat and knife. They needed to start running fingerprints though the system ASAP. Jackson went back to the kitchen to hear what Gunderson had to say.

The medical examiner knelt next to the teenage boy. From the back, with his short gray ponytail and black shirt, Gunderson looked more like an aging artist than an investigator. Yet his attention to detail often made the case.

"I need a time of death," Jackson said, knowing Gunderson would do it first anyway.

"Give me a minute."

With gloved hands, Gunderson pulled back the elastic waistband of the boy's shorts and plunged a large thermal probe into his hip. While he waited for a reading, Jackson took in more of the kitchen. The countertops were cluttered, but overall the space was clean. A black baseball glove, like the kind worn by batters, was on the end of the counter near the door leading to the garage. Had the boy come in from batting practice and left the glove and bat in the kitchen?

A moment later Jackson noticed the pigs. Ceramic pigs in assorted sizes, colors, and moods nestled among the countertop appliances. The largest one, a happy, white-speckled creature with a contrasting pink lid, caught his eye. Jackson lifted the top and inside was a palm-sized silver handgun.

Instinct told him it belonged to the family. Why had they not used it to protect themselves? Had the attacker or attackers broke in and overwhelmed them? Jackson lifted the mini-revolver and sniffed it, concluding it hadn't been fired recently. He emptied the chamber and put the gun and bullets in separate prelabeled bags. The killer must not have known it was there.

"Body temperature is 84.6 degrees," Gunderson announced. "So I'd say this boy died between eleven and twelve last night."

Ten hours ago. The killer could be in Mexico already. Even if he was still around, he'd had plenty of time to get rid of his bloody clothes and possibly establish an alibi.

"Any obvious defensive wounds?"

"He has minor nicks on his hands, so it's likely he struggled with his attacker." Gunderson bagged the boy's hands to collect any trace evidence that might dislodge during transport.

"Any head wounds?"

"None that I see."

The son hadn't been struck on the head. What did that mean? Had the boy come in while his parents were being attacked, and had he tried to stop the slaughter?

A clicking sound filled the room as the medical examiner took a dozen photos of the boy's knife wounds and position on the floor. The smallness of the room and its overpowering smells closed in on Jackson. He had to get out for a moment and breathe fresh air.

He also needed information, such as the relationship between the victims and who else lived here. He'd been assuming they were a nuclear family, but he could be wrong. He pulled his booties off at the door and headed for the sidewalk. Evans was still talking to the sister, who had calmed down a little. Quince was with the older couple at the edge of the lawn.

Jackson introduced himself to the sister, then turned to Evans. "Give me a rundown on who lives here."

"Jared and Carla Walker, and their two children, Lori and Nick Walker. The kids' cousin Shane, from Jared's side of the family, spends a lot of time here but doesn't live in the house."

Jackson looked at Rita. "How old is Shane and where does he live?"

"He's twenty, and I'm not sure where he lives now." She reached into her purse for a tissue. "He used to live with his parents, Kevin and Tracy Compton, on Windsor Circle. Tracy is Jared's sister." A startled expression came over Rita's face. "You don't think Shane was involved, do you?"

"Is he capable of something like this?"

"Lord no." An emphatic shake of her head. "He's had his troubles, but he loves his family and he's very close to his cousins."

Jackson gave Evans a slight nod. Shane would be the first person they interrogated. "What kind of trouble?"

"He used to have a drug problem, but it's in the past." Rita raised her hands to cover her face. "Shane didn't do this."

"Where does he work?"

"He worked at Country Coach until about a month ago when he was laid off."

Evans broke in. "Should I go find him?"

"Send a uniform to the Compton house and put out an attempt-to-locate. I need you here, talking to the neighbors." Jackson suspected finding Shane would require some manpower.

He turned back to Rita. "Any idea who might have done this?"

She shuddered. "None. My sister and her husband were good people. Good kids too." Rita began to sob.

"Had anything changed in their lives recently? New friends? Marriage troubles? Drug or alcohol use?"

"They both lost their jobs recently, like half the people in this country, but otherwise I can't think of anything."

"Was the front door open when you arrived?"

"It was closed but not locked. When no one answered, I opened it and went in." Rita inhaled short little gulps of air, trying to control her sobs. "I need to be at the hospital with Lori." She started to move away.

Jackson touched her arm with just enough pressure to stop her. "I understand. We'll let you go in a minute. Right now we need your help to find out what happened here." Jackson steered her toward the mobile unit. "I'd like you to go with Officer Anderson into our mobile office and sit down and write out the names of everyone connected to this family, including friends and coworkers. Make a note of the connection, please. It will be very helpful for us."

"You don't think Lori will live to tell you who did this?"

After losing that much blood, Jackson thought she might never wake up. "She may be unconscious for a while. We need to act now."

Rita nodded and followed the officer.

Jackson took a moment to assess the situation. A bad-boy cousin with a drug problem who might be a suspect—and a survivor. He started to feel a little less bleak about this case, but the image of the severed hand would be with him for a while.

CHAPTER 2

More cars came up the street, and Jackson recognized the district attorney's black Lexus. He waited while the DA parked, hurried up the sidewalk, and ducked under the yellow tape. Dressed in gray pinstripes that made him look lean and hungry, Slonecker always managed to make Jackson feel disheveled. He briefed the DA about what he'd learned so far, then let Slonecker go in and see for himself.

Evans was talking with the woman who lived next door, and Quince was still questioning the old couple. Jackson directed two patrol officers to canvass the people in the homes across the cul-de-sac. He and his team would likely question them all again later, but right now they needed to know: Did you hear anything? Did you see anyone come and go? What was he driving?

Jackson planned to focus on the family's cell phones, where he would find their most important contacts. He started for the house, then heard Sergeant Lammers call out, "Jackson, wait." She came barreling up the sidewalk, creating her own wind factor.

Lammers rarely attended a crime scene but this was no ordinary homicide.

"Sergeant."

"Are you acting as primary here?"

"I assumed I was."

"I don't think you're ready." Her hands came up to her hips and her green eyes challenged him. She was his height and matched him pound for pound.

Jackson kept his face blank. "This is a tough case. I need to run it."

"Your surgery was only five weeks ago. You still look pale."

"It's early June. Everyone is pale."

"I need your experience here and your determination, but I can't let you push yourself too hard." Lammers nodded in the general direction of his belly scar. "You can have all the help you need, except for Detectives Bohnert and Rios, because they're working the carjacking case."

"I could use more patrol units. I want to round up people and bring them here to interview."

"You've got it. Solve this quickly, please." She reached for her cell phone. "The public is jittery enough with these carjackings. The last woman was hurt badly."

More vehicles raced up the street, including the white KRSL news van. *Crap. That didn't take long.* Yellow crime-scene tape stretched across the street, but it wasn't always enough to keep the media at a distance. Especially a certain newspaper reporter who always managed to worm her way into Jackson's cases.

Jackson jogged up the driveway, not wanting to get caught by a cameraman's telephoto lens. He hated seeing the bodies again, but he needed to gather cell phones and check the other rooms in the house. To find the perpetrator of this heinous crime, he had to get to know each of the victims, to peel away the layers of their lives and see where their connections led.

Schak was still at the computer in the living room, and a crime tech lifted fingerprints from the front windowsill. Joe Berloni, the tech, had pulled the plaid couch away from the wall to make room to work. The window had sliders opening on both sides of the solid center, but the screens were still in place.

"Any sign of forced entry?"

"None in this room," Joe said, not looking up. "The front door mechanisms weren't jimmied or smashed and the screens are still in place, so no one came through the front widow. Unless they put the screen back when they left."

Jackson crossed to where Schak clicked open computer files. "Anything jump out at you?"

"Not so far. Lots of photos, music downloads, and jewelry designs. Very few text documents. This is not a family of writers."

"Are there more computers in the house?"

"There's a laptop in one of the bedrooms. McCray is looking at it now."

Jackson remembered the purse on the kitchen counter. Is that where Carla kept her phone? He braced himself and headed for the cluster on the other side of the archway. Jasmine Parker, the lead evidence technician, was bagging the severed hand, her face expressionless as always. The DA looked like a man waiting in a hospital, not expecting good news, and his assistant looked queasy. The medical examiner knelt next to the dead man and said, "He took two blows to the head. From the looks of their placement, I'd say the perpetrator was shorter than this victim."

Jackson jotted down *Perp < 6 ft tall*. It didn't narrow the field much. "Anything else I should know about the assailant?"

"The force behind these blows was very powerful. Your perpetrator may not be particularly tall, but he's exceptionally strong."

"Any idea why he left the girl alive?" The DA glanced at Jackson.

"He probably didn't mean to," Jackson speculated. "The father was likely his target. Or maybe the mother, but either way, he had to take out the father first. The kids may have been an afterthought. They probably came in to see what the commotion was about. The perp was on his way out and only knifed them because they saw him or got in his way. By then, his rage and energy were spent, and the attack on them was weaker. He may have thought the girl was dead."

Slonecker nodded and turned to the ME. "He didn't use the baseball bat on the kids?"

"The medics transported the girl out before I got here," Gunderson said, "but the boy has no head trauma."

"The girl has none I could see," Jackson added. "There might be two killers."

"We have a working theory then." Slonecker shifted his weight like a man ready to move on. "Any suspects yet?"

"We have patrol units looking for Shane Compton, a cousin who spends time here and used to have a drug problem." Jackson walked lightly around the perimeter of the room. "I'm grabbing Carla Walker's phone, then I'll create a comprehensive list of contacts for the family."

"Anything you need from us, just ask. My assistants will write all the subpoenas to save you time."

"We need records going back three months for every cell phone in this house. I'll have a list to you in a few minutes."

Jackson grabbed the denim purse, tucked it into his oversize bag, and began a room-by-room search. The first bedroom clearly belonged to a teenage girl. The bedspread was a fuzzy pale orange, and the walls held posters of Brad Pitt and a young female singer Jackson didn't recognize. Clothes covered a rattan chair in the corner and books were scattered across the desk:

a math book from school, a library book about Hawaii, and a paperback titled *Dead Girl Walking*. The room was fairly tidy for a teenager. McCray sat at the desk, perusing a small white laptop.

"Did you see a cell phone in here?" Jackson asked.

"I did a cursory search of the drawers and closet." McCray glanced over his shoulder. "No drugs, no weapons, no cell phone."

His partner's well-worn face seemed to have new worry lines. Was it the case or something personal? Now was not the time to ask. "Anything interesting on her laptop?"

"Her internet history shows recent visits to a site where people connect with roommates and several sites listing rentals in Maui. She may have been planning, or at least dreaming of, a move to Hawaii."

"Seems like age-appropriate behavior. What about e-mails?"

"Mostly to and from a girl named Jenna, no last name mentioned, and a guy named Dylan Dalka, who lives in Australia. Lori, the daughter, seems unhappy with her waitressing job and is worried about her family's finances."

"Both parents were laid off recently. We'll talk to their ex-employers tomorrow." Jackson gave the room another quick look. Nothing grabbed his attention. "Is there a purse on the desk?"

"There's this." McCray handed him a plastic evidence bag containing a small red backpack. "Her driver's license says Lori Anne Walker, age eighteen."

She was about to graduate from high school, Jackson thought. *Please let her live.* His next thought gave him a jolt. What if Lori was still in danger? If the killer knew the family, he would soon find out Lori had survived. Jackson called Sergeant Lammers, who was probably still standing on the sidewalk, and asked for round-the-clock patrol support outside Lori's hospital room.

Jackson slipped his phone back in his jacket pocket, stuffed the red backpack into his now-bulging shoulder bag, and walked down the hall. The door to the next room stood open, and the stink of rotting shoes drifted into the hallway. Clothes, papers, sports equipment, and gadgets cluttered the room like an invasive growth. Jackson was glad to be wearing gloves as he checked the pockets of the jeans on the floor, searching for the boy's cell phone. He found a pocketknife, two condoms, and a crumpled notice from school. The cell phone was on top of a tall dresser crammed with unfolded clothes. Jackson bagged the phone, then conducted a quick search of the drawers and closet.

Satisfied there was nothing pertinent in the boy's room, Jackson crossed the hall to the master bedroom. Later, they would slow down and carefully examine everything, but right now he was looking for the obvious—a bloody handprint on the wall, a discharged weapon, hate mail—anything that would give them a direction and a suspect to bring into custody.

The room was a study in contrasts. Light blue carpet for the wife, a brown-and-gray bedspread for the husband. Dozens of little perfume bottles and tiny glass sculptures on her dresser, and a pile of coins, receipts, and work gloves on his dresser. Jackson's visual search revealed nothing significant—only more ceramic pigs, presumably collected by Carla, and a stack of hunting/fishing magazines, collected by Jared. On the surface, they seemed like a normal working-class couple with two normal kids.

What the hell had happened here? Had a crazed killer chosen them at random?

Jackson noticed the bed was elevated with corner blocks. He knelt next to it and clicked on his flashlight. Underneath, a large silver container took up a chunk of the space. He grabbed the handle and pulled it out where he could get a look. The weight surprised him, then he realized it was a gun safe. The shape indicated it contained rifles, and the case had a built-in lock that opened with a key. His team would search for the key, but if they didn't find it, the evidence techs would bust open the safe at the crime lab.

Evans came into the room. "Jackson, I think we have a time frame for the crimes."

"Tell me."

"The neighbor next door on the right heard shouting around eleven o'clock. She heard someone yell, 'I'll kill you.'"

CHAPTER 3

Marlyn Beebe was striking, with large violet eyes and dark hair that looked as if it would never go gray. Sitting straight as a board, she enunciated every word carefully. Evans had mentioned on the way over that Marlyn was a librarian.

"I was in the kitchen, making some chamomile tea. It helps me sleep." Marlyn nodded between beats. "I heard shouting from the Walkers' house. That's when I heard someone yell 'I'll kill you.'" A tear rolled down Marlyn's face. "I feel terrible now that I didn't call the police."

They sat at her kitchen table, a gorgeous piece of handcrafted oak, and bright sunlight filled the space. Marlyn was drinking coffee that smelled wonderful. Jackson considered breaking his no-beverages-from-witnesses rule and accepting some. "What happened after that?"

"Nothing really. That's why I didn't call. People say that kind of thing when they're mad. Parents say it to their kids all the time. 'If you wreck my car, I'll kill you.'"

"You heard it all the way over here, so it must have been loud. Did the person sound angry?"

"Yes." Marlyn twisted a strand of hair. "I had the kitchen window open, so it wasn't that loud."

"Did you recognize the voice?"

"No." Her brows came together. "It didn't sound like anyone who lives there. At first I thought it might be the friend who comes over. I think his name is Shane, but I'm not sure. I've only spoken to him once. He wasn't shouting then, so it's hard to say."

Jackson made a note: *Neighbor heard other voice shouting. Maybe cousin Shane.* "Do they do a lot of yelling next door?"

"Not really. Sometimes I hear Carla hollering at the boy to get up in the morning." She hesitated. "There's been more volume lately." She met Jackson's eyes. "Was it a murder-suicide? Did Jared go crazy and kill his family?"

"Did he seem like the type?"

"I really don't know them. They only moved in two years ago. I chat with Carla sometimes when we're both outside, but we don't socialize."

"Renters or owners?"

"Renters."

"Do you know the landlord?"

"I think it might be Property Management Group."

Jackson made a note to contact them. "Have you noticed anything unusual lately? New people coming to the house? A change in pattern for anyone?"

Marlyn gave it some thought. "Their cars are home a lot more. I think it's because they're unemployed now."

"Let's go over last night again. Did you see any cars come or go from the Walker house?"

A little shake of her head. "I didn't get home until seven thirty after having dinner with my sister. I noticed their Subaru wasn't in the driveway."

"Did you hear the car come home at any point?"

"I took a shower, then listened to an audiobook. I didn't hear any outside noises until I went into the kitchen to make tea around eleven o'clock. That's when I heard the guy yell."

"You said 'guy.' It was a male voice?"

"Probably. I know I didn't recognize it. I wondered if everything was okay. I listened for a while and heard some movement, but no shouting, so I went back to my audiobook. Around midnight, I went to bed."

Jackson stood. "Thanks for your time. If you think of anything else, let us know."

He hurried out to the mobile unit, curious to see the list of people Rita Altman, the sister, had come up with. Before he sat down to interrogate anyone, he needed to know more about this family. He needed to know who was driving the Subaru that came home after seven thirty. More important, was someone else in the car?

The sound of sobbing almost made him turn back. Even after all the years of being exposed to the rawest of human emotions, he wasn't immune to a family's grief. He'd trained himself to push through and keep asking questions, but it was challenging to feel sharp when the person nearby was sending out palpable pain waves.

He climbed the steps, each lift tugging on his scar, and entered the crowded mobile space. The clutter would have been overwhelming if he had not spent the last twelve years in a cramped office at headquarters. Rita Altman and Officer Anderson sat at a small folding table near the front. Anderson kept his face impassive, but under the table, his leg was jumping.

"I'll take this for a while," Jackson said. Anderson patted Rita on the shoulder, then hustled out like a man in need of a bathroom. Jackson looked at the list. The writing changed midway through, as if Rita had started it, then Anderson took over. Neither had decent penmanship, but the information was substantial.

At a glance, Jackson learned Jared had been laid off from Engall's Renovation eight weeks ago, and Roy Engall was listed as his boss and friend. Carla had worked for Silver Moon Jewelry until late April, and Lori Walker worked at Appleton's.

"Does Lori drive?" Jackson asked.

"Yes. She uses her mom's car."

"Does anyone in the house play baseball?"

"They all play softball. Carla and Jared are on a city league together, and Lori plays on the high-school team." Rita stifled a sob, then announced, "I need to go to the hospital to be with Lori."

"Are you okay to drive?"

"I called my husband. He's going to meet me at our house, which isn't far from here."

"Thanks for your help." Jackson patted the back of her hand, and Rita shuffled out. They would fill in the list as they questioned everyone.

McCray pounded up the steps into the mobile unit. "Hey, Jackson. You need to look at this." The older detective had a sheet of white paper in his hand. "I think Jared Walker may have been blackmailing Roy Engall, the guy who didn't come home last night."

CHAPTER 4

Two months earlier

Jared slipped the cell phone back in his pocket. What the hell? His boss had just invited him out to breakfast. In the five years he'd been painting houses for Roy Engall, they'd never had breakfast. Plenty of beers together at the Time Out Tavern after work and an occasional burger for lunch, but whenever Roy called early in the morning, it was always to talk about the work lined up for the day.

The coffee went sour in Jared's stomach. Something was up. He pushed back from the table just as Carla came into the kitchen. Her pink pajamas were stained and her crazy morning hair was worse than usual, but his heart filled with joy every time he saw her. "Morning, gorgeous."

She kissed the top of his head, and he squeezed her butt as she padded toward the coffee he'd brewed. Jared stood and pulled on his overshirt. "I've got to run. Roy wants to meet me for breakfast."

Carla turned and scowled. "That's weird."

"I know. See you later."

"Do you think—"

"Don't even say it." Jared grabbed his keys from the hook by the refrigerator, kissed Carla, and scooted out. There was no point in speculating. He would find out soon enough.

As he reached the restaurant, the sun came up over the mountains, revealing a dark layer of clouds overhead. A late-spring chill was still in the air as Jared crossed the parking lot, which was nearly empty. He'd never seen it like this before, and he'd been coming to Shari's since it opened. Jared hurried into the foyer and spotted Roy in a booth along the front wall. He bypassed the hostess and headed straight over. The scent of maple syrup and toasty bread made his mouth water.

"Hey, Jared." His boss' fleece jacket seemed tight on his torso, his cheeks were red, and moisture glimmered on his scalp where his hair was receding. But that was Roy.

"Hey." Jared searched his face, and Roy's left eye twitched. He'd had too much coffee already. How long had his boss been sitting here, waiting?

"We should order. I'm starving." Roy tapped his plastic-coated menu.

Jared flipped through the pages, seeing the pictures and words, but not processing the food details. What was this about? Did Roy know he had started documenting the safety problems? The waitress came to the table, and they both ordered Denver omelets.

"Are we still going out to the Wetzlers' house to prep today?" Jared said, when she walked away.

"No." Roy locked his fingers together. "They canceled the job."

"Ah shit." They'd had a lot of cancellations lately. "So we'll start the Deacon Street job early."

Roy leaned toward him like a conspirator. "Jared, it kills me to tell you this, but I don't have enough work to keep you on. I have to let you go. I'd like to think it's temporary, but we all know better. This recession isn't going away for a while."

Jared felt like he'd been body-slammed. He had to pull in some air before he could speak. "Why me? I've been with you for five years."

"I let Keith go too."

"What about Tyler?"

Roy looked away. "He's Noni's kid. I'm stuck with him."

"But he's not dependable and he can't paint or sheetrock for shit." Heat and shame fought for space in his chest. "What about Darrell? He's only been with you a year."

"His wife just had a baby. They have no other income. At least Carla still has a job."

"I have two kids and a truck payment, not to mention rent. I don't believe this, man."

"I have no choice." Roy was louder now, less sympathetic. "We simply don't have enough work to keep everyone on."

Jared's mother had taught him to never raise his voice in public. He whispered loudly to make his point. "You know I can't collect unemployment!"

"You knew that when you took the job. I'm sorry."

Jared wanted to punch his smug little face. Instead, he bolted from the restaurant.

Back in his truck, he put his forehead against the steering wheel and fought the black hole trying to swallow him. What the hell would he do now? No one was hiring. He heard his mother's voice in his head, nagging him to quit working under the table and start paying into Social Security. Jared let out a bitter laugh. She got the first half of her wish.

He couldn't go home and face Carla yet. She was such a worrier. The thought of telling her he had no job made his teeth hurt. Carla counted on him to pay his share of the bills. He could not let her down ever again. They had married straight out of high school, with little Lori already on the way. Jared had not been ready for any of it, and it took him a while to settle into his responsibilities. Carla had been patient for a long time, but she had expectations now.

Jared started the truck and squealed out of the parking lot. What if Carla got that look? The one that said, *I told you this was a bad idea and now we're going to suffer for it.*

Jared had had his share of bad ideas over the years. Like the time he'd loaned six hundred dollars to Deke, this kid he knew who never lost at cards. The money was for Deke's stake in a poker game at the Eldorado. Deke was supposed to win ten grand or more and split the pot with him. Jared had planned to send Nick to basketball camp and buy Lori a used car. He'd fantasized about how happy they would be. Things hadn't turned out quite like that, and Jared had learned his lesson. He'd promised Carla "no more money mistakes."

Off to the right, the dark water of Fern Ridge Reservoir caught his eye. Unconsciously, he'd driven west toward Veneta, the small town where he'd grown up. Ten minutes later, Jared was parked in front of his mother's house. Only she didn't live here anymore. She didn't live anywhere.

Jared let the memories flood him: Playing tag with his friends in the park in the summer. Fishing at the lake with Cory. Drinking with his high-school friends behind the barn on Perkins Road.

The reality of his situation slammed back into his head. What the hell could he do? His chance of finding a job was laughable. Nobody was building new houses, and damn few people were spending money on new paint. He'd worked as a prep cook when he was younger and could apply at restaurants, but they weren't hiring now either. Jared cursed himself for working under the table all these years. An unemployment check would at least help pay the rent and the truck payment. He wished like hell he'd never bought the truck either. It wasn't anywhere near new, but they were still eight grand in debt for it. Carla had argued against the vehicle, thinking they should drive the damn Explorer until it finally died. Why didn't he listen to her? She was almost always right.

Jared checked his watch. Carla would have left for work by now. He drove home, racking his brain for a way to make a little money. Even if he sold the truck, he'd be lucky to just get out from under the payments. And he would still need transportation. He knew Carla would say he could sell the guns. Jared's jaw locked up at the thought. They were his father's hunting rifles and all he had left of the old man. What were they worth? A month's rent? He shook his head. If they ended up homeless, he'd consider it.

Jared's thoughts jumped to Roy and his nice house by the river and his fat little savings account. Part of the reason Roy had a lot of money was because he cheated everyone. He cheated the government out of taxes, and he cheated his employees by not insuring them. Jared thought he shaved their hours sometimes too. The fucker had laid him off instead of that lazy-ass Tyler. Jared was glad he hadn't drunk any coffee at the restaurant. He could feel his heart pounding with stress.

At home he pulled a spiral notebook from his bottom dresser drawer and a piece of plain white paper from the printer tray, then took them to the kitchen table. He labeled the top of the paper *Job Search*. The notebook had already been labeled *Roy Engall*. He started the job search page by listing three painting companies to go see and five chain restaurants that might have some turnover. His thoughts kept coming back to Roy and what a cheap bastard he could be sometimes. Jared had to buy all his own tools, including a sprayer. The worst of it was the lack of insurance though. No one who painted houses under the table expected health insurance as a job benefit, but he expected to be insured for on-the-job injuries. Roy Engall didn't even cover those.

Jared had only recently come across this sobering information. Six months ago, Manny had fallen off a ladder after being dive-bombed by a bird, breaking his collarbone and two bones in his right hand. Roy had insisted on driving Manny to the hospital rather than calling an ambulance. Manny had never come back to work, but months later Jared ran into him at a grocery store. Manny told him Roy didn't cover his employees with accident insurance. Roy had offered to pay half the hospital bill, then laid Manny off. Not being a legal citizen, Manny had not filed a complaint or threatened to sue.

Jared filled in more details on the page with neat printed letters. He wasn't good with cursive, but his printing was better than most. He knew he should probably type the list on the computer and save it in a file, but he didn't type worth a damn. Besides, he thought best with a pencil in his hand. He got up to look at the calendar, found the first Monday in October, and wrote *October 6* as the day of Manny's accident.

It was illegal to run a painting crew without accident insurance, wasn't it? Roy could lose his business license if the state found out. Shame filled Jared's stomach. He didn't want to put Roy out of business; he just wanted enough cash to get by while he found other work. He just wanted to keep his family together and happy. A lot of employers gave severance packages when they laid someone off. Wasn't he entitled to one?

Jared tapped his pencil. He knew there was more to Roy's dealings. If you worked for someone long enough, you learned all kinds of things about their character and business practices. He remembered something else. Roy sometimes cheated his customers too. If he thought the homeowner wasn't well-informed, he bought cheap paint and charged him for expensive paint. If someone notified all those cheated customers, they could sue Roy. The question was: What would Roy be willing to pay to keep Jared quiet about all of it?

CHAPTER 5

Monday, June 1, 2:15 p.m.

Jackson glanced at the list of Roy Engall's alleged infractions, then climbed out of his unmarked blue Impala. A half block away, the river scurried by with a soft summer song. The Engalls lived in the Centennial area, with an address in Eugene, but closer to sister city Springfield's downtown. In this neighborhood, nobody cared about zip codes. They were in their own little world, where the streets were wide, the homes were spacious, and the sound of the river lulled them to sleep on summer evenings.

Jackson strode past a blue Toyota FJ Cruiser in the driveway on his way to the front door. A tall woman with shoulder-length red hair opened it before he could knock. "What can I do for you?" Her eyes were wary, with a hint of anger.

"I'm Detective Jackson with the Eugene Police. I'm here to see Roy Engall."

"Why?"

"I need to ask him a few questions. Is he here?" Jackson wanted to see if she would cover for her husband's absence the night before.

"I haven't seen him since yesterday."

"What is your name and your relationship to Roy Engall?"

"I'm Noni Engall and Roy is my lousy husband."

While Jackson wondered how to use the information to win this woman's confidence, fear transformed her face. "Is Roy okay? Was he in a car accident?"

"I'm not here about an accident. Can I come in, please?"

She hesitated, then stepped back to let him in. Jackson followed her into a spacious living room with overhead skylights. A rosemary potpourri lingered in the air. Noni gestured for him to sit on a pale-green couch in a patch of indoor sunlight. It made him feel strangely exposed.

"You say you haven't seen Roy since yesterday. Is it typical for him to be gone overnight?"

"It happens. He gets drunk and crashes on a friend's couch sometimes."

"Did you think he'd crashed at Jared Walker's house?"

"It seems unlikely. Why?"

"Are he and Jared friends?"

Noni sighed. "Not anymore. Jared was an employee and they used to be friends. You know, have a few beers after work sometimes. Then Roy had to lay Jared off because there wasn't enough work. Jared took it badly."

"You called Jared this morning, looking for Roy. Why?"

She jumped up in alarm. "How do you know?"

"Why did you call Jared?"

"I called a bunch of people. Jared was last. How do you know I called him?"

"We'll get to that. What's Roy like when he's drinking?"

She didn't like the question. "A little obnoxious. Why?"

"Do you know where he is now?"

"He'd better be at work. He can't afford to lose any more jobs."

"He's a housepainter?"

Now she looked defensive. "Roy is a home-improvement specialist. He does consulting work as well."

"What work site would he be at today? I need an address."

"Just a minute." Noni hurried across the open space to a kitchen facing the backyard. Jackson followed, casting around for signs of Roy's presence, such as a jacket over a chair.

Noni studied a wall calendar and said, "It's 1250 Parish Lane. It's in the Coburg area, off Bailey."

Jackson realized it wasn't far from the murder scene. "What does Roy drive?"

"A white Dodge van with the name of his business on both sides." Noni pulled her hands together in front of her heart. "Please tell me what this is about. I'm starting to get really scared."

"We're investigating a crime; we want to ask Roy some questions."

She slumped into a kitchen chair. "What do you suspect him of?"

Jackson took a seat too. "I can't tell you yet. Has Roy been the target of blackmail?"

"Not that I know of." She gestured at the house. "We're not exactly rich here."

"What time did you last see Roy yesterday?"

"Around noon. We had lunch together."

"Did he call anytime after?"

Something flashed on her face, but Jackson couldn't read it. Fear? Frustration?

"I haven't heard from him."

"I'd like to look at Roy's business records and get the names of his employees."

She shook her head. "Sorry. Not without a court order."

"I'll be back." Jackson handed her his business card. "Thanks for your time. If you hear from Roy, tell him to call me immediately."

As he stood to leave, Jackson heard a vehicle pull up out front. He rushed to the door. A squat, balding man wearing slept-in clothes lurched out of a van parked on the street. The guy looked up at Jackson and jumped back in the driver's seat.

"Stop! Police!" Jackson shouted, and ran toward the van with one arm held out in front and the other on his still-holstered Sig Sauer. Roy cranked up the engine, and Jackson considered drawing his weapon. He could shoot out a tire and keep a potential mass murderer from getting away.

A boy on a bicycle rolled across the sidewalk, oblivious to the events unfolding. Jackson took his hand off his gun and the van screamed down the street. He ran for the radio in his car, as Noni shouted at Roy from the front grass. "Don't run! It can't be that bad! Roy!"

Jackson fumbled for his keys. *Radio first*, he thought. He grabbed the speaker and made the connection. "Detective Jackson here. In pursuit of a white van, traveling east on Aspen about five blocks from Centennial." He started the car as he spoke. "The van is registered to Roy and/or Noni Engall. Lettering on the side says Engall's Renovation. License plate unknown. Roy Engall is driving. I want him arrested and brought in to headquarters."

Jackson threw the cruiser into reverse and started to back out. The boy on the bike had returned and was stopped in the driveway. Jackson stuck his head out the window. "Move!"

The boy scurried out of his way, but stopped to watch as Jackson entered the street. He hauled ass to the corner, but the van was nowhere in sight. Jackson raced toward the main road, wondering if Engall would try to put distance between them or use side streets to avoid patrol cars. When he reached Centennial, he scanned the traffic in both directions. No white van.

Jackson made a left and headed for city hall. Chasing Engall was a waste of his time. He might as well meet with his detectives and let the fleet of patrol units track down the suspect.

Jackson processed the Roy Engall scenario. It seemed damn suspicious the man would disappear for twelve hours after the homicides, then run at the sight of a cop. Yet killing a whole family over a blackmail threat to his business seemed like an extreme reaction. Still, if Roy was prone to binge drinking, he could have done it in an alcoholic rage.

Jackson knew plenty about alcoholics. His ex-wife, Renee, had slid slowly into a daily drinking pattern that turned her into an unpredictable stranger. The moment he'd realized he hated her as much as he loved her, he knew it was time to make a break. Watching her mother disappear into a drunk had been even harder for his daughter, Katie. He'd finally given Renee an ultimatum: get sober or get out. She had tried and failed several times, and he'd finally been forced to pack her stuff and load it into a moving van while Katie cried and Renee called him names. It had been the worst day of his life. Almost.

Jackson shook his head to clear it. No point in thinking about the past. He had a new woman in his life and new issues to deal with, but these homicides were his priority. His first case after his suspension and he had to be brilliant. He felt a twinge of pain in his abdomen. Was it the fibrosis, or fear?

What if the slaughter on Randall Street was the work of a psychotic serial killer who moved around too much to be caught? What if he never resolved this case? The faces of the dead would haunt him. Jackson put his earpiece in, prepared to make calls while he drove. "McCray, have we heard anything on Shane, the cousin?"

"Not yet."

"Let's meet at headquarters in an hour. Tell Schak, Evans, and Quince. I'm headed there now to write a subpoena for Roy Engall's business records. He showed up while I was at the house, then bolted in his van when he saw me."

"Engall just bumped himself to prime suspect."

"Sure did." Jackson inched along Coburg Road and tried not to swear at the slow-moving traffic. "Check with Gunderson before you come in. See if he has anything new to report about the bodies."

Ten minutes later Jackson pulled into the parking lot under city hall. He hoped this would be the last year the department was in the crowded, badly constructed building. The city council had finally approved a new site, and they were scheduled to move early next year. It seemed insane for the relocation to be happening when officers and detectives were being laid off, but the money came from two separate budgets, and that was how city government worked.

Jackson hurried down the narrow hall into the violent crimes area. He wouldn't miss having eight desks crowded into a room with file cabinets crammed into every nook and cranny, leaving only narrow paths to navigate. He wouldn't miss the slats over the outside of the windows either. More stupid architecture.

Jackson eased into his chair and clicked on his computer. He wanted to check the national databases before the meeting. If a similar crime had been committed anywhere, he needed to know. He also planned to call the local FBI office and ask if they'd ever had a case with a severed hand.

Schakowski and Evans were already in the small room with the long dry-erase board. Jackson breathed in the intoxicating aroma of dark-roast coffee. They each had a tall cup, bitter black with no foaming milk or syrup. Evans picked up a third container from the floor by her chair and handed it to him. "Did you order food?"

"Sandwiches from the little deli on Park Street. They'll deliver."

"I'm glad you're running this case," Quince said, as he came in. "What a mess. There's so much to cover with four homicide victims."

"Three," Jackson corrected. "I called the hospital and Lori is still alive. She's not conscious yet, but they think she might pull though. They'll call me as soon as she's able to answer questions."

"Any word on Roy Engall?" McCray came in, carrying a steaming cup and looking weary. The lines in his face seemed to plow deeper every week and his hair was turning old-man white. The unit had been through several tough cases in the last year, then Jackson and Schak had both been on medical leave for a while. McCray had picked up some of the slack. Jackson wondered what the job was doing to his own appearance.

"We've got nothing on Engall yet." Jackson turned to the other detectives. "He never came home last night, then bolted when he saw me at his house today. I put out an attempt-to-locate for him and an interstate alert."

Evans looked confused, so Jackson added, "He's Jared Walker's ex-boss. McCray found a list of Engall's wrongdoings, likely compiled by Jared. We think Jared might have been black-mailing Engall."

"You think he killed the whole family to keep from being exposed?" Evans' expressive face telegraphed all her thoughts. At the moment, she was skeptical.

"It's just our first avenue. His behavior is highly suspicious and he's a binge drinker. I ran a background check. He's had two DUIs and one assault charge that was reduced to menacing."

Evans nodded. "I'll put him on the board."

Jackson started to tell her to let someone else handle it this time, then stopped. Evans was good at it. "Put Shane Compton under suspects too." He looked around hopefully. "Did patrol bring Compton in?"

"Not that I know of. How is he connected?" McCray tugged on his brown corduroy pants, then finally took a seat.

"He's the kids' cousin. First we need to map out the family connections." Jackson dug out the list Carla's sister had made at the crime scene. "Let's put the family members down the middle. Start with Jared Walker, then Carla, Lori, and Nick."

As Evans printed the names in neat letters on the board, Jackson read from his yellow tablet. "Jared's sister is Tracy Compton, who is married to Kevin Compton. Shane is their twenty-year-old son. List him first. They also have a daughter, Lisa, twenty-five."

"Kevin Compton?" McCray asked, surprised. "A Kevin Compton was assaulted in the parking lot of the Time Out Tavern last month. Do you suppose it's the same man?"

Jackson's heart quickened. He could feel this case getting sticky. "Considering the size of this town, it's probably the same guy. What's the story on the assault?"

"The victim called 911 before he passed out, then someone found him unconscious and bleeding and called again. The ER doctor reported it as an assault and I was assigned the case. When I questioned Kevin Compton, he said he was drunk and fell against his vehicle. I thought he was covering for someone."

"Any witnesses to the incident?"

"No." McCray shifted, looking uncomfortable. "I didn't go after it very hard. Compton didn't want to press charges."

"Whatever is going on here may have started a while ago and may involve several members of the family," Jackson said. "Dig up your notes on the case, and we'll visit the Comptons tomorrow."

He looked down to read more of the list. "Carla's sister, Rita Altman, discovered the bodies, and Roy Engall is Jared's boss."

Evans wrote *possible blackmail* under Roy's name. She turned to Jackson and said, "We'll have to call people by first names in this case."

"I'll try to remember." He gave her an indulgent smile. The door popped open and the desk officer brought in the sandwiches he'd ordered. They ate for a minute in silence.

"What did we find out from the neighbors?" Jackson set his meal aside and flipped through his notes from the morning.

Evans jumped up and began writing on the board, recounting the details from memory. "Marlyn Beebe heard shouting around eleven. She thinks someone said, 'I'll kill you.' She didn't recognize the voice as belonging to the family and she referred to the shouter as 'he.'"

Jackson added, "Marlyn also noticed when she came home at seven thirty that the Walkers' Subaru wasn't in the driveway. It looks like one member of the family was out for part of the evening."

"Speaking of cars"—Quince consulted notes—"A neighbor across the street, Rose Linley, says she saw a light-colored van parked on the street in front of the Walkers' house. She had gone out sometime after ten o'clock to set her garbage on the curb."

"Any details on the van?"

"Just light colored and probably no windows in the back."

"A work van. Like the white one Roy Engall drives."

Evans' marker squeaked across the board as she tried to keep up.

Jackson thought about the timing. "If Engall was there at ten, why didn't the shouting start until eleven? What was going on during that hour?"

"Maybe the visit started friendly, two guys having a beer, then Jared brought up the blackmail," Schak offered.

Jackson's phone rang. It was the medical examiner. "What have you got?"

"I'm just letting you know we're doing the post on Carla Walker at eight tomorrow morning. We'll do Nick and Jared on Wednesday."

"Thanks." Jackson hung up and looked at Quince. "Anything else from the neighbors? Any unusual behavior from the Walkers lately?"

Quince shook his head. "The neighbors liked the family. They all said Jared and Carla were friendly with them and affectionate with each other."

"What about their teenagers?" Jackson asked. "Any complaints?"

"Occasional loud music when the parents weren't home, and Nick once put up a skateboard jump in the middle of the cul-de-sac, which nobody liked. Typical kid stuff."

"Except the family is dead now." Jackson rubbed his forehead. "What did we get from the house besides the blackmail list?"

Schak spoke up. "I scanned the e-mails on the computer in the living room and nothing seems unusual. In the last week, the boy sent only one e-mail to a friend, asking about a basket-ball game. Carla sent out a bunch of job search e-mails with her résumé attached, but only two personal communications, one to her sister and one to a woman she used to work with. The father, Jared, doesn't seem to use the computer."

Jackson looked around at the group. "Unless this slaughter was the act of a psychotic stranger, someone in this family likely had some connection to criminals."

McCray cut in. "What about the guns? What if it was a rob-bery gone wrong?"

"It's a possibility." Jackson nodded at Evans; she wrote *guns* on the board under her motive list. "Yet they didn't take the case with the rifles or the handgun in the cookie jar."

"Still, we should look at similar crimes," McCray pressed.

"We will. In the meantime, each of you investigate a family member, and I'll talk to the suspects when they're brought in." Jackson gulped some coffee before it got cold. "Evans, take Lori. Start with her friends; find out if she had a boyfriend. I asked the nurse at the hospital if Lori had a cell phone in her clothes, but she wasn't sure. Will you follow up?" He turned to McCray. "You found the blackmail list, so you get Jared. Talk to all of the people he used to work with. Find out what you can about Engall too."

Jackson stood, needing to take pressure off his still-tender scar. "Quince, you look into the boy, Nick, and the cousin, Shane. That leaves Carla for you, Schak. If you find anything significant, call me right away. We'll meet again in the morning at ten, unless you hear otherwise."

They wolfed down the rest of their sandwiches and headed out. As Jackson stopped by his desk, his cell phone rang. It was the front-desk officer. "A uniform just picked up Roy Engall and he's bringing him in."

CHAPTER 6

While Jackson waited for his suspect to arrive, he called Kera. He'd met her eight months earlier when he'd investigated the murder of a young client at the Planned Parenthood clinic where Kera worked as a nurse. Their attraction had been instant and powerful, and they'd started dating as soon as the case was resolved. After his surgery, Kera had insisted he and Katie stay with her while he recovered. He'd woken up in her bed this morning, as he had for the last four weeks.

"Hey, Wade. We missed you at dinner tonight." Her warm, sexy voice had a touch of melancholy. But he loved it when she called him Wade, since no one else ever did.

"Sorry. We had a mass homicide last night. I went out to the scene this morning and haven't had a chance to call until now."

"What do you mean by *mass*?"

"Three family members dead and one critically injured."

"Oh no. How horrible." Kera had lost her son to the Iraq war, and Jackson hated to mention death to her. "Was it a murder-suicide?" she asked. "Did the father do it?"

"It doesn't look that way. We have a suspect and I'll question him soon. I just wanted to let you know I'll be working really late."

"Are you okay physically?" Kera couldn't help but be a nurse.

"I'm fine. Except I miss you already, just knowing how it will be for the next few days."

"Don't work too hard. There are seven other detectives in your unit."

"For now. They're laying off one of us on Friday."

"That's a damn shame. Do you know who?"

"No, but Lammers looked right at me when she announced it. If the city lets me go now, they won't have to pay my full retirement."

"No! You're only a month away from twenty years. They wouldn't do that, would they?"

"These are desperate times." Jackson didn't want to think about it. "Is Katie around? I want to say hello to her."

"She and Danette took the baby out for a walk. I have the house to myself for a moment and I'm enjoying it immensely." Danette was a college girl Kera's son had slept with before shipping out to Iraq. Nathan had died on his second day in the war zone, never knowing he was a father. A few months after the baby was born, Kera had taken in Danette and her grandson. It made for a full house.

"In that case I'll let you go. I'll be in touch."

"I love you."

"Love you too." Jackson hung up and unconsciously glanced around. The only other detective in the area was across the room on the phone. Jackson was still adjusting to Kera's openness and occasional displays of public affection, but he loved those things about her and hoped he would never stifle her. He'd rather take a little grief from his peers.

Jackson printed some of the photos from the crime scene, then went out in search of coffee. After the interrogation, he'd start on the cell phones and work until he was too tired to focus. In the past he'd taken Vivarin tablets to stay awake when he had cases like this, but Kera had strongly encouraged him to stop. Too much caffeine made his heart race. They were both a little worried about his heart now that they knew about the growth around his aorta. Retroperitoneal fibrosis, commonly called RF. The diagnosis two months ago had stunned him, and his future was uncertain. In the meantime, one small cup of coffee couldn't hurt.

He'd let Engall sit alone in the interrogation room for twenty minutes. By the time Jackson walked in, the sleazy housepainter was already rocking himself for comfort. Jackson took a seat, and the gray walls instantly closed in on the small windowless room.

"Whatever this is about, I'm not your man," Engall pleaded. "You've made a mistake."

Jackson set his digital recorder on the table and clicked it on. "Please state your name for the record."

"Roy Engall."

"You're here to answer questions about a homicide last night," Jackson said for the recorder. "Stand up, please." Jackson walked to the other side of the table and scrutinized the suspect's clothing. He saw no blood but he hadn't expected to. Twenty-four hours had passed. "Roll up your sleeves and hold out your hands."

Engall did as instructed. His fingers had a grayish tinge from years of paint stain. "Turn them over." A two-inch gash on his forearm was still fresh, the skin around it raised and red.

"How did you get the cut?"

"I work with my hands and use a utility knife every day. What's this about?"

Jackson pulled his camera from the bag and took a picture of the wound. "It looks like somebody in the Walker family fought back."

"It's a scratch! I come home with these all the time."

"I've already talked to your wife, Roy. I know you didn't come home last night. Tell me where you were."

"I was drinking at the Time Out Tavern."

"What time did you leave?"

"I don't know." Roy took off his glasses and rubbed his eyes. "I had a blackout. I woke up early this afternoon in my van in the parking lot of Value Village."

"Your statement is that you don't remember anything about last night or this morning?"

Roy hesitated. "Yes."

"I'm supposed to believe that?" Jackson gave him a look of incredulity.

"It happens sometimes."

"Who were you drinking with?"

"I had a few beers with my painting crew, then they went home. I had a few beers with another friend named Steve Zuckerman. After that I don't remember."

"It's not much of an alibi."

"Why would I need an alibi?" Engall blinked rapidly as he spoke. He was a terrible liar.

"Jared Walker and his family were murdered last night. A white van was seen outside their house, and you experienced a binge-drinking blackout. You also have a defense wound made by a knife. This doesn't look good for you."

Engall's face crumbled. After a moment, he remembered to act surprised. "Jared's dead? And his family? How horrible."

"What did you and Jared argue about when you went to his house last night?"

"I wasn't there!"

"How much blackmail money was Jared asking for?"

Engall's eyes registered a little panic. "I don't know what you're talking about."

"We found Jared's list." Jackson slid the paper across the table. He needed Engall to feel trapped.

"Jared never said anything to me. We haven't talked since I laid him off."

"Your wife called Jared's cell phone this morning looking for you. I believe you and Jared have been in touch."

Engall slumped a little. "I called him a few times last month, asking him out for a beer, but he never picked up or called back. He was mad at me."

Jackson decided to mix it up. "What have you got against Carla?"

"Nothing. I like Carla."

"Did she hit or scratch you to defend Jared? Is that why you cut off her hand?"

Engall lost a little of his natural flush. "I don't know what you're talking about."

Jackson slid an image of Carla's severed hand across the table and laid it next to the blackmail list. "She must have really pissed you off."

Engall stared at the wall.

"Look at the photo!"

"You're wrong about me."

Jackson stood. "Let me see your feet. Put one shoe up on the table."

Engall started to object, then thought better of it. He lifted his right foot to display a pair of white, paint-stained running shoes.

"Size ten?"

"Ten and a half. So?"

"The tread looks familiar. You left tracks in the blood on your way out of the Walker house. It's enough to convict you." Jackson took close-up photos of the shoes, then snapped shots of Engall wearing the shoes. He didn't have a subpoena yet to seize evidence from Engall. The blackmail list and this photo, alongside the crime-scene picture of the footprints, would convince a judge to let them search Engall's property and collect his DNA.

"I want to call my lawyer."

"First, let's get a swab of the inside of your cheek." It didn't hurt to ask. Some criminals didn't know they could refuse.

"Not a chance." Engall tried to sound tough, but his voice couldn't contain his distress. "I'm invoking my rights." He put his foot back on the floor.

"You haven't been arrested or charged. I'm just giving you a chance to tell the truth and clear yourself."

"I want to call my lawyer, and I'm not answering any more questions."

"Refusing to cooperate will not look good to a jury."

Engall stayed silent. Jackson finally took him out to the hallway and let him make his call. Afterward he made Engall sit in the interrogation room while he wrote both a warrant and a subpoena to collect his suspect's shoes and DNA.

Engall's lawyer showed up an hour later, and Jackson grudgingly released his suspect. Without a witness to place him at the crime scene or a DNA match to any evidence, he couldn't hold him. He'd arrested Engall for obstructing justice, but it wasn't a serious enough charge to book him into the overcrowded jail. Jackson would ask Lammers to assign uniformed officers to watch Engall round the clock in the meantime. He thought about the officer watching Lori Walker. He still held hope she would be alert soon and able to identify the family's attacker.

As Jackson finished the paperwork, he tried to assess Engall's demeanor during the interrogation. He had been holding back and worried about something, yet his face had shown no dishonesty when he said he'd had a blackout and couldn't remember anything. Was it possible Engall had killed the Walkers during an alcoholic rage and didn't remember it? The suspect hadn't seemed very concerned about Jared's list of infractions. Yet he was involved in this mess somehow, Jackson was certain. He would have to explore Engall's connections. For example, did Roy Engall know Jared's brother-in-law, Kevin Compton, who'd been assaulted at the Time Out Tavern where Engall liked to drink?

Had Jared been blackmailing more than one person? Did he have something on his brother-in-law too? Jackson reached in his desk for some aspirin and checked the clock: 9:12. Why did he feel so damn tired already? He pushed himself to finish the paperwork, then grabbed the evidence bags with the family's cell phones. He started on Jared's first.

He found the *Recent Calls* menu, then scrolled through the *Sent Calls* option, which held the last twenty calls Jared had made. Most were to his wife and kids, two were to the Employment Division, and three had no ID available. Jackson entered the numbers in the Lane County database and came up with three businesses: Caldwell Construction, Olive Garden, and Umpqua Credit Union. Just a man looking for work. He would call each business to ask about Jared's contact, but he didn't expect much. He would have to wait for the cell-phone records to see if and when Jared Walker had called Roy Engall. Maybe Jared hadn't called his ex-boss at all. Maybe he'd made the blackmail threat in person.

The *Received Calls* menu showed more of the same, mostly calls from Carla. At the end of the list was a call from Kevin Compton, made Friday at 5:32 p.m., two days before Jared was murdered. Jackson made a note, curious to see if Kevin would mention the call when he questioned him tomorrow. The call seemed a little unusual. In Jackson's world, brothers-in-law didn't chat on the phone. They saw each other at family gatherings and made small talk three times a year.

As he slid Carla's cell phone from its evidence bag, his own phone rang, startling him. "This is Alisha. I'm the nurse you talked to earlier. I found Lori Engall's cell phone in the ER. You should come get it now. She's starting to regain consciousness."

CHAPTER 7

Monday, June 1, 9:55 p.m.

Northwest McKenzie was still operating downtown near the University of Oregon, but construction had been completed on a new hospital at the edge of Springfield near the McKenzie River. Most of the staff would make the move later that summer. The massive new complex was in a wide river plain, not far from the newspaper's new home on the Eugene side of the boundary. Jackson was sad to see the major institutions leave the heart of Eugene. The city was losing its core.

Because it was late, he found a space in the small parking lot next to the hospital. He tried to hurry inside, but his legs felt tired and his scar hurt. The receptionist in the middle of the huge lobby told him Lori Walker was on the third floor in the critical-care unit. He took the elevator and in a few minutes was pleased to see a patrol officer sitting in the waiting room outside critical care.

"Anything to report?"

"No, sir. Only her aunt has been here to see her. She's in there now. Room 317."

Jackson pushed through the double swinging doors, then entered the quiet corridor lined with rooms where people were trying not to die. The smell of disinfectant hung heavy in the air. He spotted Rita Altman sleeping in a chair in a room midway down. Next to her, Lori was covered to her neck by a white blanket, her eyes closed and a tube running out of her nose. Both arms held IV lines. The pale teenager did not look as if she were regaining consciousness. Under any other circumstances, he would have walked away and let her rest. But this girl might know the identity of a homicidal maniac. Jackson eased close to her bed. "Lori, can you hear me?"

Her lips moved in the smallest response.

"Lori, I need you to wake up for a minute. I need to ask some questions."

Her eyes stayed closed and her lips were still.

"Detective Jackson?" A nurse in yellow scrubs had come into the room behind him.

"Are you Alisha?"

She smiled and motioned with her head that he should follow. "I have her phone in a bag at the nurses' station."

Jackson walked with her down the hall. "Do the doctors think Lori will pull through this?"

"They're optimistic. The knife missed her celiac artery, so her blood loss was slow, which is why she survived at all. There is some concern she may have suffered brain damage."

"Has she spoken yet?"

"Not really. She mumbled a little when her eyes were open earlier. That's when I called you." They reached the desk, and she retrieved the cell phone from a zipped plastic bag.

"What about her clothes?"

She grimaced. "They were cut from her body in the ER, then discarded with the medical supplies used during her revival."

Jackson hated the loss of trace evidence, but with three other victims in the morgue, he hoped he wouldn't need anything from Lori but her testimony. "When she regains consciousness again, please have the officer in the lobby take a statement from Lori. It's very important and I may not be able to get here quickly enough."

"I'm going off duty soon, but I'll let my replacement know."

Jackson started in the direction of the swinging doors, then changed his mind. He turned and headed back to Lori's room. He might as well try again while he was here.

Her aunt woke up when Jackson came into the room. "Hello, Ms. Altman."

She pushed her hair out of her eyes. "Lori's still not awake, but the doctors think she'll make it."

"I'm happy to hear that. Has she spoken to you at all?"

"She woke up and mumbled something an hour ago. It gave my heart such a lift."

"I'd like to ask you some questions."

Rita braced herself. "Okay."

"Does Carla have any other relatives in town?"

"Our parents live in Veneta."

"Did Carla ever say anything to you about blackmail?"

"What?" Rita scowled. "Why would anyone blackmail the Walkers?"

"Was Carla having an affair?"

Rita made a scoffing noise. "Not a chance. Carla loved Jared, no matter what he did."

Jackson heard the implication. "What did Jared do?"

"Nothing serious," Rita said quickly. "He's just never been good with money."

"Had Carla seemed different or worried about anything?"

"She was worried about being evicted." Rita started to get teary eyed. Jackson gave her a minute.

In the quiet, Lori made a moaning sound.

"Lori?"

She didn't respond.

Jackson gently picked up the girl's hand and stroked the back, being careful of the IV line. "Lori, can you open your eyes?"

She rolled her head as if to say no. Jackson couldn't believe this girl was eighteen. Her blonde eyelashes and pale skin with a sprinkling of freckles made her seem younger. "I need to ask you some questions. Just a few, then you can rest again." Her eyes came open, made direct contact with him, then closed again. "Lori, I need to know who did this to you."

Her mouth tried to form a word.

"Who did this to you, Lori?"

A small "shhh" sound came from her lips.

Jackson leaned closer. "Who did this? Say it again, please."

"Shane."

CHAPTER 8

Tuesday, June 2, 12:08 a.m.

Jackson pulled into Kera's driveway and cut his headlights and engine. The house was dark and he hoped everyone was sleeping. Except Kera. If she woke up when he climbed into bed, it could turn out well. He was exhausted but he would find the energy for sex. For weeks after his surgery, he'd been in too much pain. With all the young people in the house, they'd had to be sneaky and look for opportunities to be alone. Their relationship was still in the honeymoon phase and he wanted her all the time, but their family members were always present. Sometimes he resented all of them—Katie, Danette, and little Micah—for their intrusion into his intimacy with Kera. The last few years of his marriage to Renee had been angry and mostly sexless, and he was tired of doing without.

Jackson hurried though the big house, guided by the night-light in the hall. In the kitchen he made himself half a peanut-butter-and-grape-jelly sandwich and washed it down with a diet Dr Pepper. It was Kera's preferred soda and he'd come to like it too.

As he stood at the sink, Kera slipped into the room and into his arms. He kissed her neck and breathed in the sweet melon scent of her body wash. Now he felt like he was home. "I've missed you." She responded with her lips on his. Jackson loved Kera's tall, strong body, her long copper hair, and her exotic face with its prominent cheekbones. Most of all, he loved her full generous lips.

The baby began to cry. Kera stiffened and pulled back.

"Danette will take care of him." Jackson drew her to him again, but Kera resisted.

"Sometimes Danette's slow to wake up."

"Micah will be fine. Let's go to bed."

Neither moved. Danette was still struggling with postpartum depression and posttraumatic shock, and the prescriptions she took made her a heavy sleeper. Jackson tried to cut Danette a lot of slack. First her boyfriend had been killed in Iraq, then she'd been left pregnant and alone. While struggling with a newborn baby, Danette had been kidnapped and nearly sold into sexual slavery. After her ordeal, Kera had taken her in and Danette was recovering, but slowly.

The crying grew louder and Kera hurried away. Jackson sighed and went to bed.

The alarm went off at five thirty and Jackson bolted out of bed. His head pounded and his abdomen burned with pain as he rushed for the bathroom. After swallowing his prednisone, he slipped the pill bottle into his shoulder bag, deciding to keep the medication with him. In the shower, he alternated between hot and cool water, trying to clear his head after three hours' sleep. By the time he dressed, strapped on his weapon, and hurried into the kitchen, Kera and Katie were already there.

"What are you doing up so early?" he said, kissing his daughter's forehead. Still in her pajamas, Katie had one hand on the open refrigerator door. Her dark curly hair was tangled from sleep and she seemed to be losing weight again. Kera, wearing workout clothes, made coffee and smiled at him.

"We have a graduation-planning session before school this morning." Katie pulled out a carton of eggs and set it on the counter.

"Do you need a ride?" Jackson poured himself a cup of coffee.

"Emily is picking me up."

"Emily doesn't drive."

"I mean Emily's brother Jason is taking us."

Jackson chose his words carefully. "Have I met him?"

Katie let out a sigh. "I thought we were past that."

Last fall, Katie had been involved with a group of kids who had some very adult ideas. Two of the girls had ended up dead, and one was pregnant when she died. Jackson had watched his daughter more closely ever since. "You can't get into a car with a boy I haven't met."

"That's ridiculous! I'm almost in high school."

"All the more reason for me to know the people you hang out with."

"Fine," she snapped. "Come out and meet him when they get here at seven."

"I'll be at the department by then. Sorry." Jackson had driven Katie to school since they'd been staying with Kera, but he needed to start work earlier today.

"I'll take her," Kera offered. "First I'll make scrambled eggs. Who wants some?"

"Not me." Katie left in a huff.

Kera gave Jackson a gentle smile. "It may be time to ease up a little. Jason is important to her and she's earned some trust."

"I don't think so." Jackson poured his coffee into a travel mug.

"Are you staying for breakfast?" Kera asked. In the back of the house the baby let out a wail.

He shook his head. "I have to get going. Three people are dead, and I still have no idea why."

Kera looked a little hurt. "Good luck with your case."

He gave her a quick kiss, grabbed his shoulder bag, and got out of there. Once he was in the car, he felt a little guilty. Kera had been wonderful to him, especially the first few weeks after his surgery. She'd also welcomed Katie with open arms. Yet they had different ideas about how to raise kids. Kera's openness about sexuality was great for him and it suited her well as a Planned Parenthood employee, but he wasn't sure it was good for his daughter.

Hell, he didn't know what to think. A boy would have been so much easier.

At such an early hour, the violent crimes area was empty, and Jackson was glad for the quiet. He sipped his coffee while he examined the contents of Carla Walker's purse. The blue denim bag had an ink stain near the bottom and the strap was frayed on the edges. Jackson dumped out the contents and decided Carla was the kind of woman you'd like to sit next to on a long bus ride. She carried a little pack of tissues, a penlight, a notepad and three pens, a small book of crossword puzzles, aspirin, Rolaids, spearmint gum, earplugs, and reading glasses.

In a zipped pocket, he found her wallet and checkbook. Jackson opened the notebook with a small hope Carla had left him a clue. Instead he found a short grocery list; a reminder, *iron good blue blouse for interview*; and a collection of names, addresses, and phone numbers scribbled hastily on various pages.

One entry caught his eye: *Dr. Dubois.* Jackson thought he'd heard the name but couldn't remember when or where. He keyed it into his Word file and kept going. He would look up the doctor later. He had an autopsy to attend an hour from now, then a task-force meeting right afterward. He wanted to examine all these personal items before he met with the other detectives.

Jackson picked up Carla's wallet. She had eighteen dollars in the cash pocket, a single credit card, and a fat stack of coupons and receipts. Jackson added a reminder at the top of his file: *Check Walkers' bank accounts for unusual activity.* He flipped through Carla's receipts. Nothing interesting until he came to one for Westside Buyers, a pawnshop on Highway 99. The amount was $1,700 and the date was April 25. What had Carla sold for that amount of money? Had she cashed in a piece of jewelry to get them through a tough financial spot?

Jackson added the pawnshop to his list of things to check out, packed Carla's things back in her purse, and started on Lori's red backpack.

At a quarter to eight, Sergeant Lammers burst into his space. "Good, you're here. We need to talk." She kept moving, right past his desk, a wall of muscle and political ambition that could not be ignored or denied. Jackson followed her down the hall.

"The media is reporting these homicides as a home invasion," she said as they entered her office. "We're swamped with calls from hysterical citizens. Tell me you've got a suspect." Lammers motioned for him to sit.

"I have two suspects, both with personal motives. Roy Engall, the dead man's ex-boss, was being blackmailed by the dead man, and Shane Compton, his nephew, is a former drug addict."

"What's his motivation?"

"I don't know yet." Jackson pulled his shoulders back and tried to feel confident.

"Was he a meth user?"

"I assumed so, but I'm not certain."

"Is Shane Compton in custody?"

"Not yet. We're looking for him."

"What about the other one? Engall?" Lammers tapped her pencil.

"We have him under surveillance."

"You think he killed the whole family because someone was blackmailing him?" She was as skeptical as Evans.

"I don't know yet. It's only been twenty-four hours."

"It's weak, Jackson. All of it. I want someone in custody before the day is over. If it turns out to be the assholes who are doing these carjackings, you can have your pick of assignments for a year."

"I'll do what I can." Jackson left, thinking he had a better chance of winning the lottery than bringing in the carjackers in connection with this case. He laughed at the notion that picking his assignments was some kind of reward. He would always choose cases like this.

Jackson hurried into the downtown hospital for the second time in twelve hours. Autopsies, or "posts," as the new pathologist called them, were conducted in the basement in a small room called Surgery Ten. It was only his fifth postmortem in this convenient location. Until recently he'd had to travel to Portland for autopsies, taking up a good part of the day. Lane County had finally hired its own pathologist, Rudolph Konrad, and Jackson was still developing a working relationship with him.

"You're on time. I appreciate it." Konrad gave him what counted for a smile. Jackson had seen the man's résumé and he knew the pathologist was at least forty, but he looked younger.

It must be the thick blond hair and chubby cheeks, Jackson thought as they shook hands.

The medical examiner came in behind him, and the dingy basement room felt even smaller. One wall was taken up by a bank of huge stainless-steel drawers and a hint of rubbing alcohol hung over everything. "We started with the woman because of her extreme blood loss," Gunderson said, pulling on a gown. Jackson suited up as well, including booties.

"Do you plan to attend all three family members' posts?" Konrad asked, then continued without waiting for an answer. "I ask because there may not be much to discover during the autopsies themselves."

"I like to see the trace evidence even if the cause of death is obvious."

"We'll get started."

Konrad pulled back the white covering, and there was the hand in its own little plastic bag, resting innocently on Carla Walker's pale stomach. The toast and coffee in his stomach roiled at the sight. "Can we do the hand first, then put it away?"

"Is it creeping you out?" Gunderson, all in black, seemed mildly amused.

"A little."

Konrad reached for the appendage. "The only other case I've seen like this was a high-school boy who drowned after losing a foot in the propeller when he fell out of his boat. The foot was still hanging by some skin when they pulled him out of the water. The ME at the scene detached it for safekeeping."

Jackson wanted to tell him to shut the hell up. Instead he nodded as though it were an interesting tidbit. The last thing he needed was a rumor spreading through the department that he was squeamish about severed appendages. For some of his coworkers, practical jokes would be impossible to resist.

"I believe her heart was still pumping when the hand was severed," Konrad said in his flat voice. "But not at full capacity. The single blow to her head probably knocked her out, but didn't kill her. The bat found at the scene is the most likely weapon."

"Are there defense wounds on her hands?"

"There are none on this one." Konrad held Carla's left hand under a bright table light and began taking scrapings from under the nails. "I don't see any obvious trace evidence either."

"Was the hand severed with the same knife that killed the boy?"

Gunderson spoke up. "It seems very likely. The wounds are all consistent with that weapon, but we won't know for sure until we do the boy's post tomorrow."

Jackson had learned to live with the vagueness of autopsies. Very little was ever completely conclusive, except when things didn't match up.

Konrad took his time conducting an inch-by-inch search of Carla's body. He noted the sprinkling of moles on her shoulders and the uneven sizes of her breasts. The reddish-purple livor mortis on the back side of her body indicated she'd lain face up since her heart stopped, and had not been moved.

The internal examination was longer and slower. After forty minutes, Jackson felt jumpy and ready to get out. He'd learned almost nothing except that Carla had a significant scar on the inside of her lower right thigh. Konrad guessed it had been made by a barbed-wire fence long ago. The pathologist had opened Carla's body cavity and examined her organs, which revealed a healthy woman with no obvious disease or damage.

"This is surprising," Konrad said, without sounding surprised. He had both hands in her lower abdomen.

Jackson waited.

"Her uterus is enlarged and I think she was pregnant."

CHAPTER 9

Six weeks earlier

Carla woke up in a good mood. Sunlight slanted through the blinds, and a light breeze delivered the smell of morning dew. She loved this time of year, when the world seemed fresh and bright again. She threw back the covers, put her feet on the floor, and pushed out of bed ready to start the day. She promptly felt nauseated and bolted for the bathroom.

What the hell was that about? Carla wondered after upchucking what little was in her stomach. Feeling slightly better, she padded into the kitchen to make coffee, thinking she would let Jared sleep in. He'd been getting up for work at the crack of dawn since they'd been married and he deserved a break.

Not much of one though. He had to find a new job immediately. The seven hundred dollars they had in savings would be gone in a month, without his paycheck coming in. Carla pushed the worry away. She couldn't change reality by making herself sick over it. They would survive this. In fact, if Jared ended up with a job requiring him to pay into Social Security and unemployment, they'd be better off in the long run.

The coffee didn't sit well in her stomach. She dumped the rest, then showered and dressed for work. Carla heard Lori's radio playing softly and knew her daughter was getting ready. Thank god one of her kids liked to get up early and work hard in school. She was proud of her daughter for holding down a waitress job during her whole senior year as well. She couldn't believe Lori was graduating from high school in a month. Where had the years gone?

She opened Nick's door. His alarm blared and he slept right through it. "Nick!" She shook his shoulders. He sat up, slammed off the alarm, then grinned at her. "I'm up."

"I'm going to work early. Don't forget to turn in your homework. Love you."

Carla heard the shower running in the hall bathroom, said good-bye to Lori through the door, and headed out. As she reached her car, Shane pulled up in his small white Toyota truck.

"Morning, Carla."

"Hey, Shane. You're a little early. No one's ready for school yet."

"No problem. I'll make sure Nick doesn't go back to bed."

"Thanks."

Carla watched him lope up to the house. Since Shane had been laid off, he'd had more free time and was taking the kids to school and bringing Lori home from softball practice. Carla appreciated the help and couldn't wait until Lori could afford the used car she was saving for.

Carla hopped in the Subaru, and as the engine roared to life, she said a little thank-you to God or whoever was in charge. The last thing they needed was car trouble, but so far the Subaru had been very faithful. Carla kept coming back to the idea they should sell the truck, but she hadn't said anything to Jared. He was so down about being unemployed, she couldn't kick him with that reality yet.

Silver Moon Jewelry had expanded soon after she started, and the new work site was bigger and nicer, but she wasn't crazy about the location off West Eleventh. Not that it mattered, Carla reminded herself, as she hurried into the long narrow building. This was her dream job. She was designing jewelry! She had never been this happy.

Two years earlier, the *Willamette News* had laid her off after fifteen years of selling classified ads for them. Craigslist had cut the paper's classified business in half and Carla, having been there the longest, was the highest paid and the first to go. The loss of income and security had knocked her off her feet for a few days, but by the end of that week she'd started to feel liberated. Nobody enjoyed selling classifieds. Good grief. Every day had been a challenge to get through, but she'd stayed because of the health-insurance benefits for her family.

Carla said good morning to the receptionist and trotted up the stairs to her shared office with a big window overlooking a little canal. She loved this space and this job. She'd started out in sales because that's what her résumé said she could do. She had targeted this business specifically because it designed and manu-factured beautiful jewelry. Long ago, Carla had wanted to attend college and major in art. Instead, she'd gotten pregnant with Lori her senior year in high school and everything had changed. She had tried to bury that part of herself because it wasn't practical. The layoff had opened the door just a crack and Carla found a way to push through it.

She sat down at her desk, still excited by the huge monitor they'd given her two months ago when she shifted to full-time designing. Her office partner wasn't in yet and Carla had a few moments to herself. She pulled off her sweater and opened her e-mail. The top message was highlighted in red, meaning priority. Carla opened it, scowled a little. Helen wanted to see her right away. Could she make herself a cup of tea first?

She decided against it, grabbed a notepad and pen, and hurried down the hall to the owner's corner office. Did they have a new big order? Was there a problem with one of her designs? Sometimes manufacturing challenges forced the designers to make changes.

"Hi, Helen. You wanted to see me?"

"Yes. Close the door, please." Helen, wearing her usual velour jacket and yoga pants, smiled tightly, then set her face in expressionless mode.

Carla's stomach lurched. Closed door? What did it mean?

"Carla, I have some bad news. We lost the Lacey account, which means we lost half of our business, just like that." Helen snapped her fingers. "It's the damn economy. Everyone is cutting back, tightening their expenses." Helen averted her eyes and bit her lip. "This is very difficult for me to say, but I have to let you go. I'm cutting five people in production too."

Too stunned to speak, Carla sat unmoving. *This can't be happening. We can't both lose our jobs.*

"I'm sorry." Helen's expression pleaded with her to understand.

"Do you think it's temporary?" Carla's voice felt weird, as if the words were getting stuck in her dry throat. She should have made the damn tea.

"I don't know. Either way I have to cut payroll immediately to stay in business. This isn't personal; you just happen to be the newest designer."

"Can I go back to sales?"

"I'm cutting someone in sales too."

Tears built up and Carla fought for control. "Jared was laid off recently too, you know."

"Oh shit." Helen looked like she might cry too. "I'm so sorry."

Carla wondered if she was meant to go home right now. She couldn't bring herself to ask. "I'll clear out my personal files, then get out of here."

"Take your time. Everyone will want to say good-bye." Helen blew her nose as Carla walked away. Tears burst from their wells and she hurried into the bathroom to cry in private. For a few minutes she let herself sob, without thinking, without recriminations. When it was out of her system she repaired her makeup as best she could and began to plan. She could find a job in sales. There were always sales jobs. She had to be employed or the kids wouldn't have health insurance. First she would file for unemployment. How much of a weekly check would she get?

Before she made it out of the bathroom, her stomach revolted and she was once again hanging over the toilet. Rinsing the sour taste from her mouth, Carla wondered if she had a flu bug. Or was she getting an ulcer? Teenagers could do that to you. Lori had been especially moody lately, and with Jared laid off, Carla had been worrying herself into a frenzy.

Still, it was unlike her to vomit. She couldn't remember the last time she'd thrown up. Carla headed for the door, then stopped dead in her tracks. Oh shit. She'd just remembered the last time she'd lost her breakfast. Fifteen years ago, about seven months before Nick was born. *No!* This couldn't be happening. Her doctor had assured her the IUD was effective. She'd reluctantly gone off the pill after fifteen years because her doctor was worried about the long-term effects on her health.

She was thirty-six, for christ's sake! And unemployed. No longer needed in the building. Pregnancy was not an option.

Being the kind of person who rips off a band-aid rather than peel it slowly, Carla strode to her desk and made short work of deleting personal e-mails and files. She grabbed a box from the mailing room, packed her Christmas cactus and family photos, and marched out of the building, head held high. She smiled and waved but didn't stop for hugs. She was done crying—and puking—for the day.

Two nights later, Carla took a lasagna out of the oven and calculated it had cost her twelve dollars to make. They were headed over to Tracy and Kevin's for a potluck dinner and she had to bring something nice. Jared had wanted to buy steaks, but she'd vetoed the idea. Her unemployment check would be $310 a week. After paying rent they'd have $400 left for everything else. She couldn't even buy groceries for a month with that paltry sum. Twice Carla had picked up the phone to call her mother, then set it back down. Her parents lived on Social Security in a two-bedroom trailer in Veneta. She couldn't ask them for anything.

Lori came into the kitchen and hugged her from behind. "Smells great, Mom."

"Thanks. I used real Italian sausage like everyone likes."

"I wanted to remind you I'm going to the WOW Hall after dinner to see a show. I'd like to take the Subaru."

"You can. Lori, I have to talk to you about something."

Her daughter crossed her arms but she didn't roll her eyes. Carla was grateful. Lori had never treated her with contempt the way some teens did with their parents.

Carla sat down at the kitchen table, which they'd stained and assembled themselves, and waited for Lori to do the same. "I know the money you make at Appleton's is yours. You work hard for it and you're entitled to spend it how you like. However, this family is in a bad situation, and if it gets much worse we could get evicted."

"That's not right."

"Still, that is how it works. If we get behind on the rent they'll kick us out."

"What are you saying? I have to give you my paychecks?" Lori's sweet angel face twisted with disbelief.

Carla wanted to crawl in a hole and die rather than continue the conversation. Yet she plunged ahead. "You don't have to hand them over but I'm asking you not to spend them. Just stick the checks in the bank in case we need to borrow money for rent down the road."

"You said *borrow*. You and Dad will pay me back?"

"Of course. This situation is temporary. Your dad had an interview this afternoon, and I'm optimistic about it. I'm just asking you not to buy any more concert tickets or clothes. Put your money in the bank, please."

"Okay." Lori stood. "I don't understand how economies work or why this is happening. We've been talking about it in civics class but it's too weird for me."

"Me too, sweetie."

"Are you okay, Mom? You don't hum anymore. It used to drive me crazy but now I think I miss it."

"I'm fine. We'll get through this."

"Jared, did you decide?" Carla glanced in the backseat at Nick, who still had his earphones in, listening to music. They were headed across town to have dinner with Jared's sister, who lived in the south hills near Churchill High School. The neighborhood had been considered upscale until all the huge houses on Timberline and Skyridge had been built, leaving those below feeling a little more working class. Carla had given up hope of owning a home long ago and now she was glad for it. Being evicted as a renter was less heartbreaking than losing your home to the bank.

Jared reached over and squeezed her hand. "Stop worrying. I'll ask Tracy. She'll tell me she has to talk to Kevin, but it'll be okay. They'll loan us some money."

"How did your interview go today?"

"The guy kept throwing around cooking terms I didn't understand. How can you pay someone eight fifty an hour and expect them to have chef training?"

"It's a different world now. People are educating themselves online, and employers expect a lot more for their money." Carla bit her lip, then said it anyway. "You should take some internet classes at the employment office. I think it would help."

Jared sighed and didn't look at her. "I know you're right, but it makes me feel stupid to have some twenty-year-old kid showing me stuff that seems like a foreign language and then acting like it's nothing."

"I know what you mean." Carla looked up to see they'd missed their turn. "We just passed City View."

Jared gave her a sad smile. "Some things never change."

They'd eaten outside on the big deck with the pond and mini-waterfall providing a soothing background. Now they were drinking beer, eating homemade apple pie, and enjoying the sunset. Carla loved this backyard, at least to visit every once in a while. She wouldn't want the pond in her own yard. It would be too much work and too much money, but she loved sitting here on an early summer evening.

After the kids went into the house to check out Shane's new CD and Kevin went to the kitchen for more beer, Jared announced, "We're in trouble, Tracy. We're hoping you and Kevin can loan us some money."

"How much money?" Tracy tried to sound casual, but she didn't pull it off. She was the polar opposite of Jared: short, dark, and tense. But like Jared, she had a good heart.

"Two thousand. Just enough to pay the rent for a couple months while I look for work." Jared took a long slug of beer. Carla noticed he'd been drinking more than usual, but she understood.

"I'll have to discuss it with Kevin. His business hasn't been great lately either." Kevin owned Pacific Pool & Patio, and Carla could imagine that people were spending less money on backyard luxuries.

"My business has plummeted in the last two months," Kevin said, coming out of the sliding-glass door. "So if you're thinking of asking us for money, please don't. I have employees and health-insurance premiums to pay no matter how few hot tubs I sell."

A long moment of silence followed. Carla ached for Jared. She could feel his humiliation and she wished she hadn't pushed him to make the request. "I'm sorry to hear your business is down," she said to Kevin, giving him an appropriate look of sympathy. "I hope it's temporary."

Jared asked about a basketball game coming up and Carla excused herself. Someone was in the hall bathroom, so she rushed through the master bedroom and into the private bathroom, closing the door behind her. She needed to be alone for a moment. Sitting on the edge of the tub, she pulled in long, slow breaths and tried not to cry. Unemployed, broke, and pregnant. How could her life have turned to such shit so quickly?

Without a job she didn't even have health insurance. She couldn't afford to see an obstetrician, let alone a hospital stay. She had to get an abortion. As much as the idea appalled her, she had no choice. By the end of the summer they could be living out of a van parked on some side street. She couldn't bring a child into such circumstances. She couldn't even take care of the kids she had now. How would she pay for an abortion? It would take every dime they had in the bank. Then what?

Carla took more deep breaths and willed herself to go back out there, smile, and pretend everything was okay. As she crossed the plush-carpeted bedroom, the top shelf of a small bookcase caught her eye. Five baseball cards, each encased in a plastic frame, were proudly displayed. Valuable baseball cards. She'd heard Kevin talking about them. One in particular was worth several thousand dollars. Carla peered at the cards. They seemed rather inconsequential.

Without thinking she grabbed the card in the middle, stuffed it into her purse, and bolted from the bedroom. Her legs trembled and threatened to collapse as she hurried up the hall. Good god, what had she done? She hadn't even formed an idea about stealing the card. It just happened.

Carla stopped in the hallway. She had to put the card back. This was insane.

"Carla? We've got to go!" Jared called to her from the dining room. "I'll get the kids while you say good-bye."

Carla stood frozen. Their hosts followed Jared into the house. As her husband barreled down the hall calling for the kids, Tracy gave Carla a hug and whispered, "I'm sorry." Carla squeezed her back, unable to speak.

CHAPTER 10

Jackson bought coffee on his way back to headquarters, then sat in the small conference room waiting for the other detectives to show up at ten. He expected the task-force meeting to be brief, unless someone came in with something unexpected.

Evans showed up first, looking fresh in pressed black slacks and a pale-blue jacket. Her face had no visible signs of sleep deprivation. "Morning, Evans. You look great. Still taking that buzz drug when you work cases like this?"

She flushed a little and rolled her eyes. "Provigil isn't a buzz drug. You're just jealous because I have a prescription and you don't." She sat and put her oversize black bag on the floor. "Now that you're seeing a doctor, you could ask him to write you a prescription."

That reminded Jackson to take some naproxen. "Excuse me for a moment," he said, getting up.

He hustled into the restroom at the end of the hall and dug the little pill bottle out of his bag. The steroids he'd taken earlier controlled the growth of the fibrosis, and he would cycle on and off the medication, probably for years. The naproxen was an anti-inflammatory that suppressed the pain he was still feeling from having his belly flayed open like a fish and his plumbing rerouted. He swallowed the tablet with a mouthful of water from the sink and headed back to the conference room. Before his diagnosis, he might have taken aspirin in front of his coworkers, but now that he had this RF thing he couldn't let anyone see him take any medication. It would just remind them that he was less than vigorously healthy. In the world of law enforcement, a perception of vulnerability could derail your career. Jackson worried about the prednisone. One of the side effects was mood swings and/or depression, but he hadn't experienced either yet.

Schak and Quince had come in and were still standing, sipping tall coffees and talking about a TV show they'd both missed the night before. When McCray showed up a few minutes later, they all sat and pulled out notepads.

"What's that smell?" Schak said. "It's fruity or something." He turned to McCray, whose under-eye bags were especially puffy this morning.

"It's herbal tea." McCray's voice projected false confidence.

"Tea? Since when?" Schak asked.

"I quit coffee about a week ago. It was ruining my sleep. My tossing and turning was keeping the wife awake too. I miss it but I feel a hell of a lot better."

"You look like shit."

"Thanks."

"Let's get started," Jackson said. "Schak, your turn to take the board. You might as well go first and tell us what you've learned."

"Not a damned thing." Under Carla's name, Schak wrote *well liked*. "Carla Walker was respected by everyone at Silver Moon Jewelry where she worked. She has no enemies and no secrets I can find."

"She was pregnant," Jackson announced.

"No shit?" Schak turned and stared. "The autopsy?"

"The pathologist says six to eight weeks."

Victor Slonecker rushed into the room. "Who's pregnant?" The district attorney put his briefcase on the floor and tugged up the pant legs of his pinstriped suit before sitting down. His dark hair was perfectly groomed and his sharp features made him look intelligent and intimidating. He delivered on the promise.

"Carla Walker, one of the murder victims," Jackson answered. "Thanks for coming." The DA, or sometimes an assistant DA, sat in on at least one task-force meeting at the beginning of each case.

Schak wrote *pregnant*, then said, "I wonder if Carla knew."

"Could the baby have any bearing on the case?" Evans interjected. "A secret lover who killed Carla when he found out she was pregnant?"

Schak shook his head. "It seems unlikely. Everyone says Carla and Jared were very happy together, still in love after eighteen years of marriage."

The room was quiet for moment.

"How sad," Evans said, voicing what they were all thinking. "I found out a few things about Lori, but none of them seem critical."

"Let's put it all on the board anyway."

"Her friend Jenna Larson says Lori's been stressed lately because her parents lost their jobs, and she's been giving them her tip money. More important, the manager at the restaurant where Lori works has been sexually harassing her. I'm going over there to see him right after this meeting."

"What's his name?" Slonecker asked, pulling out a notepad.

"Greg Blackwell."

Jackson hoped the DA would follow through. Assholes like Blackwell who harassed teenage girls in the workplace pissed him off. His daughter, Katie, might soon be one of those employees. Jackson handed over Lori's cell phone, still in its plastic bag. "I picked this up from the hospital last night but I haven't had a chance to look at it. It'll be interesting to see if her boss was calling Lori or leaving messages."

"Was she conscious? Did you get anything from her?" Evans sounded as fresh and eager as she looked.

"Lori was partially awake, and I asked her who had done this to her. She clearly said 'Shane.'"

Slonecker's eyes lit up. "Who is Shane?"

"The cousin with a drug problem," Evans responded. "I knew it."

"Hold on," Schak said. "Let me catch up." His writing had started out messy and was getting nearly illegible.

"I assume that's who she meant. Did any of you ask about Shane? Do we have any clue where he is?"

Quince leaned forward. "I spoke with Jared's sister, Tracy, last night. She's Shane's mother and she hasn't seen him for days. She says it's typical though. He often stays with his friends and only crashes with them when he has to."

"Did you get the friends' names?"

"I asked but Tracy wasn't forthcoming. I sensed she was protecting her son." Quince scowled. "I also asked about his drug problem and she said it was all in the past. Then she promptly hung up on me."

"Did you run a background?"

"Of course. He had two known associates from previous arrests. Tyler Gorlock and Jeff McIntyre. McIntyre is in the state prison in Salem, but Gorlock lives in a trailer in Springfield. I was out there this morning and no one was home. Or they were hiding."

"Get a search warrant," Jackson said. "Now that Lori has named Shane as the killer, we should be able to search any home he's known to reside in."

"I'll have an assistant write it up," Slonecker offered. "Maybe Trang will even get it signed for you if he has time."

McCray spoke up for the first time. "You said Lori was only partially conscious. If she doesn't pull through to testify, a defense attorney will shred her statement."

"True enough, but it gives us leverage with a judge for now." Jackson took a long drink of his lukewarm coffee. "What did you find out about Jared?"

"I've talked with two of his coworkers so far. They said he was always upbeat and friendly." McCray glanced at his notes. "When I asked about Jared blackmailing their boss, they seemed stunned by the idea."

"What do they think of Roy Engall?"

"They like him too. One complained about working for the same wages for three years, but neither mentioned any problems."

"They want to stay employed," Evans commented, making a face.

"Have you talked to Jared's sister?" Jackson turned to McCray.

"She's not answering her phone."

"Find Tracy, wherever she is. Ask her about Jared's blackmail and about the attack on her husband last month. Pressure her if you have to. I think Tracy Compton has key information." Jackson stuffed his notes into his bag. "I'll track down Kevin Compton and see what he has to say. Our other priority is finding their son Shane. If he's using meth and it caused him to lash out violently at his family, then he's an extreme danger to others as well." Jackson stood, ready to get moving.

"You think it was Shane who attacked his father in the parking lot?" McCray got up too. "That would explain why Kevin Compton didn't want to press charges."

"It's a working theory. Nothing else about this case makes sense."

As they headed out Slonecker asked, "What about Roy Engall?"

"We have detectives from vice watching him round the clock. That reminds me. Evans, will you take this warrant to a judge? Let's bring in every pair of shoes Engall owns and get the crime lab to compare them to the bloody footprints in the foyer."

"I'm on it."

On his way to the underground parking lot, Jackson called Katie, knowing she would soon be out of class, and left a message: "Want to have lunch with Dad today? I'll buy waffles and bring them to the school. We'll eat in my car. Call me."

Katie called back while he was pulling up to a little restaurant called Off the Waffle, where two bushy-haired Israeli brothers made the best waffles he'd ever eaten. Jackson doubled his order and added bacon—surprisingly recommended by the young owner—then headed south. Seeing his daughter would set him back thirty minutes, but it was worth it. Now that she was a teenager and feeling more independent, it seemed critical to stay present in her life, even for short periods of time when he was working homicides.

He eased into his usual place at the end of the parking lot and saw Katie waiting for him under the oak tree. She wore shorts and a tank top, which seemed inappropriate for school, but it was June and Jackson had learned to pick his battles. As long as she didn't dress like a hooker, he didn't comment on her clothes. She was still a little too short and thick to get away with the bare-midriff look and he was glad. But he knew all that would change soon.

Katie hopped in the car. "Hey, Dad. Thanks for bringing waffles." She peeked in the bag. "Bacon. Thank you. I'm so tired of eating healthy."

It was a backhanded complaint against Kera, but Jackson sympathized. He was just glad Katie wasn't dieting. Those were not good times. "I only bought these because I'm on a complex homicide and don't have time for anything else."

Katie laughed. "Yeah, I buy that." She pulled out the bacon-and-cheese-stuffed waffles and handed him one. "It's nice to have some time with just us."

"I agree." Jackson reached over and gently touched her dark curly hair. "You got my message yesterday, right? You knew I was working late?"

"Of course." Katie put down her waffle. "I have to ask you something important."

Jackson tensed.

"Mom wants me to spend the summer with her. I was supposed to let her talk to you about it first, but this seemed like a good time to bring it up."

Jackson felt blindsided. "I don't think so." Katie started to argue, but he cut her off. "Hear me out. I think it's reasonable to spend some extended periods of time with her while you're out of school. I'm just not committing to the whole summer."

"What's the big deal? Other kids with divorced parents do this."

"Your mother is still struggling to stay sober. That's why she's taking the anti-anxiety medication. I don't think she's ready for the full-time responsibility."

"I'm not a little kid. I take care of myself." Katie tried to sound offended.

"You're an amazingly self-reliant young woman." Jackson smiled softly. It was true. Katie had matured early because her mother was an unreliable alcoholic and he was a workaholic. Feeling guilty, he said, "Renee and I will talk about it and work something out."

"Can I go stay with Mom while you work this case? Tomorrow's my last day of school anyway."

Jackson finished his waffle. "Okay, but let me talk to Renee first."

Pacific Pool & Patio sat on an ugly stretch of Highway 99, halfway between Eugene and Junction City. Jackson arrived at the low-slung stucco building just before one o'clock and hoped the owner would not be at lunch.

A salesman led him through a crowded showroom filled with hot tubs and pool accessories to a small office in the back. Kevin Compton sat at a cluttered desk and was slow to look up when they entered the room. His lean, muscular body said forty-something, but his thick gray hair made him look older.

"Kevin, a police detective is here to see you."

The man looked up, revealing hazel eyes and a tanned face with no expression. No surprise or concern. "What can I help you with?"

Jackson took a seat on a plastic chair. The salesman shifted on his feet. "I need to be out in the showroom until Ray comes back from lunch."

Kevin nodded. "Go. I'll be fine." The salesman left, looking uncomfortable.

Jackson was confused by their dynamic but he plunged right in. "I'd like to know where you were Sunday night between nine and midnight."

"When my brother-in-law's family was killed?"

"Yes."

"I was home with my wife."

"What about Shane? Do you know where he was?"

"We haven't seen Shane for a few days." Kevin spoke slowly, carefully.

"Do you have any idea where we can find him?"

"Sometimes he stays with Tyler or Damon." Still no expression. Did he use Botox?

"What is Damon's last name?"

Kevin shook his head.

"Do you know where he lives?"

"No.

"How about where Damon works?"

"I think he's at Golden Temple, where they make cereal."

"Who else would Shane stay with? Especially if he was worried?"

Kevin blinked and gave a small shake of his head.

Who was he protecting? Family, of course. "You have an older daughter, correct? Is Shane staying with her?"

"Unlikely."

"Tell me where to find her."

Kevin pulled his cell phone from his shirt pocket, located Lisa's phone number, and read it to Jackson. "She lives on Pleasant Street in Springfield. I don't know the exact address." Kevin's expression never changed, his voice was eerily flat, and his speech was slow.

Jackson realized Kevin had some kind of neurological problem. "Tell me about the assault on you last month at the Time Out Tavern."

"I got drunk and fell down. I hit my head on my SUV. End of story."

"Why don't I believe you?"

Kevin didn't even shrug.

"What did the emergency-room doctor say about your head injury?"

"He said to take it easy for a few days." Discomfort flickered in Kevin's eyes.

Jackson struggled for a diplomatic way to ask if the *fall* had caused brain damage. "Did you recover fully from the injury?" he finally said.

"Not really. What does this have to do with the murders?"

"You tell me."

"What are you getting at?"

"We have an arrest warrant for Shane. If you know where he is and don't tell me, I can arrest you for obstruction of justice."

Kevin's eyes blazed but the rest of his face was immobile. "Shane didn't kill anybody. Just because he has a history of drug use…" His voice trailed off.

Jackson suspected he'd lost his train of thought. Jesus. The poor man. "Do you have any idea who would kill the Walker family?"

"No. The whole thing is too bizarre." Kevin's eyes started to water. "My wife is devastated and Shane must be too. His cousins were like siblings to him."

"I know this is a painful time for you and your family, but I'm trying to find the perpetrators and I have a few more questions."

Kevin took a long, slow breath and stared straight at him.

"Was Jared capable of blackmail?"

"I don't think so. He's not too bright, but he's a good man."

"What do you know about his ex-boss, Roy Engall?"

"Not much, except he pays his employees under the table." Every sentence was a struggle for Kevin.

Jackson felt bad for the man but he had to continue. "How did Jared feel about Roy Engall?"

"Like any boss. He liked him but he got irritated about some things."

"Ever hear of any violence from Roy?"

"No, but he's quite a drinker."

Jackson glanced at his notes. "You called Jared on Friday at 5:32 p.m. What did you talk about?"

Kevin hesitated. "We were planning a family get-together for Lori's graduation. A barbeque."

Jackson didn't believe him. "What else did you talk about?"

"Nothing."

"Does Shane know Roy Engall?"

"They've met, but that's it."

Jackson shifted on the hard chair. Why couldn't he make solid connections here? He knew Kevin was covering for his son but his face was impossible to read. "If you hear from Shane, please call me." Jackson handed him a business card. "The sooner we talk to him and verify his alibi, the sooner we can clear him."

Back in the car, Jackson called Lisa Compton and left her a message asking her to call right away. As he started to dial McCray, his phone rang. *Sophie Speranza.*

Jackson closed his eyes and weighed his options. She would just keep calling and leaving messages if he didn't talk to her now. The TV reporters had long ago given up trying to interview him directly. They called the department's spokesperson and settled for whatever canned statement she made, but they were only looking for a sound bite. Sophie was always after *the story*. As much as she annoyed him, Jackson had come to respect her tenacity. She pursued her newspaper job with the same diligence he pursued his investigations. Sometimes, he grudgingly admitted, she even managed to help him.

He picked up. "Hello, Sophie."

"Hey, Jackson. I'm glad you're back at work. Kera says you're recovering nicely."

Jackson cringed. Sophie had met his girlfriend a few months ago when Kera was looking for her missing daughter-in-law. Now Kera and the reporter were friends. It still made him uncomfortable. "I'm fine. What can I do for you?"

"I assume you're working the mass murder. Do you have suspects?"

"We do."

"Is anyone in custody? Anyone you want to name?"

"Not yet."

"What's your theory? Home invasion gone horribly wrong? Or was it someone who knew the family?"

"It's too early to say, but when I do have information I'll call you." Jackson started to say good-bye but Sophie broke in.

"I heard the mother had one of her hands chopped off. Will you confirm?"

Shit. How did she know? "I can't discuss the victims yet. Other family members are still in shock, and I don't want to add to their grief."

"What does Lori Walker say about what happened?"

"She's still in intensive care and isn't able to talk yet."

"Can you give me anything?"

"We have some viable suspects and we're working round the clock to make an arrest. Meanwhile, the public should be as cautious as ever about locking their doors and watching out for their neighbors. I've got to go now."

"Thanks. Call me with news when you have it."

Jackson hung up and wondered who Sophie was talking to for inside information. It had to stop. For now he put the reporter out of his mind. He would investigate the leak later.

Next he pressed speed dial #7. How much time did he spend in his car on the phone? Jackson wondered. "McCray, have you talked with Tracy Compton yet?"

"I'm headed to the hospital now. Tracy is there visiting Lori." McCray chewed something as he talked. They all ate meals and made calls in their cars. It was the only way to work a case efficiently.

"Lori is conscious?"

"I don't know. I think her aunts are taking turns staying with her."

"I'll meet you there."

"I'm not leaving Lori's room. Someone needs to be here in case she wakes up." Tracy Compton looked as if she hadn't slept, showered, or put on makeup, yet she projected a strength that was bigger than her small-framed body.

"We'll talk here."

McCray hung back near the entrance like someone ready to vanish. Tracy stood up from the only chair in the crowded ICU room, where much of the small space was taken up by medical equipment. The nurse had not looked happy to see the two of them and had suggested they go somewhere else to talk.

"Is this really necessary?" Tracy whispered. "My brother and his wife are dead. My nephew is dead, and my niece may never be the same. I'm not doing well right now either."

"I'm sorry, but it is necessary. We're trying to find the killer."

"What do you want to know?"

Jackson wanted to ask about Shane, but decided to start easy. "Tell me about the assault on your husband last month."

Her slender body retracted as if she'd taken an invisible blow. "There was no assault. He fell."

Tracy kept her face and eyes immobile, and Jackson knew she had just lied to him. "Who are you protecting? Shane?"

"Kevin had too much to drink and stumbled in the parking lot," she insisted. "Why are you asking about this?"

Jackson kept his voice low too, but he wanted Lori to hear them. He wanted her to wake up. "What do the doctors say about Kevin's brain damage?"

Tracy's lower lip quivered. "They say it could be permanent. He starts cognitive therapy next week."

A wave of sympathy washed over Jackson. This poor woman had taken some hard hits and there were more to come. Still, he had a job to do. "Where is Shane?"

Her face tightened and her eyes signaled fear. "I don't know. I haven't seen him in a few days. Why are you asking about Shane?"

"When did you see him last?"

"He went out Thursday morning to look for work and didn't come back."

"Did that worry you?"

"Not at first. He often stays with friends." She glanced over at the girl swaddled in white sheets.

"I want names and addresses."

"Shane has a lot of friends, but I don't know where they live."

"You do know their names."

"He's been hanging out with someone named Damon lately." Tracy's voice pitched higher. "Why are you asking about Shane?"

"Lori named him as the killer."

"No!" Tracy burst into tears. "You heard wrong. Shane did not do this."

"If he has an alibi for the time frame, he needs to come forward and tell us."

Tracy came into his personal space, her voice begging. "Don't railroad my son for this heinous crime just because you're stumped. If Shane's fingerprints are in the house it's because he hung out there with his cousins."

"Is Shane using drugs again?"

"No." She looked away, then spun back. "Get out of here, please. I can't handle this right now."

A low moaning came from the bed. They both pivoted toward Lori, whose eyes were open.

"Lori. You're awake." Tracy gently touched the girl's face.

"Aunt Tracy?" Lori's voice was scratchy and weak.

"I'm here, honey. You're gonna be okay." Tracy fought back tears.

"Why am I in the hospital?" Lori's eyes darted around, frightened and confused.

Tracy glanced at Jackson. He wasn't sure how to respond.

McCray stepped up to the bed. "Something happened at your house on Sunday night. Do you remember it?"

"What do you mean?" Lori squeezed her eyes closed, then opened them again. "Why does my stomach hurt? What happened?"

"You don't remember?" Tracy reached for Lori's hand.

"I was at work," Lori said, her voice a whisper. "Was I in a car accident on the way home?"

CHAPTER 11

Tuesday, June 2, 2:38 p.m.

After they left the hospital, McCray headed for the Golden Temple factory to look for an employee named Damon, and Jackson drove to the Sweet Life Bakery where Shane's sister worked. The yellow-and-purple restaurant was nestled in a little area on the edge of downtown where it butted up against the low-rent Whitaker neighborhood. Lisa Compton worked as a baker in the converted warehouse down the alley. When she'd returned his call, she'd given him instructions on how to find her, and Jackson was glad he didn't have to enter the restaurant where he would be tempted by a display of luscious snacks.

He strode down the alley and entered the bakery. The aroma of spice cake—nutmeg, cinnamon, and other things he couldn't name—filled his senses. Next came images of his mother in the kitchen, wearing an apron and smiling as he trotted in carrying schoolbooks. He didn't let himself think about his parents very often, but ever since his RF diagnosis, they kept surfacing. Now was not a good time though.

A pretty woman in her twenties looked up from one of the giant stainless-steel tables and hurried over. "I'm Lisa Compton. Are you Detective Jackson?"

He shook her outstretched hand, warm from the ovens. Lisa was taller and bigger framed than her mother, but they had the same short dark hair and intense eyes. "Is there somewhere private we can talk?"

"Let's go outside. There's a break table we can sit at."

The day was temperate and cloudy, but Jackson was glad for the fresh air. "I know this will be hard for you, but we have to talk about your family." Jackson took a seat at the rusty metal table.

Lisa lit a cigarette. "You probably think it's weird that I'm at work today, but I can't just sit at home and think about everybody in that house being slaughtered. I have to keep busy."

"Do you know who killed Jared and his family?"

She looked stunned. "Of course not."

"What happened to your father in the parking lot at the tavern? I mean the *real* story." Jackson wanted to keep her off guard. He had a feeling this woman wasn't good at hiding things.

Lisa looked away, stared at her cigarette. "I don't know. My parents won't talk about it."

"Let's go down to headquarters and have this conversation." Jackson stood, prepared to follow through.

"Oh, come on." Lisa held out her hands. "I'm not sure, but I think Dad and Uncle Jared got into a fight. My mother quit talking to Uncle Jared when she realized Dad had brain damage."

"What did they fight about?"

"I don't know." Lisa glared at him. "You don't think my dad had anything to do with the murders, do you?"

Jackson hadn't envisioned that scenario, but now he wondered. "What does your dad drive?"

"A van with his business name on the side."

"What color?"

"The front is white and the sides are covered with pale-blue pool water."

Damn. It could be the light-colored van the neighbor had seen. Had Shane borrowed his father's van or had the father and son worked together? "Where can I find your brother?"

Lisa shrugged. "No clue."

"The fact that no one knows where he is makes me think he's using again. Is he?"

"I don't know." She grimaced. "He was in a methadone program and doing great, then he lost his job and everything went to shit."

"The Recovery Health clinic? He's a heroin addict?"

"Yes." Lisa pressed her lips together. "Shane started pulling away from us a few weeks ago. I called the clinic but they wouldn't tell me anything."

"Have you ever seen Shane get violent with anyone?"

"Don't even *think* it." Lisa stubbed out her cigarette and stood up. "Dad didn't kill anyone, and neither did Shane. No matter how bitter they are." Lisa walked back into the building and Jackson let her go.

He loved family loyalty, even when it was misguided. Walking up the alley to his car, he tried to take stock of the investigation. He had three possible suspects, all of them connected to Jared Walker, who seemed to be the primary victim. In the past month or so, Jared had fought with his brother-in-law, causing him brain damage, and possibly blackmailed his ex-boss. Were these events connected?

The blackmail was clearly about money. Jared had lost his job and needed cash. He may have also been bitter toward Roy Engall. *Bitter.* Lisa had said Kevin and Shane were bitter too. He had assumed she meant toward Jared for causing Kevin's brain injury, but Shane could have been bitter about many things.

Jackson climbed in his cruiser and called McCray. "What have you got, partner?"

"Damon was surprisingly candid. He says Shane has been showing up to crash at his place, but not last night. He claims Shane is devastated by the death of his family members and, I'm quoting here, 'not in his right mind.'"

"Any idea where to find him?"

"At his dealer's, a guy named Zor, who lives on Eighth Avenue between Polk and Almaden."

Jackson started the engine and rolled slowly down the alley. "No address?"

"Damon says it's a blue house on the north side of the street. I'm only six minutes away and I'll meet you there."

Two dark-blue Impalas parked at the end of the street would have made any drug dealer nervous—if he stepped out to notice. Dealers were not typically outdoor people. Their clients came to them, they conducted their business in dark shabby rooms, and they rarely let clients hang around for any length of time. Jackson was skeptical they would find Shane at the house. It was all they had though, and Shane was their primary person of interest. Jackson needed to get him into custody so he could step back from this case long enough to see his family. Maybe sleep a little.

He climbed out of the car and felt the familiar painful tug. He'd forgotten to take his second dose of naproxen this afternoon. He had some in his bag, but it would have to wait until he had a moment alone. Besides, they had a suspect to arrest.

Small older houses lined the street, which was almost treeless compared to adjacent blocks. The sun was low in the sky but the air was still warm. The smell of beef grilling in a backyard made

Jackson salivate. Two young boys skateboarded down the side-walk as they approached the only blue house on the north side. The paint peeled in long strips and the front yard had a faded layer of bark mulch instead of grass.

Jackson's hand was on his Sig Sauer as he rang the door-bell. Drug dealers were unpredictable. A forty-something, potbellied man in a wheelchair opened the door. For a moment, Jackson thought they had the wrong house. "Are you Zor?"

"That's what my friends call me. Are you a cop?"

"Detective Jackson, Eugene Police Department. This is Detective McCray. We're looking for Shane Compton."

Zor hesitated. Jackson watched him calculate the possibilities. Give up a friend-client or get arrested for possession with intent to distribute? Zor chose the former. "Shane's here, but he's sick. Obviously, I can't do much to help you with him."

"We'll handle it." Jackson started to step forward but Zor didn't move.

"You're not coming in without a warrant."

Jackson felt a flash of heat and fought for control. If the man had not been in a wheelchair, he would have pushed his way in. "We don't need permission. We know Shane is here and we have a subpoena for his DNA. Get out of our way or I'll arrest you for obstruction."

After another pause Zor rolled back. He was protecting his stash but Jackson didn't care about it. A vice detective would visit Zor soon enough. Jackson strode into the small living room, glanced around to see no one else was present, then headed for the open door in the short hallway.

Shane was on his knees in the bathroom vomiting.

* * *

Lara Evans hurried out of Judge Cranston's courtroom with a freshly signed warrant to collect every pair of Roy Engall's shoes she could find on his property and in his vehicles. Cranston had barely read the paperwork. As soon as she mentioned the mass killing, his face had changed and he'd been ready to sign anything.

On the five-minute drive to the Engalls place, Evans called Doug, the artist she'd been dating for a few months. "Hey, what's going on?"

"I'm heading out to teach my last class for the term. Are you working?"

"That's why I called. I can't make our dinner date. I'm working the mass-homicide case and it's pretty intense." The traffic on the bridge came to a near stop and she braked hard.

"What mass homicide?"

Evans' teeth clamped together. How could he not know? "Three members of a family were killed and the fourth member is critically injured. It happened Sunday night and was all over the news yesterday."

"You know I don't watch the news."

"You really should check the headlines every once in a while."

Doug laughed. "That's why I see *you*. Do you want to reschedule our dinner or just come over here and slide in bed with me when you have a chance?"

Evans visualized the scenario and got a little jolt. "As tempting as it sounds, I probably won't see you for a few days."

"I'll be here."

She clicked her cell phone closed and eased into the right lane. If it weren't for the occasional great sex, she would break up with Doug. They had nothing in common. She had worked as a paramedic before becoming a police officer, and in her free time she volunteered at WomenSpace, a center for abused women. Evans lived for the adrenaline rush and sought out high-energy situations. Doug's idea of excitement was discovering a new favorite color to paint with.

What had Jackson said when she and Doug first started dating? *You won't be happy until you end up with a cop.* He was right. But the cop she wanted to end up with was in love with a tall gorgeous woman named Kera. Jackson had been in the middle of a divorce when Evans was first transferred to the Violent Crimes Unit, and she'd fallen hard for him, even knowing it was a bad idea.

His voice had grabbed her first. Deep, smooth, and sexy. He'd been patient with her, explaining his process and how he approached cases. Of course, his looks had pulled her deeper in. She loved his near-black eyes, his chiseled features, even the scar through his eyebrow. In the long run, it was Jackson's integrity and dedication that made her fall in love.

He'd never shown any romantic feelings for her and she'd fought her own attraction, but she couldn't help how she felt. She kept dating other men, hoping to shift her affection to someone else, but they never measured up. Never even came close. Maybe she should start dating police officers. Unfortunately, the good ones all seemed to be married.

Evans pulled up in front of the house on Aspen Street and felt a pang of jealousy for their nice home near the river. She remembered the Engalls were in a lot of trouble and money hadn't bought them long-term happiness. If there were such a thing. She spotted a patrol unit across the street and nodded at the officer, who seemed to be in a daze even though his eyes were open.

She jogged across the street, feeling the weight of her weapon. The officer rolled down his window. It was Anderson, who'd discovered the bodies yesterday. Another thing she loved about Jackson; he always tried to keep first responders involved in the case, giving them a chance to earn some experience and attention. "Hey, Anderson. Anything to report?"

"Engall hasn't left his house since we started watching it. He came out this morning to yell at the dog pooping on his lawn, but that's the only time I've seen him."

"I'm here to search for shoes. Hopefully, we'll arrest this shithead in the next day or two."

"Go get him."

Evans trotted across the street, stopping briefly in the driveway to look in the back of the white work van. Ladders, drop cloths, sprayers, and five-gallon paint cans filled the entire space. No visible shoes. She would come back later and check it thoroughly, but first she would search the house and take the shoes off Engall's feet.

He opened the door wearing a blue bathrobe and reeking of booze. Evans instinctively looked at her watch: 2:17. If he'd been a functional alcoholic before, he had rapidly devolved into a dysfunctional mess. She introduced herself and held up her paperwork. "I have a subpoena to search your property and vehicles for all your shoes, and to collect those shoes as evidence. You're welcome to read it."

Engall grabbed the stack of paper and made a show of skimming through it. His eyes watered and his body swayed. Evans braced for his fall with no intention of catching him. She'd learned at family gatherings that when drunks got wobbly it was best to get the hell out of the way. They rarely got hurt, but someone else always did. She glanced at Engall's feet and saw he was wearing slippers.

"Let's start in your bedroom."

Engall led her down the hall to a large, bright master suite opening onto a private patio with a hot tub. Another pang of jealously as she envisioned the duplex she rented in West Eugene, with its small windows and standard-height ceiling. With the market down, she had hoped to become a first-time home buyer soon. Lammers had crushed her hope with her announcement about layoffs. Being the new kid in the department, Evans knew she was the logical choice. What would she do next—move where she could work in her field?

A huge closet filled nearly all of one wall and held mostly women's clothes and shoes. A single pair of men's dress shoes nested in a corner. They were not the shoes he'd worn and wouldn't match the crisscross prints, but she pulled on gloves and bagged them anyway. She turned to Engall, who stood in the middle of the room watching her. "Where are your work shoes?"

"You find 'em, you're the cop."

She located them in a bedroom across the hall, along with Engall's paint-stained coveralls and sweatshirts. She bagged and tagged two pairs of running sneakers, a pair of brown sandals that looked as if he never wore them, and a pair of brown leather boots. Evans made a note of her inventory and carried the bags to the Impala, then went back into the house to conduct a thorough search of every closet.

In the end she found one other pair of men's slip-on loafers on the floor in the family room with the giant TV. Engall had gotten bored with following her around and was watching a recorded David Letterman show. As she bagged the loafers, Evans asked, "Is your van unlocked?"

"Is it in your warrant?"

"Yep. Unlock it for me please."

A search of the van didn't turn up any shoes, but under the seat she found a blackmail note, presumably from Jared Walker. The note was still in the envelope, which didn't have a stamp or a postal seal. Jared must have delivered it in person. The communication was on plain white paper and had been produced with a computer and printer.

"Hey, that's not in your search warrant," Engall shouted, his words slurring. He stood next to the garage door, positioned so cars passing by couldn't see him.

"Read the fine print," she hollered back.

Evans scanned the text of the blackmail note. Jared had listed Roy Engall's infractions with bullet points, using bold to highlight the major ones such as *failure to carry job-site accident insurance.* Evans didn't know if it was against the law but Jared must have thought so. At the end Jared demanded five thousand dollars and closed the note with *Your former employee.* He hadn't used his name anywhere, which was kind of smart. Except he'd underestimated Engall's reaction.

She looked up to see that he'd gone into the house. Evans slipped the note back into its envelope and dug out another pre-marked plastic evidence bag. She only had one left. The task force had gathered more pieces of evidence in this investigation than she had in all her solo cases combined. The crime lab had to be overwhelmed.

She climbed out of the van and spotted a tall green trash container on the cement walkway next to the garage. Feeling queasy that she'd almost missed it, Evans hurried over. She flipped the hinged lid back and was hit with an overwhelming blast of paint-remover smell. The giant bin was stuffed with empty cans, paint-smeared plastic, paper bags full of kitchen scraps, and a load of other junk. The bastard didn't recycle a damn thing.

Evans pushed the container over and upended it, spilling its contents on the walkway. If she had to search this mess, she was going to make it easy.

"What the hell?" Engall shuffled up, clutching a fresh mixed drink, bathrobe flapping. "You could have used a tarp!"

Evans ignored him and began to pick through the crap. The gloves protected her hands, but her cuffs were soon smeared with yellow paint. *Damn.* It was her favorite jacket. She wished she'd taken it off. She also wished she'd grabbed a cloth face mask from her shoulder bag before starting.

A few minutes later, she found, in a brown paper bag stuffed mostly with kitchen scraps, a knotted white plastic bag. Evans used the jagged edge of a tin-can lid to rip open the plastic. Inside was a pair of white, paint-stained tennis shoes. The dumb fucker had been too drunk or too lazy to find a public trash can to dispose of his guilt.

"I didn't kill anyone," Engall shouted, drunk off his ass and near tears.

Evans ignored him and stuffed the shoes, still inside the white plastic, into her last evidence bag. She would have the note and the shoes to report at the task-force meeting tomorrow morning. Jackson would be pleased.

On the ride downtown, Shane seemed to be in the half-sleep euphoria of a junkie who'd shot up more than he could handle. Jackson's plan was to leave him in the soft interrogation room, under supervision, while he grabbed some dinner. He hoped Shane would become clearheaded in an hour and be able to answer questions.

Jackson had called Kera and she'd agreed to meet him at Sweet Basil for a quick Thai dinner. Jackson walked the six blocks to stretch his legs and revive himself. His three hours of sleep were wearing off and his body felt heavy. His brain felt congested too, as if all the information in this case was so jammed together it wouldn't bounce or crystallize.

The restaurant, tucked into a block of downtown buildings, was half empty. Good for him but not for the business. Jackson sat near the windows in front, looking out at Pearl Street, enjoying the tangy scent of basil coming from the kitchen. After a minute,

Kera pulled into the parking lot across the road. He ordered a pot of jasmine green tea and a side of spring rolls.

Kera breezed in, wearing a purple blazer and smiling brightly. Several customers looked up and smiled back. People always noticed Kera and she always made them smile. Well, almost always. She was also tenacious as a bulldog about getting what she wanted, especially if it meant helping young women, veterans, or homeless people.

"Hey, Jackson." She kissed him on the mouth, then sat across from him. "Thanks for meeting me. I know you don't have much time."

"I'm trying to be more balanced, even when I'm on a case."

She laughed softly. "Define *balanced*."

"Never mind. I'm here."

The waiter brought the tea and they ordered without looking at the menu.

"Is Katie at the house?"

"She and Danette are making homemade pizza with pesto and artichoke hearts."

"Glad I missed it."

"It's my recipe." Kera touched the back of his hand. "Remember the first time we ate together?"

"Jung's Mongolian Grill. We ran into each other while I was working Jessie Davenport's case."

"You were pissed at me because I wouldn't tell you whether she was a client at the clinic."

"I still thought you were hot."

"I liked your face but your intensity scared me a little." Kera smiled and shrugged. "You saved my life, and I decided you were okay."

Jackson squeezed her hand. "*You* saved me."

The waiter came up to the table, so they pulled back to let him set down the spring rolls. They ate in silence for a moment, then Kera said, "How's the case going?"

"It's a little frustrating. I have two suspects but nothing solid on either."

"I can't imagine who they are. Who would commit such a heinous act?" Kera sipped her tea and held back from asking more questions. Jackson appreciated the sacrifice. She was intellectually curious about everything and would have loved to discuss his cases. Renee, on the other hand, had never wanted to know about his work.

"Are you coming over after you wrap up tonight?"

"Probably not. It will be easier to just sleep on the couch at the department for a few hours."

"You'll go back to your house to shower and change?"

"It's closer to the department."

Another long silence. The waiter brought their orders, spicy beef massaman for Kera and sweet-and-sour chicken for him. After a moment Kera said, "Are you still thinking of moving in with me permanently?"

"I am. I'm just not sure Katie is ready."

"She's been there for five weeks and seems to like it fine."

Jackson felt himself closing up. He wasn't ready to talk about this. Or about Katie wanting to spend the summer with her mother. Or the idea he could lose his job on Friday. "When I'm on a homicide, my job goes into overdrive. It only happens three or four times a year, but it's intense and I can't really think straight about anything else."

"I understand."

He couldn't talk about his case either. They ate mostly in silence except for Kera's chat about baby Micah. For the first time, Jackson wondered how much his job, his silence, had contributed to his ex-wife's drinking problem.

Later, at the department, Jackson escorted his still-somewhat-groggy suspect from the big room with the soft brown couch to the cramped interrogation space with the scarred table, gray walls, and harsh lighting. The walls had once been pale pink, meant to have an emasculating effect on suspects, but it had bothered some detectives enough that they repainted. Jackson didn't care about the color; it was the eight-foot-square space that made him jumpy after a half an hour.

He considered uncuffing Shane, then changed his mind. The young man was built like his father, with broad shoulders and big bones. If Shane had never been a drug user, he'd probably weigh more than Jackson. Instead he looked as if he hadn't eaten in a week. Still, he was their prime suspect in a triple homicide, and it was enough to make Jackson uneasy.

"We're recording this interview. Please state your name."

"Shane Compton."

"Shane, are you coherent enough to talk to me?" Jackson said for the camera.

"Yes. I told you, I'm sick, not high." He looked around as if he'd just realized where he was. "Why am I here? They usually just take me to jail."

"You're here to answer questions about Sunday, May thirtieth. Where were you that night?"

"May? How am I supposed to remember?" His speech was slow and soft, like someone sleepwalking.

"It was two days ago."

"Oh. Sunday." His forehead creased for a moment, then he broke into a shy smile. With his blond hair, big green eyes, and prominent cheekbones, Shane was probably what Jackson's daughter would call a hottie. "I was with a friend," Shane said. "We drove to Corvallis and didn't get back until midnight."

"Why Corvallis? You couldn't find any heroin here in Eugene?"

"We went to see a friend about a job."

"I need names."

"Aaron Priest is the guy who drove. I don't know the guy we went to see. He's Aaron's friend."

"This is important, Shane. Three people were killed Sunday night and we think you did it."

His smile was gone in a blink and his head fell forward. "Don't say that. I love my cousins. I love Aunt Carla. She's like a second mom to me."

"Sometimes people get mad at their family. It happens to all of us." Jackson used his soft, empathetic voice. "Why don't you tell me what happened? You'll feel better if you get it off your chest."

Shane began to weep. Tears rolled down his face and his body shook, but he made no sound. "Everything is so fucked up."

CHAPTER 12

A month earlier

The clinic opened at five but Shane had never made it in that early, even when he'd been working. This morning he'd shown up around eight and people were waiting on the big porch outside. Shane squeezed past into the lobby and signed in. He wished he could go outside and smoke while he waited, but they had rules about not smoking on the property, not leaving the property after you signed in, and how long you could loiter after you dosed. Recovery Health had rules about everything!

He leaned against a yellow wall and waited in the small, funky lobby with the other addicts. The clinic was on the corner of Seventh and Jefferson in an older house that had been converted into a medical space. They hadn't done much. The rooms were still small with low ceilings, and you had to climb the narrow stairs to see the counselors.

Shane didn't care. He loved coming here and getting his dose. He felt better the moment he swallowed the pink liquid, knowing it would take the edge off and he would make it through the day without using heroin. He even enjoyed the one-on-one sessions with Dr. Hunt, where they talked about his future. Shane loved having a future to look forward to. He loved being able to imagine his life five years from now. He visualized a nice little house in his parents' neighborhood with a wife and a baby son to take care of. The weekly group sessions had grown old, but even those helped keep him grounded. He was moving forward with his life, finally. Or he had been until Country Coach laid him off.

The nurse called his name and Shane started for one of the dosing rooms. "You have to see admin this morning," she said, pointing down the hall, avoiding his eyes.

"Okay, Alice." He smiled as he passed. She was a good person. Everyone who worked here was a good person.

The door was open so Shane waltzed through. "Good morning, Mary."

"Hello, Shane. How are you?"

"Not bad. What's up?"

"It's May third. Your payment was due on Wednesday. Do you have the money?"

"I have forty dollars." Shane pulled the two twenties he'd borrowed from Damon out of his pocket and handed them to her. Even the paperwork people wore latex gloves.

"This doesn't even cover what you owe for last month." Mary glanced at her computer monitor. "You still owe fifty-five dollars for April and now two sixty-five for May. We can't dose you until you pay."

Panic flooded his body. He could not walk out of here without his dose. "I can get the money. I just need some time." Shane gave her his most charming smile.

"I'm sorry, but that isn't how it works. You know because we were very clear when you were screened and accepted. We are not a charity. We try to be compassionate and flexible, but considering our clientele, we have to be firm."

"You can't just cut me off. You know what it's like." His heart raced and he fought the urge to yell. "The pain will kill me. I'll be too sick to look for work. "

Mary pressed her lips together. "I sympathize, but there's nothing I can do. You have to be financially responsible for your treatment."

"You know I lost my job. I'd only been working at Country Coach for six months, and my unemployment checks are only seventy-five a week. If I don't pay my probation fees, I'll go back to jail."

"Can your parents help you out for a while?"

Shane shook his head. His parents had paid for the methadone for the whole first year he was enrolled in the clinic. They'd told him up front that was all they would commit to. They wanted him to get off the stuff and kept pressuring him to start on a withdrawal schedule. His doctor at the clinic thought it was too soon. Dr. Hunt said the longer he stayed on methadone, the less likely he was to relapse. Shane trusted Dr. Hunt because he'd been working with addicts for twenty years. After Shane had been laid off he'd started cutting back his dose, knowing he couldn't afford the clinic for long. Even at an accelerated rate, they told him it would take six months to go from an eighty-milligram dose to zero…without horrible suffering.

"Maybe White Bird can help you," Mary said. "There are also some free residential clinics in this state."

"They have waiting lists. I'll be lying on the floor moaning by this afternoon."

"I'm sorry, Shane. As of right now, you are no longer a client of this clinic and I have to ask you to leave." Mary looked past him, not making eye contact.

Shane wanted to grab her hands and beg for his life. He wanted to chain himself to the desk until she relented. He knew it was pointless and would burn his bridges here. "Can I have my forty dollars back? Since you're not gonna dose me."

She pushed the twenties across the desk. "Good luck, Shane."

"I'll need more than luck." He grabbed the cash and bolted from the room.

Shit. Shit. Shit. He was shaking by the time he hit the parking lot. Pure fear. The withdrawal symptoms wouldn't start for a few hours. He wasn't going to let it happen. He'd experienced it once when he'd spent a day in jail because he'd missed a meeting with his probation officer. The pain had been like a sharp-toothed creature eating him from the inside. Followed by nausea and sweating and dizziness. He'd spent the night on the holding-room floor, making noises he didn't know humans could make. It had been the longest twenty-four hours of his life. It would take up to ten days for his body to fully adjust. Methadone was the most addictive drug in the world.

So he had no choice. He would make some calls and find someone selling methadone tablets. Some doctors prescribed it for pain and there was always someone with a prescription who didn't use all of it and didn't mind making a little money on the side. His forty dollars might buy him two days' worth if he took half a dose.

Then what? Street methadone would eat up his unemployment checks faster than the clinic did. Shane walked south toward the bus station downtown. He would find someone with a cell phone. Hell, he might even find someone with a connection. He knew it was dangerous to call his old drug buddies, but what else could he do? If he went cold turkey he'd end up in the hospital. Or shooting up again. He couldn't let either of those things happen. He had to stay functional and find a job and get back into the clinic. He had a life plan now and his girlfriend was counting on him. He wouldn't let her down, even if he had to go back to his parents and beg. He would do everything else first, though.

Two minutes later, Shane came across a guy outside the WOW Hall using a cell phone. He waited until he was done, then asked to use it. "Make it quick, I'm expecting a call back." Shane dialed an old number from memory. Tyler Gorlock would know someone who could help him.

The connection hadn't worked out, but Tyler had kept his forty dollars, claiming Shane owed him. By five that afternoon he was in the parking lot where his mother worked, lying on the ground next to her car, shaking. He'd vomited once in the grass nearby and was now taking short rapid breaths like a woman in labor. He hoped none of his mother's coworkers would see him. The last thing he wanted was to embarrass his mother. He also prayed she would come out soon.

"Shane, what's going on?" Her worried face gave him his first glimmer of hope for the day. If it were in her power, his mother would help him. She knelt on the blacktop and stroked his face, not caring about her nylons. "Let's get you in the car."

"The clinic kicked me out because I couldn't pay. I'm in withdrawal." Shane struggled to his feet, climbed in the backseat, and lay down.

"Do you need to go to the ER?"

"I need to borrow forty dollars and buy some methadone."

His mother started the car and headed out. "You mean from a dealer?"

"Yes."

"That's not a long-term plan."

"I know."

She drove in silence and Shane knew she was taking him home. The thought gave him little comfort. Nothing but methadone, or some other opioid, would take away the withdrawal pain.

At the house, his mother urged him to come inside but he stayed in the back of the car. There was no point in suffering the trip inside. If his parents agreed to start paying for the clinic again, he would numb the pain with alcohol and survive until the clinic opened in the morning. If they wouldn't pay, he would have his mother take him back downtown. She would probably give him enough cash to get a dose for today. He had another idea about where to score methadone.

After a few minutes, both parents came out to the car and his father opened the back door and stared at him. Shane tried to suppress the little animal sounds but he couldn't. The pain was making him feel suicidal.

"Oh, christ." His father sounded worried and disgusted at the same time. He turned to Shane's mom. "This is emotional blackmail. If we pay for even one month of methadone, then it becomes our responsibility again. And if Shane doesn't find a job, we'll have to pay again next month and the next month. I want him to get off the damn stuff."

"What is your plan?" His mother was emotional now too. "We can't leave him like this."

"This will pass. He'll be okay."

"What if he starts using again? Do you want that on your conscience?"

Shane wanted to die. He hated being the source of his parents' fights. His father was a good person, but he just didn't understand. Holding his stomach, tears rolling down his face, Shane climbed out of the car and stumbled down the driveway. He would find another way.

CHAPTER 13

Tuesday, June 2, 8:05 p.m.

After an hour in the interrogation room, Shane began to vomit again. He finally admitted he was in withdrawal from methadone, but Jackson didn't know what to believe. So he decided to book him into the jail where he would get medical attention. The county deputies who ran the jail would not be happy with the burden, but tough shit. Jackson wasn't about to let Shane go unless they confirmed his alibi, which seemed highly unlikely. Meanwhile he wanted Shane to have a doctor on standby in case something extreme happened. Drug addicts were known to have heart failure from losing potassium through vomiting.

Jackson walked him downstairs to his cruiser under the building. Shane was still cuffed and his nose dripped mucus, but he seemed okay for the moment. No crying, no puking. The kid had been through a very tough time lately, but Jackson couldn't let himself sympathize. The pile of bloody bodies was still fresh in his mind and Shane was the primary suspect. He'd been a little out of it during the questioning and Jackson didn't trust anything he said.

As they walked across the underground parking lot filled with cop cars, Jackson said, "I noticed you said you loved your cousins and your Aunt Carla. What about Jared? Why didn't you love Uncle Jared?"

"I used to. He took me and Nick fishing all the time when we were kids."

"What happened?"

"He harassed my dad one night at the tavern. I don't even know what about. They got in a fight and my dad got hurt." Shane stopped and gulped in air. Jackson hoped he wouldn't start puking again.

"What happened next?" Jackson nudged him toward the car.

"Dad hit his head and now he's like a different person. It's weird and sad. The guy who used to be my dad is gone, and I miss him."

"You blame Jared, don't you?"

"I did, but now he's dead. I don't know how I feel."

Jackson remembered Lisa saying her brother was bitter. "You were still mad at Jared when you went over there on Sunday. Did you argue with him?"

They reached the car and Jackson opened the back door. Shane started to cry again. "Two months ago, we were a happy family. Now everything is all fucked up."

After booking Shane into the jail, Jackson drove back to headquarters and searched for Aaron Priest in the database. The name was an alias for Adam Palmer, who had been convicted of possession, distribution, and various forms of theft. Another addict. Jackson put out an attempt-to-locate and asked for a patrol officer to check the last known address for Priest/Palmer, realizing it was probably a waste of time. Looking for an addict was like looking for a runaway dog. He could be two blocks away, living with the first person who'd fed him, or in a car a hundred miles down the road.

Jackson leaned back and closed his eyes for a moment. He kept thinking the fight in the parking lot between the brothers-in-law had to be connected to the murder of Jared and his family. Had Kevin and Shane gone over there together and confronted Jared? Those two as perpetrators would explain why two of the victims had been hit in the head with the bat and two had not. They probably hadn't intended to hurt the kids until Nick and/or Lori tried to defend their parents.

He needed to talk to Tracy and Kevin again and get the whole story. Jackson checked his watch: 9:10 p.m. They wouldn't like him showing up this late, but it was a homicide investigation and he needed information. Nick and Jared's autopsies were scheduled for tomorrow and would take up a big chunk of his day. He also had a conference scheduled at the crime lab to reconstruct the murders based on blood spatter, position of the bodies, and various other factors. He was not looking forward to it, but he needed the experts' opinions about how many perpetrators were involved and who was killed first.

Jackson resisted stopping for coffee on his drive out to Windsor Circle in southwest Eugene. He hoped to head home after this and get a few hours of sleep. The Comptons' house was a large split-level near the top of Windsor Circle, where it intersected with Wilshire. Even in the dark, Jackson could see it was well maintained.

Lights were on all over the house and two cars occupied the driveway, a silver hybrid Prius and the white van with the wavy pool water on the sides. Jackson wondered how the family was holding up. First the economy must have hit their business hard, then Kevin suffered the brain injury. Now Tracy's brother and his family were dead and her son was suspected of the murder. To get a confession out of Shane, Jackson needed his parents to tell him everything.

He rang the doorbell and a dog started barking. Jackson tensed. A dog had given him the scar through his eyebrow. Tracy's voice came through the closed door. "Who is it?"

"Detective Jackson. I have Shane in custody and we need to talk."

The barking got louder as she opened the door. The noise came from a small, fluffy dog the size of a stuffed toy. Tracy reached down and grabbed the dog's collar to keep it from jumping on Jackson's leg.

"Will you put the dog in another room while we talk?" Jackson waited while Tracy came back from a bedroom, then followed her to the dining room, where Kevin was going over paperwork at the table.

"I'm sorry for the late-night visit," Jackson said, "but I need to know what happened between you and the Walkers." He sat down across from Kevin and stared, trying to get his attention.

"They have Shane in custody," Tracy said, sitting close to her husband. She bit her lip and squeezed his shoulder.

"Is he okay?" Kevin finally looked up at Jackson.

"More or less. He seems a little strung out, but he'll get medical treatment in jail."

"Oh bullshit." Tracy shuddered in anger. "They give addicts antinausea medicine and that's it. They don't even put them on suicide watch unless the inmate says he feels suicidal when he's booked in."

"You've been through this a few times." Jackson gave her a sympathetic look. "I wish we had a better system." Neither parent was moved by his compassion. "Your daughter, Lisa, says Shane was bitter."

"Shane didn't kill anyone." Tracy's eyes begged him to believe her.

"Tell me about the confrontation with Jared in the parking lot at the Time Out Tavern." Jackson kept his focus on Kevin. He wanted to hear Kevin's version.

"Jared was pissed off because the cops arrested Nick."

"His fifteen-year-old son?"

Tracy and Kevin exchanged a look.

"Why was Nick arrested? And why would Jared be mad at you about it?"

"Nick stole Kevin's Lou Gehrig baseball card," Tracy said in a rush. "It's a 1934 Goudy worth at least two thousand dollars, so Kevin called the police. I wish like hell we could take it back."

CHAPTER 14

A month earlier

Both cars were gone and Nick felt a little surge of joy. He rushed into the house and headed straight for the kitchen. First he cut a paper-thin piece of cheese, wrapped a slice of bread around it, and wolfed the snack in three seconds. He chased the skinny sandwich with a gulp of milk and a single Taffy cookie. He would have liked to have eaten several more, but resisted. His mother had always monitored the food somewhat, and got pissed if he ate things that were supposed to be for dinner, but now that his parents were unemployed, she had become a Nazi about it. Frustrating as it was, he understood the money situation and tried to be reasonable.

Once he'd fed the growling pit in his stomach, Nick hauled his backpack to his room and dug out the pot he'd scored from Brian in exchange for two math assignments. He'd taken his first toke at Brian's house last week and wondered why he'd waited so long. Nick finally understood what *take the edge off* meant. And why shouldn't he? He had a lot of new edge in his life lately. Like the constant worry his family could end up homeless and living apart from each other. He'd heard his parents talking about it one night. Dad had said the kids could go stay with his sister Tracy, but he and Mom would trade the truck for a van and live in the van. Picturing his parents as homeless was too stressful to think about. Nick rolled a crappy-looking joint and headed to the back deck to take a hit or two. He knew to be careful and not get all bug-eyed and zoned out.

Halfway through his first inhale, he started coughing. The more he coughed, the more his lungs hurt, and the worse it got. Worried the old couple next door would hear him, Nick went inside and gulped down some water. He hadn't coughed like this last time.

The brain softness crept in, but this time Nick didn't like it nearly as much. He felt stupid and guilty and wished he hadn't brought the pot home or smoked it. He should be out looking for a fast-food job or mowing lawns to help his parents. He decided to get on the computer and make a yard-work flyer to pass out in the neighborhood.

As he shuffled toward the desk in the living room, he heard the doorbell ring. A tingle of fear crawled up his spine. Who would ring the doorbell in the afternoon? His friends always knocked once, then barged in. Should he ignore it? Definitely. Nick took two steps toward his room, then stopped. Was the pot making him paranoid? He'd watched enough stoner movies to know it could happen. The doorbell rang again. What if it was something important, like a package delivery? His parents would be irritated if he didn't handle it.

Nick grabbed a banana, ate one bite to cover the pot smell in his mouth, then tossed the rest on the counter. He hurried to the front of the house, wondering what his parents had ordered. He pulled open the door and his heart nearly stopped. Two cops waited impatiently on the front patio.

Shit! Nick's heart pounded so loudly he was sure the cops could hear it. What did they want? Did they know about the pot? Were they here to arrest him? He tried to form a response, but his brain wouldn't focus or make words come out of his mouth.

"Are you Nick Walker?"

"Yes."

"We need to talk to you. Can we come in?" The guy cop asked the questions. The girl cop came in close and sniffed. Her blue shirt was stretched tight over big breasts. Nick tried not to stare.

"Let's go inside," she said, sounding mean.

"My parents aren't home."

"We can talk here or we can talk at the police department."

Oh shit. Nick wished he hadn't gotten high. He couldn't think straight. He knew he didn't want to get into the back of a cop car. Ever. After what seemed like an eternity of bouncing thoughts, he reluctantly let them in.

"Let's sit at the table," the woman said, heading through the house like she owned it. "I'm Officer Freemont. This is Officer Gibson."

Nick's legs shook as he followed her and he was glad to sit. He hoped it would help him concentrate too.

Officer Gibson, an older guy with bad teeth and breath, leaned toward Nick and said, "We're here about the baseball card. The Lou Gehrig you stole from your uncle. Do you still have it?"

"What?"

"Don't bother to bullshit us. Kevin Compton wants his card back. The more you cooperate, the less likely you'll end up in Serbu."

Every young man in the county knew Serbu was the juvenile-detention center, but Nick had no idea why they thought he had Uncle Kevin's baseball card. "I didn't steal anything."

"The card disappeared while you were in their house. Try again." Gibson's eyes drilled into him.

"I didn't take it. Really." *Lame!* The sound of his own voice made him cringe.

"You won't mind if we search your room?" The woman stood and gestured for him to follow.

Shit. The pot was in there. Or was it in his pocket? "I do mind," Nick stammered.

"You smell like marijuana," she said with an evil smile. "We have just cause to search the entire house for illegal drugs based on the reasonable assumption that you're currently using them. Are you sure you don't want to just give up the baseball card?"

"I don't have it." The words came out in a squeal. Nick thought he might run for it. Just charge out of the house and get away from these cops before they ruined his life. His legs shook, his heart felt like it would explode, and he had to pee so bad his bladder hurt. Unwillingly, he followed them down the hall where they instinctively found his room.

As the girl cop—he couldn't remember her name—began to dig though his sock drawer, Nick realized he should call his parents. He started to turn around and head for the phone in the kitchen, then he remembered they had canceled their landline. Nick glanced around his room, looking for his cell phone. Why couldn't he keep track of it?

Gibson picked up his backpack from the floor, pulled out a stack of old homework assignments, and tossed them on the bed. The cop rummaged around in the bottom of the pack and came up with the crust of a peanut-butter-and-honey sandwich.

Nick watched as they searched, knowing they would eventually find the little baggie, but he was too paralyzed with fear and brain softness to do anything. *Oh shit.* His parents would freak out when they found out about the pot. Especially if there were fines involved.

Nick spotted his phone on the bed. The cop had tossed it out of his backpack and was now searching the closet. *The closet.* He'd hidden the pot in the closet. Nick lurched forward and grabbed the phone. "I'm gonna call my parents."

They ignored him and kept searching.

Mom or Dad? Nick stared at his speed-dial choices. Mom. She would be calmer, less likely to start yelling. For only the second time he could remember, his mother didn't pick up when he called her. Nick left her a shaky message: "I'm in trouble. The cops are here searching my room. Can you come home?"

Moments later, Gibson found his pot. "Here we go." The other cop looked up from her search as Gibson said, "You're under arrest for possession of a Schedule I controlled substance." He spun toward Nick. "I could cuff you, but if you cooperate, I won't."

"What do you want me to do?" Nick's bladder was on fire.

"Get the baseball card and turn it over to us."

Nick shook his head and felt a tear roll down his face. "I don't have it and I don't know anything about it." He stuck his index finger in his mouth and bit down hard. The pain distracted him. It looked stupid but it was better than crying. "I have to pee."

"I'm coming with you."

Having a cop watch him pee was only the first of his humiliations. Before his parents finally showed up at the police station, he had been hauled away in the back of a cop car, fingerprinted, and grilled again about the baseball card. Eventually, he was given a court date and allowed to go home. On the ride, his parents were mostly silent, which was worse than being yelled at. If they yelled, they got over it and not much more would happen to him. The quiet meant they hadn't yet figured out how to punish him.

He knew they were thinking about the cost too. The cops had said the judge would probably mandate a treatment program instead of sending him to Serbu. Nick was relieved, but his father had given him a look that made him want to disappear. Treatment programs cost money and they didn't have any.

His mother would not look at him.

CHAPTER 15

Wednesday, June 3, 5:23 a.m.

Jackson pulled into his bungalow on the corner of Twenty-Fifth and Harris just as the sun was coming up. A sense of nostalgia mixed with a little loneliness crept into his bones. His home, snuggled among giant oak and birch trees, was older and smaller than Kera's, but it was charming in a different way. Her house up on the hill was bright, open, and minimalist, while he had cozy rooms with arched entries and dark crown molding. He wondered what it said about their personalities.

He put on a pot of coffee and headed straight for the shower. Around two that morning, after adding the day's notes to his file, he'd stretched out on the couch in the soft interrogation room and slept for three hours. He'd driven home to shower, change, and brew coffee. As much as he wanted to see his family and eat a real breakfast, he couldn't afford the distraction right now. He had to stay focused on this case. He would fill his tall travel mug with coffee and eat some toast on the way out the door.

Jackson entered the morgue for the second time in two days. Nick Walker was on the table this morning and Jackson willed himself to stay in the room. Autopsies on kids were hard to take. He always ended up thinking about Katie and how he would feel if she were killed.

"Are you okay?" Konrad said, making eye contact.

"I'm fine." Jackson avoided looking directly at the body. Nick Walker had fallen on his stomach after being stabbed, and the blood had drained to his front side. Face to ankles, he was dark red with lividity. "Tell me about the defense wounds on his hands," Jackson said.

"His right hand has multiple tiny cuts." The pathologist paused and thought for a moment. "It's possible these wounds were made by the square edge of the knife blade found at the scene."

"You're saying he had the knife in his hand at one point?"

"Or he struggled for possession." Konrad was still examining Nick's hand. "He has quite a bruise around his wrist too. I'd say someone gripped him very tightly."

"He wasn't struck with the bat?"

"That's probably why he was able to fight the attacker." Gunderson, the ME who had been at the scene, offered the information.

"The knife wound is in his back," Jackson countered. "So he must have lost control of the knife and turned to flee." He knew the pathologist liked to conduct the autopsies methodically, but he needed to get some information and get out. "Can we look at the wound on his back? Can you tell me how tall the assailant is?"

Konrad sighed. Gunderson stepped up to the table and the two men rolled Nick over on his stomach. Jackson mentally mapped out the rest of his day while he waited for Konrad to examine the gaping hole in the boy's back.

"The wound is to the right of center, so the attacker is likely right-handed." Konrad used a stainless-steel pathology ruler to measure the gash. "It's 6.4 centimeters long and 4.4 centimeters deep and angles downward. I'd say the attacker is a couple of inches taller than this victim."

"Nick is five-seven," Gunderson said. "I measured before I put him in the cold drawer."

"How tall is Jared Walker?" Jackson asked.

"Six-one."

Jackson put it together. "Based on what you said at the scene about the attacker being shorter than Jared, we can assume our perpetrator is somewhere between five-eight and six feet."

"As are most of the men in this country," Gunderson noted with an edge of dryness.

Jackson tried to visualize Shane Compton and Roy Engall. Roy fit the short end of the range and Shane was around six feet. *Crap. No help.* Jackson watched Konrad probe the wound, then decided his time would be better spent elsewhere. "I have a meeting to attend," he said. "Will you call me if you find anything significant?"

Gunderson gave him a quizzical look. "Sure."

The task force wasn't scheduled to meet until ten. Jackson had time to stop for another coffee and sit at his desk for twenty minutes. He closed his eyes and pushed a dozen questions out of his mind. Sometimes, if he shut down his brain and stopped thinking for a while, answers would come to him later. He refused to call it *meditation*, but it was effective.

This time he made the connection almost immediately. Carla Walker had a receipt for seventeen hundred dollars from a pawnshop, and Kevin Compton was missing a baseball card valued at around two grand. Carla had stolen the card. Or Nick had stolen it and Carla had pawned it for cash. Had Kevin and Shane Compton killed the whole Walker family over a damn baseball card? Jackson didn't want to believe it, but there was the brain injury too. First, one of the Walkers stole Kevin's valuable card, then Jared Walker permanently injured his brother-in-law in a fight about it. Maybe it was a cumulative reaction. Maybe Shane had committed the murders by himself in a drug rage to avenge his father.

Jackson saw Evans get up from her desk and move toward the hallway, so he followed her. He hoped the other detectives had something to report at this meeting, because he sure didn't have much.

He strode into the conference room and his muscles tensed. The windowless space felt cold this morning and the names of the dead on the board jumped out at him. Day three of the investigation and they had nothing solid. Why hadn't the crime lab called? As he and Evans waited for the others, Jackson pressed speed dial #10. When Jasmine Parker picked up, he said, "Jackson here. What have you got for me?"

"Give me a moment." There was a pause, accompanied by the sound of paper shuffling. "None of the prints from the front door or windows matched anyone in CODIS, but a partial print on the baseball bat matched a local drug offender named Shane Compton."

"Is it good enough to take to court?"

"It's only one partial print. The most prominent latents are from family members Lori and Nick Walker, but even those are smudged and inconclusive."

Crap. No help. A defense attorney would claim Shane had played baseball with his cousins. "Let's reconstruct the crime scene this afternoon. Do you have the blood-spatter analysis completed?"

"Not quite. Is three o'clock okay?"

"See you then."

Schak, McCray, and Quince had come in while Jackson was on the phone. None of them looked as tired as he felt. Should he delegate more of the work? He hated to step back from the most important elements of a case, especially the interrogations. "Good morning," he said, slipping his phone into his pocket. "Who brought me coffee?"

Schak rolled his eyes in mock disgust. "You had a little nip and tuck. I had a heart attack. If anyone deserves the prima donna treatment, it's me."

McCray grinned. "If I can call you 'prima donna' I'll buy you all the coffee you want."

"Where's Quince?" Evans headed for the board.

"He's tracking down Shane Compton's supposed alibi. It's critical to close the net around Shane as much as we can." Jackson scanned his printed notes, looking for the name of the guy Shane had given him. Aaron Priest. "I arrested Shane for possession and booked him into jail where he could get medical treatment. He's a troubled young man, and I think we'll eventually get a confession."

"What exactly do we have on him?" Schak wanted to know.

"When I asked who attacked her, Lori named Shane. His prints are also on the bat used in the assault." As he said it, Jackson realized how weak their case was.

"Lori was only half-conscious when she spoke to you," Evans shot back. "Shane also spent a lot of time in the house and probably played baseball with his cousins. The print may not be worth much. Do we have any DNA evidence?"

"Not yet, but we're meeting at the crime lab today to reconstruct the scene. Be there if you can." Jackson nodded at Schak. "What have you got?"

"I have a dozen little details about Carla Walker, such as her appointment at Planned Parenthood, but nothing that helps this case." Schak glanced at his notes and grimaced. "She was well liked by everyone. Her sister and her best friend think she's a saint. No one could give me a single reason anyone would want Carla dead."

"I think she stole and pawned a valuable baseball card that belonged to her brother-in-law Kevin Compton," Jackson said.

"No shit?" Schak's mouth fell open.

"I found a receipt in her purse for Westside Buyers, dated April twenty-fifth, for seventeen hundred dollars. I talked with all the Comptons yesterday, and Tracy finally admitted they thought Nick had stolen the card. They reported it to the police and Nick was arrested for possession of marijuana." Jackson glanced at his notes. "Four days after Nick's arrest, Jared Walker confronted Kevin Compton at the Time Out Tavern. Both men were drunk and they fought. Kevin got knocked against his van, struck his head on the door handle, and ended up with brain damage."

"How bad is it?" Schak asked. "Would it make him angry enough to kill?"

"Kevin seems subdued, but Lisa described her brother and father as bitter. She also said Shane had been in a methadone program, then may have started using again after he lost his job." Jackson waited for Evans to catch up with writing everything on the board. "My best working theory is Shane got high, then killed Jared and Carla in a vengeful rage. The kids just got in the way."

"I thought Shane was a heroin addict," McCray countered. "Heroin addicts aren't violent."

"They're not picky either. If they can't find H, they'll take whatever they can get."

Evans turned to face Jackson, eyes wide with disbelief. "You think all of this was about a baseball card?"

"It's a working theory." Jackson felt defensive.

"What about Roy Engall?" Evans looked around. When no one responded, she said, "Jared was blackmailing him, he has no alibi, and his van matches the description we got from the neighbor."

"We haven't ruled him out," Jackson shot back. "Did you get his shoes and DNA?"

"I not only picked up the four pairs in his closet, I dug through his garbage bin and found the pair he'd wrapped in plastic and thrown out." Evans grinned. "Why would he throw away the shoes unless he was worried about them?"

"Well, hell. That changes things." Jackson felt a little blind-sided. "You should have called me."

"Sorry. I knew we were meeting this morning."

"If the lab finds a match, we'll bring him in. And yes, you'll get the arrest."

"There's more," Evans said, suppressing a smile. "I found a blackmail note." She pulled the evidence from her bag. "I thought you would want to see this before I took it over to the lab."

Jackson slipped on latex gloves and scanned the white sheet of paper. Jared hadn't signed his name, but the bullet points matched the list they'd found in his home. The lab would likely find his fingerprints too. "This definitely brings Roy to the front of our investigation."

"I hate it when cases ping-pong like this," Schak complained.

Jackson had learned the hard way not to focus exclusively on one, or even two, suspects. They had to question and process everything. He turned to Evans. "What did you learn about Lori's restaurant boss?"

"He's a little creepy, but I questioned two other young women who work there, and they both denied being sexually harassed. They said Greg Blackwell, the manager, had seemed a little too friendly with Lori lately though." Evans jotted *boyfriend?* on the board and turned back. "One of the young women said Lori had mentioned a new boyfriend recently."

"Did you get a name?"

"No. In fact the waitress said Lori acted secretive about it and wouldn't say who he was. I called Jenna, her friend from school, and she didn't know anything about a boyfriend." Evans wrote down *why secret?* "She says Lori hasn't dated anyone in a year. It's a little odd Lori would keep the information from her best friend."

"Unless she's screwing her best friend's boyfriend," Schak offered.

"Look into it a little more, would you?" Jackson was skeptical about its relevance, but he never ignored anything that seemed odd. He asked McCray, "Did you find out anything new about Jared?"

McCray shook his head. "His coworkers liked him fine. They also like Roy Engall, even if he is cheap." McCray made air quotes when he said *cheap* and it made Jackson smile. "I looked at the Walkers' bank statements too," McCray continued. "No infusions of cash. Not even the seventeen hundred you said Carla got from the baseball card. They recently closed out their small savings account and were down to their last three hundred dollars."

"It might explain why Carla took the card," Evans commented. "Desperation."

Jackson remembered something else. "Carla was pregnant. Maybe she needed the money for an abortion. That might explain why she had an appointment at Planned Parenthood."

"The poor woman." Evans wrote *abortion?* on the board under Carla's name. "What if it wasn't Jared's baby? What if she was having an affair with Engall? It would give Engall motive to kill the husband and wife."

"Why would Engall cut off her hand?" McCray scowled, his forehead wrinkles deepening into crevices. "The hand bothers me. It's some kind of message."

"Maybe Carla fought back and hurt one of the attackers, so he cut off the hand that struck him," Jackson speculated.

Evans bounced on her feet. "Can we get a DNA test on the fetus?"

"I've already asked for it." Jackson tucked his notes into his shoulder bag. "Let's get back out there. Meet me at the crime lab at three, unless you're on to something important. In that case, call me."

As they stood to leave, the desk officer opened the door. "Detective Jackson, I'm sorry to interrupt, but there's someone here to see you."

"Who is it?" Jackson noticed the officer looked uncomfortable.

"It's your wife, sir. I mean, your ex-wife."

"Oh crap."

Schak slapped him on the back. "That's the problem with bad wives, they make bad ex-wives too."

"It's probably about Katie." Jackson's heart pounded as he hurried toward the front of the building. Renee had hardly ever come to the department when they were married, and her presence here now disturbed him. This had to be about Katie. Jackson pushed through the security door into the small foyer on the other side of the plexiglass.

The sight of his ex-wife stunned him. She'd cut off her curly dark hair and now wore it mannishly short with spiky bangs in front. Her weight loss since their divorce had been steady, but today she looked almost gaunt in a black pantsuit. She stood by the door, staring at the fingernail she had just chewed. That hadn't changed. Renee looked up and breathed a sigh of relief. "Thank god you're here, Wade. I've been trying to connect with you for days."

"Is Katie okay?"

"She's fine. Why didn't you answer your phone?"

Jackson instinctively reached for his cell phone. How had he missed her calls? "Do you have a new phone number?"

"Yes."

"That's why I didn't pick up. I didn't recognize the number, and I've been very busy. Let's go into the conference room next door." He stepped outside and started across the breezeway.

"You don't want Schak and the others to see me, do you?"

"I just want some privacy."

Jackson used his ID card to enter a small conference room in the building they shared with city hall. The department's internal investigators had offices over here. Jackson couldn't decide if keeping them separate from the other officers was brilliant or potentially crippling. He and Renee took seats on opposite sides of the table.

His ex got right to the point. "We need to resolve the issue of the house."

"I thought we were going to wait a year."

"Did Katie tell you I got laid off?"

The information surprised him. "She didn't. I'm sorry."

"We lost the Safeway account and they laid off fifteen people." Her face twisted in a bitter grimace. "They cut everyone at the top of their pay scale." Renee had worked as marketer for a design firm for almost a decade. Through all her years of drinking, she'd managed to keep her job.

"You're collecting unemployment, right?"

"Of course, but it's only about sixty percent of what I was making and it won't last forever." Renee started on another fingernail. "Nobody is hiring PR people in this economy."

"What do you want from me?" He knew she'd come here with a specific request.

"I want to sell the house and split the equity."

Jackson knew it was coming, yet it still slammed him. "I think the timing is wrong." He drew in a deep breath. "First, the housing market here has bottomed out. If we're lucky enough to sell it, we won't get anywhere near what it's worth. Second, that house is my and Katie's home. I'm not sure I want to move." He wanted to point out he had invested more of his earnings into the house than she had, but he didn't say it. Not yet.

"You've been staying with Kera. What's the big deal?" Renee's voice took on an edge.

"I was recovering from surgery. I'm back at the Harris Street house now."

Renee sat back, arms crossed. "This isn't fair to me. I paid half the mortgage for twelve years. I want to be compensated."

Guilt and stress fought for control of his emotions. Jackson knew she was right, but he was not ready to sell the house. "Our divorce agreement says I have a year from the final decree before making a change."

"My life has changed." She lurched forward, hands flat on the table. "I'm divorced, living in a condo, and now unemployed. You've got the house and Katie. Work with me, Wade."

Options bounced around in his head. "What if the house doesn't sell? What is your plan B?"

"You were going to start buying me out, remember? Making payments on my half of the equity."

Oh crap. "I'm already struggling to make the mortgage by myself. Even if I could start paying you, it wouldn't be much."

"It has to be something. I don't want to get lawyers involved." Renee reached over and squeezed his hand, but not in a comforting way.

"A hundred dollars a month," Jackson offered. "It's all I can give you. I have to pay twenty percent of my surgery costs and the bills are still coming in."

"A hundred a month is not enough. I have fifty thousand in equity in the house."

"You *had* fifty thousand. In this market, it's more like thirty."

"At a hundred a month, it will take you twenty-five years to buy me out." Renee's ability to do math instantly in her head had always been a little creepy.

"I can't afford any more."

"There is another solution."

He could tell by her tone he wouldn't like it. "What?"

"I could move back in. That way Katie would get to live with both parents and we would both pay the mortgage and benefit from the house we own together."

Jackson fought the urge to laugh. "We're not getting back together."

"I know. We'd just be roommates."

"I don't think so." Jackson stood.

"Will you put the house on the market?"

"I don't know." His legs were shaking. "I have to get going. I have an investigation."

"You always have an investigation." Renee, as usual, got the last word.

Jackson grabbed a burrito from a cart vendor across the street, then headed for his car in the underground lot. He sat in the dark space and wondered: *How many meals have I eaten in my car over the past twenty years? How many dinners have I missed with my daughter?* After a couple of bites, his stomach protested and he put his food aside. He couldn't stop thinking about money. His share of the medical bills, including the trip to the emergency room and the stent procedure, was just under twelve grand, and he only had about forty-five hundred in accessible savings. He'd already contacted the accounting department at the hospital, and they'd given him sixty days to pay in full before they turned the bill over to a collection agency. The news had stunned him. He was still weighing his options, none of which he liked. The most obvious was to sell his '69 GTO, lovingly restored over a period of five years and painted a shimmering midnight blue. It broke his heart just to think about watching some other guy drive away in it.

Jackson started his city-issued Impala and headed for the hospital. The sky had turned brilliant blue in the last hour and the temperature was climbing. Pedestrians and cyclists were everywhere, wearing shorts and looking happy. A motorcycle roared by on a cross street and Jackson thought about the trike, sitting there in the garage, nearly finished. He and Katie had been building the three-wheeled motorcycle for eight months. All that was left were a few wiring issues to work out, but his surgery had brought everything to a standstill. He and Katie had hoped to take the trike out for its first cruise this weekend. It seemed unlikely now.

Jackson pulled into the hospital's parking structure and hurried across the sky bridge. He hadn't called ahead but he expected to find Lori still in the ICU. He wanted desperately for her to remember something about the attack. It might be the only way they would ever convict Shane…or Engall. If she couldn't recall anything, he needed to know if the amnesia she was experiencing was a protection mechanism that would fade in time, or if her blood loss had resulted in permanent memory impairment.

Either way, he had to keep Lori safe. The idea that she might be in danger had started small but now seemed real and imminent. Would it help to release the information about her amnesia to the media? If the killer thought she had no memory of the murders, he might not worry about Lori's testimony. Jackson wondered if he should tell the reporter Sophie Speranza about the amnesia, give her some exclusive information, and get her off his back. The profile she'd written about him had been published while he was suspended. People had called and e-mailed the department in his support and Lammers had reluctantly lifted his suspension. Once again, Jackson owed the feisty little pain-in-the-ass reporter a favor.

Jackson grudgingly dialed Sophie's cell-phone number. After five rings, he started to hang up, then Sophie came on the line. "Detective Jackson. I can't believe you called. What's going on?"

"I've got an exclusive for you. Lori Walker has amnesia and doesn't remember anything about the night of the murders."

Sophie was silent for a moment. "Is this true? Or are you using me to protect Lori?"

"It's true, but telling the public also protects Lori."

"Thanks. Any other new leads or breakthroughs?"

"Not yet."

In the waiting area Jackson saw an older woman with a young baby, and a teenager with a buzzed head and a nose ring. He did not see a patrol officer. The punk kid watched him as Jackson looked around and waited by the swinging doors. The uniformed officer came hurrying up the hallway. She was in her late twenties and Jackson had never seen her before. With the weapon, flashlight, and radio on her waist, she looked burdened by her uniform. "I'm Detective Jackson. Why weren't you at your post?"

"I had to use the restroom, sir." She sounded unapologetic.

"Has anyone been here to see Lori Walker?"

"Her aunt was in the room when I came on shift at eight this morning, and two high-school students stopped in around noon." The officer pulled a small tablet from her pocket and read the names. "Jenna Larson and Mason Black. I frisked them for weapons and watched them for a few minutes in the room, but they seemed harmless."

"Thank you." Jackson pushed open the double doors and walked softly past the rooms with unconscious patients. Older people who looked like they would not walk out.

A nurse was changing the dressing on Lori's abdomen, so Jackson waited in the hall for a few minutes. The smell of diarrhea lingered in the air, then a cart went by with the aroma of applesauce. He grimaced. As often as he was in the hospital to question victims or suspects, he never got used to the weird combination of smells.

"You can go in now," said a nurse in yellow scrubs as she came out. "Physically, Lori is doing much better, but she's emotionally fragile. Please be gentle."

"Of course." *Did he look like a prick?*

Lori pulled up her blanket and her lips quivered. He stood back from her bed to give her some space. "I'm Detective Jackson. I was here last night. Do you remember me?"

"Yes."

"I'm investigating the crime that took place at your home Sunday night. Can you tell me what happened?"

She closed her eyes and Jackson felt guilty for even being there. Lori may have been a legal adult, but lying there in the hospital bed with her milk-white skin and traumatized expression, she looked Katie's age. Jackson waited.

Finally Lori said, "I don't remember that night but my aunt told me what happened. I know my family is dead."

"I'm sorry for your loss. I know this a horrible time for you but I need your help."

"I can't help you. The only reason I'm not hysterical is the tranquilizers they're giving me." Lori looked as if she would cry at any second.

Jackson pressed ahead, feeling like a prick after all. "What is the last thing you remember?"

"I was at work, having a crappy day."

"Your boss was sexually harassing you?"

Her eyebrows arched, then she glanced away. "I don't want to talk about it."

"Does your boss know your family? Is it possible he did this?"

"No." She shook her head. "He's grabby, but he's not a monster."

"What route did you take to get home?"

"I always take Delta Highway."

"What was the weather like that night as you drove?" Jackson's theory, his hope, was if he led her gently through that evening, her memory might start to come back.

Lori's mouth trembled. "I remember it was nice outside when I was working and I hoped there would still be daylight when I got off."

"Did you stop anywhere on the way home? A store? Maybe to buy gas?"

Another scowl. "I remember stopping to see a friend, but I think that was another day, maybe last week."

"What time did you get home?"

"I don't know. I don't remember." She stared out the window.

"What does your doctor say about your memory?"

Lori turned back. "She thinks I have trauma-induced amnesia and my memory will come back someday. I'm having a CAT scan this afternoon to see if my brain is okay."

"What's your doctor's name?"

Lori's face was blank. "I don't know."

"When I was here yesterday, I asked you who hurt you and your family. You said 'Shane.' Did your cousin do this?"

"No." She looked horrified. "He would never hurt me. Or anyone. I can't believe I said that."

"You said his name twice."

She shook her head. "It doesn't mean anything."

"What about Shane's friends? Can you think of anyone he hangs out with who has criminal connections?"

Lori glanced over at the chair where her aunt had been, saw that they were alone, and said softly, "Shane used to hang out with Tyler Gorlock sometimes, back when he was using. Tyler is a thief, a dealer, and a jackass, but he's never been arrested."

"Would he have any reason to kill your family?"

Lori shivered. "My dad has guns."

A whole new scenario played out in Jackson's head. "How does Shane know Tyler Gorlock?"

"Tyler is Roy Engall's stepson. Shane and Tyler both painted for Roy last summer." Lori started to cry. "My dad never liked Tyler either."

"I'm sorry I upset you. " Jackson gave her a moment. "Thanks for this information. If you start to remember what happened that night, please call me."

She nodded. "I'm sorry I can't help you."

They were both quiet for a moment and Lori started to drift. Suddenly her eyes flew open. "Will they come back for me?"

"Probably not now, but we've had a patrol officer stationed outside the ICU since you arrived."

"What happens to me after I leave here? Will the police still protect me at Aunt Rita's house?"

Good question, Jackson thought. "We're going to find these guys and put them in jail so you don't have to worry."

Lori didn't look reassured, and he didn't blame her. "Will you get my nurse? I need more medication."

"Sure."

Jackson flagged the first person he saw, a guy in gray scrubs who said he would find Lori's nurse right away. Jackson went back to her room and stayed until a nurse came. It took seventeen minutes.

CHAPTER 16

Twenty days earlier

Lori stopped at the intersection and rolled down her window. The old homeless guy with the little dog hustled over, gave her a nearly toothless grin, and snatched the dollar out of her hand. "Thanks, miss. You have a good day."

Not very likely, Lori thought as she drove onto the freeway. Giving away the dollar and seeing his battered face light up had become the best part of her day—a talisman she hoped would keep everything else from being unbearable. Lori turned on the radio to distract herself. She had trained herself to not think about her job on the way. Walking into the restaurant feeling stressed just made Saturdays longer. She tried to start each shift with an open mind; her customers would be nice, she would be organized and efficient and make everyone happy, and her boss would be too busy to bother her.

The illusion was shattered twenty minutes into her shift. A family group of twelve sat in her station, taking up three tables, asking questions at the same time.

"One at a time. Please!" Lori knew her tone would cost her some of her tip, but she had to get control or this group would turn into a disaster. They quieted down, and she answered their questions as best she could. "Yes, the Cobb salad comes with bacon, and yes we can leave it out. No, you can't substitute onion rings for fries, and I don't know if the dressing has MSG, but I'll ask."

Of course, by the time she got back to the kitchen to start making their drinks she forgot about the salad-dressing issue. Lori watched some of her coworkers in amazement. They were cheerful about the job and good at it. They laughed and had fun with their customers and never seemed to forget anything or get flustered. It was like watching aliens perform an incomprehensible feat. Lori knew she was not cut out to be a waitress and desperately wanted to quit.

It was not an option. Her parents were so stressed about money right now, they would freak out if she quit or got fired. Lori gave most of her tips to her mother every day for groceries. Cash that should have been going into her savings account for her move to Hawaii. Getting out of Eugene was more important than ever, but everything was working against her. The whole new scene at home was too weird. Sometimes it felt good to help her parents, like she wasn't a needy kid anymore, but most of the time it felt stressful and so unfair. Her mother had become a fanatic about not spending money, and her dad was lost. The only bright spot in her life was the time she spent with her sweetie, but things were not good for him right now either. Lori dreaded the day her parents found out about their relationship. If they could just get to Maui and start their own life together, everything would get better.

"Lori, we're out of to-go boxes up here and it's your station's responsibility." Gina, a skinny woman who looked eighty but was probably not, hollered at Lori from the dessert bar. As lead waitress, Gina bossed everyone around, but she also helped Lori when she got too far behind. Lori tried not to think mean thoughts about her.

"I'll get them." She walked away from her half-finished drink order and hurried to the closet where paper products were kept.

"Bring some napkins too!"

Another thing she hated about this job; it was too damn loud in the restaurant. The roar of the dishwasher, the whine of the blenders going all the time, food servers shouting at each other just to be heard. The constant chaos wore on her nerves.

She loaded her arms with two sizes of to-go boxes and grabbed a big sleeve of napkins. From the corner of her eye, she saw the manager slide out of his office. *Oh shit.*

"Need some help?" Greg slid up behind her in the narrow hallway and reached for the napkins she was holding. His breath tickled the back of her neck, warm at first, then cooler as he inhaled deeply, taking in her scent. His hand slid over her right breast, pausing slightly, then slipped lower.

Lori jerked away and lost her load of paper products, which tumbled to the floor. *Shit.* She shot Greg a dirty look, then squatted and started to gather up the boxes. He knelt to help her, his face level with her breasts. "I need to see you in the office after your shift." His voice was a slithery whisper.

Lori pretended not to hear. She gathered the last of the packages and scooted away. Her heart pounded in her ears and her legs shook. The bastard. God, she hated him. What would happen if she didn't go see him after her shift? Would he cut her hours? Or fire her?

Lori stashed the boxes and napkins in the space below the soda fountain. When she reached for the drink tray she'd started, she realized someone had taken the two chocolate shakes she'd already made. *Oh shit.* She'd have to start over. The day's endurance contest had begun.

CHAPTER 17

Wednesday, June 3, 1:55 p.m.

Jackson squared his shoulders and walked into Surgery Ten for the third time in two days. Spending this much time with the dead was unnerving. He didn't know how pathologists handled it and was glad the autopsy was on an adult male this time. Women and children were harder to watch. Dead *men* often had it coming. Everything he'd learned on this case pointed to the notion that Jared had somehow brought this on his family. He had stepped outside of the bounds of socially acceptable behavior, and someone he associated with had reacted violently.

Rudolph Konrad's cheeks were flushed pink, popping out of his pale round face. Had the pathologist slipped a little bourbon in his coffee at lunch? Jackson had never seen the pathologist in the afternoon before. The medical examiner was not in the small room. "Where's Gunderson?" Jackson asked, grabbing a white overcoat from the wall hooks.

"He's out on a call." Konrad rolled the narrow table toward the stainless-steel drawers. "An older woman was found dead in her bathroom. Probably natural causes, but that's the ME's job to determine." The pathologist opened the door on the left, then looked back at Jackson. "I could use a hand."

Jackson ignored the signals his body was sending and stepped up to the sliding drawer. He had handled plenty of dead bodies. Why was he feeling squeamish? Was it the prednisone? His doctor had warned him it could play havoc with his emotions.

Using the sheet for leverage, they pulled Jared's two-hundred-pound body from the drawer tray to the wheeled table in a quick, concentrated effort. Jackson noticed Jared's well-defined stomach muscles and large quads, indicating he was athletic, perhaps even a runner. The three gaping wounds on the corpse's chest held his eyes though. They overlapped, digging a hole straight into the man's heart. The only other body Jackson had seen with this much knife damage had been a homeless man who'd gotten into a fight with another vagrant. None of the homeless guy's six knife wounds would have killed him if he'd made it to a hospital.

"I'll look for trace evidence first," Konrad said, rolling the table under the bright overhead light. He lifted Jared's left hand and took scrapings from under the nails. A white stripe circled the finger where Jared's wedding ring had been, and dark grease rings filled the lower curve of his fingernails, as if he'd done some engine repair recently. The victim's face and arms were tanned from working sleeveless outside, but the rest of his body had never seen the sun.

"The victim has no defense wounds, no blood under his nails, and no extraneous hair or fiber." Konrad's voice now had a little more energy than it had this morning. Was he finally warming up to him?

Jackson forced himself to keep quiet and wait until Konrad had finished his inch-by-inch scrutiny of Jared's skin and head. As the pathologist examined Jared's torso, he said, "This is a recent wound. Maybe in the last few weeks."

Jackson leaned in over the body. A few inches from Jared's navel was a roundish dark-pink scar where something small and sharp had penetrated the skin. "What do you suppose caused that?" Jackson said.

"I have no clue."

CHAPTER 18

Sixteen days earlier

Jared pulled into the driveway, relieved to be home. He'd spent the afternoon at the employment office, sitting through a class about job interviews. He'd learned a few things, such as to come prepared with questions for the employer and to answer in complete sentences, but overall it was not worth the time. The class about improving his résumé had been better. Until that point, he hadn't had a résumé.

As Jared trotted into the house, Nick called out, "Hey, Dad."

"Hey, son. How's your day?" Carla didn't like them to yell across the house, but Jared thought it was friendly. He was grateful his son still liked him.

In the kitchen Nick stood in front of the refrigerator. "I'm just getting a glass of Kool-Aid."

"Pour me one too." Carla had stopped buying soda after she was laid off. She said they had to save their food budget for food.

Carla had also decided Jared couldn't spend any money on beer either. She was right about the priorities, but it annoyed him. Now he drank more at the bar and less at home.

"A letter from the court came today," Nick said, pointing to the table.

"Oh boy." Jared opened the envelope and scanned the thickly worded paragraphs. "Your first session at Looking Glass is next Tuesday, but we're supposed to go in beforehand and fill out the paperwork."

"I'm sorry, Dad." His son apologized for the tenth time. "Bringing the pot here was stupid. I didn't even like it."

"It's okay, Nick. I know you're not a stoner. And if we can't pay for the program, they'll just kick you out. They can't send you to juvie because we don't have money." Could they? Jared didn't really know, but it didn't seem fair and he still trusted the system to be fair. Especially to kids. "How was school today?"

"The same."

"It's almost summer break. Let's plan a camping trip."

Nick's face lit up. "Waldo Lake?"

"Sure. You can bring a friend too. We'll leave the women home this time."

Nick shifted from one foot to the other. Jared waited him out.

"I didn't steal Uncle Kevin's Lou Gehrig card. I want you to believe me."

"I do believe you, son." Jared smiled and tried to look convincing. This was one of those situations where he simply didn't know what to believe and might never know the whole truth. The card had not been found and no charges were filed. Jared had decided to let the whole thing go. Nick needed his trust and he would give it to him. Jared thought it was more likely Shane had taken the card, and Kevin was mistaken about when he saw it last.

They heard Carla's car pull in, glanced at each other, and scooted out of the kitchen. Jared grabbed a sports magazine and headed to the back porch. He wanted to sit in front of the TV and watch something mindless, but it made him feel guilty to watch television during the day when he should be working or looking for a job. He glanced at his watch: 4:12. He had stayed out there putting in applications for as long as he could.

Carla came outside and sat in the lawn chair next to him. "How'd your day go?"

"Crappy. I turned in three applications at restaurants that weren't hiring and spent the afternoon learning how to get through an interview I won't be called for. How was your day?"

"Even crappier."

Jared reached over and held his wife's hand. He was plenty worried, but Carla took it all into her heart and let it eat away at her. There was nothing he could do or say to comfort her. He had tried.

After a moment, she said, "I'm worried about Lori."

"Me too. She seems unhappy."

"She told me yesterday someone was sexually harassing her."

A bolt of adrenaline shot him forward in the chair. "Who?"

"Lori wouldn't tell me, so I think it's someone we know. Someone she's protecting."

"When I find out who it is, I'm gonna kick his sorry ass."

Carla sighed. "That is why Lori didn't give me his name. She knew you'd react this way. She mostly wanted to know how to handle it."

"What did you tell her?"

"I told her to say 'sexual harassment' to him anytime his behavior was inappropriate and to stay away from him as much as possible."

Jared didn't want to know, yet he had to ask. "What exactly is happening? Is he grabbing her ass?"

"Lori was pretty vague."

"Goddammit." Jared jumped up and paced the small porch. "Is it that mama's boy manager at the restaurant?"

"I asked her and she said no." Carla pushed her hands through her hair.

"Who is it? A teacher?"

"School is almost over for the year. Maybe this will resolve itself."

"And if it's not a teacher? Where else is Lori hanging out?"

"She's at Jenna's sometimes." Carla bit her lip and looked away.

"What are you thinking?"

"She's been over at Tracy and Kevin's a lot lately. The last time we were over there, I thought I saw Kevin looking at her that way."

"No shit? Are you sure?" Jared had never warmed to Kevin, even after all these years, but Kevin was his sister's husband. This could cause huge trouble between him and Tracy.

"It was just a look, Jared," Carla said, trying to soothe him. "I don't know what was in his mind. Forget I said anything." His wife patted his knee. "Why don't you go watch some TV and forget about everything for a while. I know you want to." She gave him one of her special smiles. For a moment, Jared's heart felt light because Carla still loved him. She went inside to get on the internet, while he kept thinking about the jackass who was coming on to his daughter.

Later, Jared had to get out of the house. When he was working, all he wanted to do was come home and relax. Now that he was unemployed, he was restless and constantly wanted to leave. He kissed Carla, told her not to worry, then hustled out to his truck, which now had a *For Sale* sign in the window. He'd told Carla he was just going for a drive, but he knew he would end up at the Time Out Tavern. One beer, he told himself. A single beer wouldn't make or break their budget. Maybe he'd run into a friend who would buy him a second beer.

The tavern was on a side street in West Eugene in the middle of an industrial area. The location was genius, catching factory workers as they left their miserable jobs. Once you started drinking in a certain place and got to know everyone, you kept coming back, even if you quit the factory or moved across town. Jared had been coming here since his brief employment at Whittier Wood Products nearly fifteen years ago.

The bar was nothing special. Dark, noisy, and crowded, like any drinking hole. The pool tables and dartboards were a nice addition because they got Jared off his bar stool every once in a while. Usually the moment he crossed the threshold he felt better. Someone always called out his name and the bartender poured him a Miller from the tap without even asking.

Tonight was no exception. Yet neither of those things took the edge off. Jared nursed his beer and chatted with Charlie, an old-timer who'd been coming to the tavern longer than Jared.

Around eight, Roy Engall walked in with two of his crew. It was the first time Jared had seen Roy since his layoff. Adrenaline rushed into his gut. Jared had typed up the blackmail note but hadn't delivered it yet. He'd been holding out, hoping he'd find a job. There were no jobs and they hadn't paid their rent this month.

He and Roy nodded at each other and Roy went to the other side of the room. Darrell and Tyler, his ex-coworkers, stopped by and asked friendly questions about his job search. Jared appreciated the gesture, but he didn't care to be around Roy's stepson Tyler. A little later, the bartender set another beer in front of him and said it was from Roy. Jared felt a pang of guilt. He planned to deliver the letter tomorrow, maybe leave it in Roy's truck. He didn't want Noni to see it first.

Jared drank the beer and played a game of pool with Darrell. His fellow painter sunk the eight ball too early and bought him another beer. Jared drank half, then decided to go home. A moment later, his brother-in-law walked in. They hadn't spoken to each other since Nick had been arrested. Tracy had called and Jared had responded politely, but his sister was on his shit list too. Jared nodded at Kevin, then turned away. He knew he should leave the bar immediately. Yet he didn't.

He kept his eye on Kevin, watching him flirt with the cocktail waitress. When had his brother-in-law become such a shit? Jared would never forgive him for calling the cops on Nick and accusing his son of stealing, especially when Kevin's own son was an addict and consequently had once been a part-time thief. Now Kevin was humiliating Jared's sister by openly flirting with every woman in reach. Had the dog fucker also touched his sweet little Lori?

He eyeballed Kevin for nearly an hour. Jared was just getting up to go home when he saw Kevin pay his tab at the bar. Jared slid off his bar stool and strode toward the door, feeling a little unsteady. How many beers had he drunk? It would be good to get outside for some fresh air. After he talked to Kevin, he'd go home. Maybe take a walk first to sober up or call Carla to come get him if he had to.

In the parking lot he found Kevin's van and leaned up against the driver's side door to wait. Jared thought about the *For Sale* sign in the back window of his own truck and felt a fresh wave of anger.

He heard the crunch of gravel and looked up to see Kevin. "What do you want, Jared? Say what you have to say, then get out of my way. I'm not in the mood for trouble." Kevin stopped four feet away.

"You've sure caused plenty of it."

"I didn't start this shit." Kevin's breath reeked of cigarettes. He had supposedly quit years ago.

"Why the hell did you call the police on Nick? That was out of line."

"He stole my Lou Gehrig. It's worth two grand. I'm supposed to let that go?"

"You're supposed to talk to us. We're family."

"You would have denied it then like you're denying it now."

"He didn't do it." Jared lurched forward, closing the gap between them. "You're mistaken about when you saw the card last."

"Bullshit."

"What about Shane? We know he's stolen things in the past. He's been arrested for it."

"Only when he was using, and *never* from us."

"Maybe he's using again."

"He's not." Kevin's jaw locked in place.

"You're so fucking blind when it comes to Shane. I know he's your son, but get real." Jared let the anger swell and his voice got loud. "The police searched our house and arrested Nick. He had a joint in his pocket and now he has a possession charge."

"I didn't mean for any of that to happen." Kevin didn't sound sorry.

"I think you wanted it to happen so Shane wasn't the only kid in the family with a record."

Kevin came toward him and was now in striking range. "Leave Shane out of this."

"I don't want Shane at my house anymore."

"He's a legal adult. I can't control where he goes."

"That's the problem." Jared reached over and tapped Kevin's chest to make his point. "You've never been able to control your own son."

Kevin grabbed Jared's hand and squeezed. "Don't touch me. You'll regret it."

Jared jerked his hand free. "Speaking of touching. Keep your hands off my daughter."

"What the hell are you talking about?"

"I'm talking about Lori. You've been sexually harassing her and it better goddamn stop."

"That's crazy! Did she tell you that?"

"She told Carla someone was getting grabby with her and Carla has seen you looking at Lori."

"Bullshit!" Kevin's eyes flared with a wild look. "You're the one who needs to keep Lori out of my house and away from Shane."

"What are you saying?"

"Lori is after Shane, you idiot. She's been trying to seduce him for months."

Jared lunged forward and grabbed Kevin's T-shirt with both hands. The blood vessels in his temples wanted to burst. "You lying sack of shit! You touch her again and I'll beat you into a coma."

Their faces were inches apart.

"Wise up, Jared." Kevin pulled free and turned away. Before Jared could respond, Kevin wheeled around and sucker punched him in the gut. The sharp blow made him suck in his breath. What the hell? As Kevin stumbled back, Jared saw the key sticking out of his fist. The fucker! Jared clenched his hands and lurched forward, ready to pulverize him. His brother-in-law saw the look on his face and scrambled to get away. Kevin's feet slipped in the gravel and he fell back.

Smack! Kevin's head slammed into the door handle on his truck and he collapsed on the ground.

Oh shit! Jared's heart hammered like overworked cylinders. "Kevin." He knelt down and shook him. "Kevin." Blood soaked through the prone man's hair. Jared fumbled for his cell phone, flipped it open, then heard a moan. "Kevin, tell me you're okay."

Kevin opened his eyes but didn't respond. Jared scanned the parking lot and didn't see anyone coming or going. He reached into Kevin's shirt pocket, pulled out the cell phone, and dialed 911. "This is Kevin Compton. I need help." Jared paused for effect. "I'm in the parking lot at the Time Out Tavern on West Fifth." He clicked the phone closed and put it back in the pocket.

Jared jogged to his truck, his heart still racing. Kevin would be fine, he told himself. He was just a little dazed. Jared climbed behind the wheel and waited a moment for his legs to stop shaking. His stomach throbbed and he no longer felt too drunk to drive. Adrenaline had burned through his buzz and he was sick with worry. He started the engine, backed out, and barreled toward the side exit. In the rearview mirror, he saw Darrel and Tyler coming out of the bar. Would they recognize his truck in the fading light?

Thoughts jumbled in his head as he drove. It wasn't his fault. He'd never even touched Kevin. In fact, Kevin had punched him. Jared pressed his fingers against the wound and felt a little blood. Why had Kevin hit him? Kevin was the ass-grabbing, lying sack of shit. He couldn't believe what his sorry brother-in-law had said about Lori. Such crap. Kevin was just trying to distract him from the real situation: his brother-in-law coming on to his daughter.

A moment of uncertainty came over Jared. Could it be true? Lori and Shane had sure spent a lot of time together lately. No. They were cousins. Jared rejected the idea they could be sexually involved. Still, he wouldn't let Lori go over to the Comptons' house by herself again. It would break his sister's heart, but he had to protect Lori from whatever was going on.

Jared sped down the road, trying to put it all out of mind. His heart didn't stop pounding until he saw the lights of an ambulance coming the other way.

CHAPTER 19

Wednesday, June 3, 3:48 p.m.

The new crime lab had been built in an old railroad neighborhood with a hodgepodge of ancient businesses and houses begging to be torn down. City officials had chosen the property because it was cheap, with the idea the public would never need to visit. The gray-brick exterior had no markings except for the street number above the door, which faced a small side parking lot.

Jackson drove up to the gate and flashed his ID at the camera mechanism. When the gate slid open, he drove onto the property and parked near the first bay door. Once inside, he headed for the check-in room, where he placed Carla's purse and Lori's backpack into a locker. The back side of the locker opened into the evidence-processing lab. The system allowed officers to securely drop off evidence without disrupting the lab technicians. Jackson logged the items into the computer terminal, then went upstairs to meet with Parker.

He found her in the hallway outside her office. Dressed entirely in chocolate brown, she looked taller and thinner than usual. "Detective Jackson, you're early."

Did he detect a hint of amusement on her stoic face? "We have some things to go over before we reconstruct the scene. Do you have a minute?"

"Of course. I'm glad you're here." Parker walked away, pulling on a white lab coat. "I have something to show you."

The main lab, about the size of a large living room, had equipment along three walls and a stainless-steel table in the middle. The "super-glue dryer," where they processed large items for fingerprints, took up a big chunk of space. A pair of white, paint-stained running shoes sat on the table, surrounded by oversize photos of bloody shoe prints. The photos he'd taken when he first entered the crime scene.

"The prints match Engall?"

"Distinctly. See this circular pattern here? And this crisscross pattern here?" Parker touched one of the prints with gloved hands. "It'll be obvious even to the laypeople on the jury. There are probably thousands of pairs of size ten-and-a-half white Adidas in this model, so it's only one piece of circumstantial evidence." Parker gave him a small smile. "I also found a tiny bit of blood on the shoes. They'd been rinsed off, but there were trace amounts in the grooves. I sent the sample to the state lab to compare to all the Walkers' blood."

A sense of lightness came over Jackson, as if he'd lost ten pounds. "Excellent." He gave Parker's shoulder a squeeze. "I need to step out and make a phone call." Jackson called the officer watching Engall's house, who had checked in with him earlier. "We'll be out to arrest Engall very shortly," he said. "If the suspect even steps outside, cuff him and stick him in the back of your car."

Next he called Evans, who picked up instantly. "Hey, Jackson, I was just going to call you. What's the word?"

"The shoes you dug out of the trash match the prints in the foyer at the crime scene. It looks like Engall is our killer. Or one of them. Why don't you go make the arrest?"

"I'm on it. Damn, it's good to be right every once in a while."

Jackson resisted the urge to remind her they still had a lot to prove. "Good work, Evans. I'd like to be there for Engall's interrogation. I'm at the crime lab now, but I can meet you at headquarters in an hour or so."

"See you then."

Jackson went back into the brightly lit lab. "Has any of the DNA analysis come back?"

"Not yet, but they promised me some results this afternoon."

"Let's head to the conference room and get this reconstruction started. The more I know about how the assault took place, the more effective I can be when I interrogate Engall again."

Quince and Schak showed up at the crime lab around two o'clock. McCray had called to say he was talking to the Walkers' neighbors again and getting conflicting information. They gathered in the conference room, a long narrow space with a long dry-erase board in front of a similar-shaped window. Photos, blood-spatter maps, and computer-generated schematics covered the board. Jackson noted the plush chairs and wondered why he and his detectives were still meeting in a closet with fold-up metal chairs. They would be moving to the new building soon, he reminded himself. *If he still had a job.*

Jackson turned to Quince. "What did you find out about Shane Compton's alibi?"

"Aaron Priest says he was with Shane on Sunday, but will not commit to a time frame. He says he was too loaded to remember much. His testimony is worthless either way." Quince pulled out a large yellow notepad. "I've never seen a crime-scene reconstruction. This should be educational." Quince had worked property crimes, then vice, and was now training in the Violent Crimes Unit. Over the years, his blond hair had darkened and his baby face was starting to show his true age.

"We don't do this very often and usually it's to build a case against a suspect we've already charged." Jackson took out a notepad as well. Schak sipped coffee and made no move to write anything down.

As Parker came into the room, Jackson said, "By the way, the shoes Engall tossed in the trash match the bloody footprints in the foyer of the Walker house."

"No shit? Evans was right?" Schak grinned.

"Looks like it. There was blood on the shoes too, but we don't have DNA confirmation yet."

Quince cut in. "So Engall went over there, drunk on his ass, to confront Jared about the blackmail and ended up killing everybody. Well, almost." Quince shuddered. "Yet alcohol is legal and socially acceptable."

"Don't get started on that," Schak warned.

"Hey, the statistics are there. Alcohol kills thirty-five thousand people a year. This is just one more extreme example."

"That doesn't mean we should make all drugs legal," Schak shot back.

"Let's get rolling." Jackson signaled Parker. He'd heard this debate before and didn't want to be distracted by it. "Tell us what happened."

Parker stood at the board in her white lab jacket with her dark hair pulled tightly back. Jackson was reminded of his seventh-grade science teacher, who all the boys thought was sexy, but in a creepy way. Parker announced, "I believe Jared Walker was killed first." She pointed to a photo in the middle of the board. "The blood spatter on the floor here and near the countertop is clearly identifiable and contains only Jared's blood, which we know because he's type O, and the rest of the family is type A. We don't have DNA comparisons yet."

Parker paused, as if expecting questions. When none came, she continued. "We don't have the postmortem report on Jared either, but the pathologist says the blows to his head came before the knife wounds to his chest. The head trauma to both Jared and Carla slowed their heartbeats, resulting in considerably less spatter than if they had been knifed first."

She glanced over her glasses at Jackson. "I talked with Konrad this afternoon. He thinks Jared took the first two blows standing up, then fell to his knees and was struck with the bat once more. The attacker plunged a knife into his heart four times. That's the blood pattern you see on the floor here." Parker pointed again.

"Where did the bat come from?" Schak asked.

"The prints on the bat belong to family members Lori, Nick, and Shane. Our best guess is the bat was in the house, lying somewhere nearby."

"So they were arguing in the kitchen and the attacker went for the nearby bat." Schak shook his head. "Are Roy Engall's prints on the bat?"

"No."

The detectives all looked at each other. "He wore gloves," Quince offered.

"Is it possible there were two assailants?" Jackson was thinking of Tyler Gorlock, Engall's stepson.

"It's very possible." Parker took off her glasses and rubbed her eyes. "This scene is a mess, and I have to admit I've never worked anything like it."

"We'll call in help if we need to," Jackson said. "For now, let's continue." He was eager to confront Engall again.

Parker went on, sounding less confident. "The biggest question is whether the assailant put the bat down to stab Jared, then picked the bat up again to strike Carla, or if he made all the blows with the bat first, then picked up the knife. The knife, we've determined, comes from the set in the kitchen."

"The evidence doesn't tell you which order?" Jackson was disappointed.

She shook her head. "Joe and I went over everything together. There's no way to know for sure. Based on the lack of blood on the bat, my best guess is he made all the blows with the bat first to get control, then used the knife to ensure they were dead."

Jackson's cell phone rang. He slipped it from his pocket and looked at the caller ID: *Sergeant Lammers*.

"We have a home-invasion situation in southwest Eugene. The SWAT team is on its way. I'm calling you because the perps are driving a van registered to Roy Engall."

"Holy crap. What's the address?" Jackson was on his feet.

"It's 3219 Stratmore. We think there's a woman and a toddler in the house. A neighbor got suspicious and called it in."

"I'm on my way." Jackson knew the others were salivating to know what was going down, but he had to wrap up this meeting first. "Parker, can you quickly summarize what you've determined about the scene?"

Her shoulders gave the tiniest shrug. "I think there were two assailants; one used the bat and the other used the knife. Jared was attacked first, followed by Carla, then the two kids. Lori was likely last and the assailant was in a hurry by then."

"Why only one set of footprints in the hallway?"

"The man with the bat may have gone outside before the blood was spilled and waited for the other to finish the job."

"Thanks. Keep me updated as the DNA comes in." Jackson reached for his bag. "There's a home invasion going on in South Eugene, and the perps are driving a van registered to Roy Engall."

"I'll be damned." Schak jumped up. "Isn't Evans picking up Engall right now?"

"That's what I thought. I don't know what this new development means." Jackson followed Quince, who was already headed for the door. As they strode down the stairs, he called Evans, but she didn't pick up. He left her a message: "Where are you? There's a home invasion on Stratmore involving a van registered to Roy Engall. Schak, Quince, and I are headed over. Don't get in the middle of anything. Call me."

"You think Evans is already at the scene?" Quince asked.

"I hope not."

By the time they reached the parking lot, they were running.

CHAPTER 20

The SWAT unit had set up a command post in the middle of the dead-end street a hundred yards from the hostage house. Close enough to strike, but out of the perpetrators' line of sight. The deep-purple armored truck, affectionately called Barney, sat in the middle surrounded by dark-blue patrol units, like a mother spider with her babies. A big box van carrying breeching equipment, radios, and shields sat off to the side, and the crisis negotiation team's bread truck was also on the street. Men armed with Remington 700s quietly made their way to sniper posts on either side of the hostage house. The tranquil neighborhood in the south-hills forest had been transformed into a battle zone.

Jackson parked behind a patrol unit, then went around to his trunk and retrieved his Kevlar vest and a pair of binoculars. He took off his suede jacket and pulled on the vest, which he only wore a few times a year. He would not likely get near any action, but it didn't hurt to err on the side of caution. The extra weight was cumbersome as he jogged to the command post. His surgery area was none too happy either. He still hadn't taken his afternoon dose of anti-inflammatory.

"Get back in the house!" An officer yelled at a teenage boy who'd come out on his front porch to check out the excitement. The officer rushed toward Jackson. "This area is sequestered, sir. Please get in your car and leave." Jackson didn't recognize him either.

"I'm Detective Jackson. Sergeant Lammers requested my presence. I may have useful information." He strode past the officer and headed for the person in charge, the lieutenant who commanded both SWAT and the crisis negotiation team. Don Bruckner and his perimeter team were looking at street maps and house plans, spread out over the hood of his cruiser. The gorgeous June weather worked to everyone's advantage. If it had been a rainy day in November, SWAT would have taken over someone's house as a command center.

Jackson glanced up the street. Men armed with submachine guns crouched behind cars parked across from the hostage house. They were the hasty team, ready to charge the home at a moment's notice. The snipers he'd seen a moment ago would soon be in place on the roofs of adjacent houses and in the living room of the home directly across. Other SWAT members were stationed on every property around the suspect house. In response to a callout, twenty-two patrol officers and sergeants dropped whatever they were doing and rushed to the compound where the SWAT vehicles were stored. Jackson had taken the training and been part of the unit when he was younger, but once he'd made detective he'd backed out. Being on call 24/7 had been too much of a demand with his violent-crimes caseload and a young child at home.

Still waiting for Bruckner's attention, Jackson scooted to the far side of the street and trained his binoculars on the two-story, cream-colored house with the hostages. An older white van, a Dodge, Jackson thought, sat in the driveway next to a gray Toyota Camry. It was not the same van Roy Engall had been driving the day he'd run from Jackson. Was Engall even here? Jackson had doubts. Who else would be using a vehicle registered to Roy Engall? The name came to him in an instant. Tyler Gorlock, the stepson.

Jackson approached the group of men huddled around the command-post car, each wearing a Kevlar vest under his dark-blue uniform and carrying a Heckler & Koch 416 in addition to the .45 Sig Sauer strapped to his waist. All that firepower made Jackson realize someone could very likely die today. He hoped not. He needed the suspects alive for questioning,

"Jackson." Bruckner clapped him on the shoulder as he stepped into the circle. "Glad you're here. What can you tell us?" Bruckner was seasoned law enforcement, an ex-military officer who'd given five years to the army and twelve to the Eugene Police Department, with a year off to work security for Blackwater in Iraq. Bruckner was a wall of muscle with a shaved head and a sweet smile that was nowhere in sight today. Jackson had worked with him years ago when they'd both been rookie SWAT members.

Jackson worried he had little to offer. "The van in the driveway is not the same vehicle Roy Engall was driving the day I picked him up for questioning. My suspect may not be directly involved. What's the situation here?"

"We believe there are two perps in the house, men the neighbor describes as in their early twenties. They seem to be holding a woman and a small child hostage. There may be other hostages as well."

"Roy Engall has a stepson, Tyler Gorlock, who's in that age range."

One of Bruckner's men radioed a dispatcher in the big box van serving as their communications post. "Run a background on Tyler Gorlock."

"Have they communicated with you?" Jackson saw Quince and Schak coming up the sidewalk. They were stopped and turned back. They would have to wait on the perimeter with the first-responder patrol cops who'd also been pushed back by the SWAT team.

"We sent the armored truck up to the door with the hailer and a cell phone, but so far, silence." Bruckner kept his expression neutral, but Jackson sensed an underlying frustration. "This is what we know," Bruckner continued. "The neighbor saw two suspicious guys go into the backyard of the house next door owned by John and Sheila Northrup. The neighbor called the police and reported it, then called Sheila to warn her. Sheila didn't answer." Bruckner's jaw tensed. "Officer Whitstone responded to the dispatch, called in the license plates of the vehicles in the driveway, and no one has seen or heard from her since."

A bolt of fear ran through Jackson. "You think she's the other hostage."

Bruckner pointed to the patrol unit parked on the street in front of the hostage house. "We ran the plates and Whitstone is commanding that vehicle today. She's here somewhere. When a second officer arrived and approached the house, he was fired on."

"Oh shit." Jackson knew Debby Whitstone. She'd been a first responder to a homicide victim in February and had helped him with the case. She also had two kids who expected her to come home after her shift. What had prompted her to enter the situation alone? Jackson had a dozen other questions but suspected Bruckner would not have answers. "Why did the perps choose this house? Why Sheila Northrup?"

"We're running the Northrups through the databases now," Brucker said. "I was hoping you could tell me something about these assholes." The lieutenant looked around. "Detective Bohnert is supposed to be here too. We think they might be the same perps doing the carjackings. Similar descriptions." Bruckner gestured at the gray home on the right. "This is our safe house. The neighbor who saw the men is in there. I'd like you to listen to her descriptions, ask a few questions, and see if you recognize anyone from your homicide case."

Jackson weaved through the SWAT officers. Behind him, an unfamiliar voice came though the portable PA system set up on the hood of the car. "We have a cop in here and we'll kill her if you don't leave."

Jackson spun back. The lone female in the cluster of flak jackets grabbed the hailer. "This is Sergeant Miller. No one is going to die today. We can work something out." Miller headed the crisis negotiation team, but was on her way up to management.

After a minute of no response, Jackson hurried into the safe house, anxious to complete this task. The door opened as he came up the walkway and an officer motioned him into the house. A woman in her sixties stood next to the front window, peeking through the closed curtains. A teenage girl was in the kitchen, talking on a cell phone to her mother, who had not been allowed to come up the street.

He introduced himself as he approached the woman at the window. "I know you've already gone through this, but please describe the men you saw next door."

"One was a little short, only about five-five." The woman kept glancing out the window as she talked. "He wore jeans and a dark-gray sweatshirt with a hood. The hood was up and I couldn't see his hair, but his skin seemed dark so he might be Hispanic." She finally pulled away from the window and perched on the edge of an overstuffed chair. "His nose was wide and flat and his eyes looked dark too, but it was hard to tell from here."

The description didn't match anyone Jackson had questioned. Certainly not Roy Engall. "What about the other man?"

"He's taller. Maybe six feet. He had on a brown jacket and he looked strong, like somebody who lifts weights. Dirty-blond hair and a pockmarked face."

"What kind of hair? Long, short, curly?" Except for the pockmarked face, it could have been Shane. Except Shane was in jail.

"Straight hair to the collar of the jacket and slicked back from his forehead."

"Anything else you can tell me?"

"The tall guy walked with a little bounce in his step."

"Thanks, ma'am."

Jackson nodded at the officer and went back outside. He didn't recognize either man she'd described. A media van was now parked near the end of the street, and he wondered if the cameraman would get close enough to film the house. Jackson checked his notebook and called Noni Engall. "What does your son Tyler look like?"

"Why?"

"Just tell me. It may save his life."

"He's five-eleven and about one ninety. He has dark-blond hair, a little shaggy, and blue eyes. What's going on?"

"Any tattoos or facial hair?"

"He has some scarring from acne."

"Thanks." Jackson hung up, thinking the pockmarks were more likely meth-sore scars. He jogged over to the command post and relayed the information to Bruckner.

"That's our guy." Bruckner raised an eyebrow. "Dispatch just told me Tyler Gorlock has only been arrested once, for disorderly conduct." They were silent while they processed the information, with everyone thinking: How did he go from disorderly conduct to home invasion without any arrests in between?

The crisis negotiator spoke into the hailer again. "Tyler, listen up. Your record is clean. If you give up the hostages and surrender now, a judge will go easy on you. Don't make this situation worse."

"Fuck you!" It was a different voice this time. The shorter, darker man.

Bruckner's cell phone rang and the buzzing voices stopped. The lieutenant picked up and listened for a long moment, nodding and pressing his lips together. He clicked off. "Dispatch again. We know what they're after."

Nobody felt like guessing.

"Weapons," Bruckner said, his voice tight. "John Northrup has three registered handguns and five hunting rifles. The perps are well armed." A murmur rippled through the SWAT officers. Jackson thought about the weapons they'd found in the Walkers' house.

"What are you thinking?" Bruckner asked.

"The Walkers had a gun safe with two rifles, plus a small handgun in a cookie jar. What if it's the same guys? And the mass homicide started as a weapons raid?"

"You're saying the perps won't hesitate to kill the hostages."

"If it's the same two intruders, they're deadly." Jackson came back to Roy Engall's bloody footprints. Was Engall part of this? Possible scenarios bounced around in his head. Did the footprints belong to stepson Tyler? If he was driving his stepfather's van, maybe he had borrowed Roy's shoes as well. If so, this case was finally starting to make sense. Except the killers had not taken the Walkers' guns. Had Jared refused to give them the key, inciting the violence? Maybe they had fled in a panic, leaving the guns.

"We have to let the hostage takers walk away," Sergeant Miller announced. "We can't risk letting them kill an officer, a civilian, and a baby." She sounded firm in her decision.

Bruckner grabbed the hailer microphone and took over the negotiations. "Tyler, are you listening? Send out the woman and child and we'll stand down."

After two long minutes, they heard the second man say, "What do you mean by *stand down*?"

"I mean the SWAT team will leave." Bruckner cleared his throat. "Here's how it will go. You send out the woman and the child. I send all the other officers away, but I stay to ensure the safety of the police officer you'll still have as a hostage. You walk out with her and get into your van. Once you're in the van, you let the officer go and drive away."

"Fuck that! The cop stays with us until we're clear. I don't want a sharpshooter taking off the top of my head as we drive away."

"You have a deal. Send out the woman and child." Bruckner clicked off the microphone, controlling the conversation.

"You can't let them drive away with Whitstone," Miller argued. "They'll kill her."

"I won't let them kill a cop," Bruckner boomed back. Despite his confidence, his eyes signaled stress. "We have four snipers in place. The perps are not leaving here alive."

"I'd like to bring one in for questioning," Jackson said.

"That's not my priority."

"Then I need to question the hostage when she comes out."

"Of course."

Bruckner radioed the hasty team and told them to expect a hostage to exit. All the SWAT members were on high alert now, weapons raised and no chatter. Five minutes passed in near silence. The sun drifted behind a cloud and a cool breeze gave them a little relief from the heat of the vests.

Jackson heard a creak and raised his binoculars to the hostage house. The front door swung open and a barefoot woman in her early thirties rushed out, carrying a boy of about three. She kept the boy's face pressed tightly against hers, eyes wide with terror, as she ran down the flagstone path. As Sheila Northrup neared the sidewalk, she cut across the lawn and headed toward the command post. A SWAT officer darted out from behind the neighbor's fence, grabbed her arm, and ran with her.

Jackson opened the back door of Bruckner's vehicle and she climbed in, still clinging tightly to her little boy. A second later she burst into tears.

"Mommy? Don't cry." The boy looked up at Jackson.

"Your mommy's fine. Sometimes people cry when they're happy." Jackson closed the door partway to give her some privacy. He would let her collect herself before he questioned her.

"Let's move out," Bruckner called to his team in a show of compliance. The thunder of heavy boots filled the air. SWAT members climbed into the back of the armored truck, then Barney and the communications van pulled away. They weren't going far. It was a show of noise and movement for the hostage takers, who couldn't see down the street without exposing themselves to sniper fire.

Jackson kept his binoculars trained on the house. Sheila's sobs began to subside, and in a moment she said, "They're going to kill that cop. I feel so bad for her."

"She'll be fine. These men are highly trained." Jackson wished he felt as confident as he sounded. He'd seen too many bodies recently.

After a few minutes movement caught his eye. The front door swung open and Whitstone stepped out. Her cherub face was a tight mask of control. Tyler Gorlock was snugged up against her, with a handgun pressed into her neck. Another movement. The second man slipped out and concealed himself behind Gorlock.

Jackson couldn't believe they were taking the risk. What the hell was their plan? They had to know cops were waiting at the end of the street.

The trio sidestepped across the cement patio in an awkward shuffle, then eased onto the short sidewalk between the patio and the driveway. Slowly, they shuffled toward the white van fifteen feet away. Jackson searched the skyline, looking for the snipers. He spotted a rifle barrel on an adjacent rooftop. For the trained officer it was an easy, close shot.

When the huddled group reached the van, they stopped. Time slowed to a crawl as they stood there looking around. What were the perps waiting for? Could they see the hasty team or the snipers? Did they have a plan for getting safely into the van?

The trio inched forward until they were next to the sliding door on the vehicle. Whitstone reached over and pulled on the handle. With her wrists tied together, she lacked strength and coordination and the door didn't budge. Whitstone tugged harder. Gorlock had the weapon in his right hand and couldn't help her. Finally he brought up his right foot and pushed. The door slammed open with a clang. Gorlock lunged sideways into the hollow of the vehicle, taking Whitstone with him.

For a nanosecond the short hostage taker stood alone, exposed. As he started to lunge sideways, the crack of a rifle split the air. A bullet hole opened in the man's forehead and he fell against the opening of the van.

Gorlock wasted no time. His foot came out and shoved his partner's body to the ground, then the van door slammed closed. The neighborhood went silent again, as if all the air and noise had been sucked out. Jackson's chest hurt and he realized he'd been holding his breath. He filled his lungs and thought, *One down.* In the car behind him, the little boy began to cry. Jackson lowered his binoculars to rest his eyes.

"What will he do now?" Sheila whispered from the car.

"I don't know. He must be panicked."

Jackson couldn't see what was happening inside the van, but he heard the engine start. He yanked the binoculars back to his face. The vehicle rolled backward down the sloped driveway. As the van neared the street, its back end curved in Jackson's direction, leaving it facing the houses at the dead end of the street. What was Gorlock thinking? Did he plan to plow through someone's yard? It made more sense than trying to outrun the cops at the other end.

The perp never had the chance. A second shot rang out from above, shattering the windshield. The side door banged open and Officer Whitstone came running, hands still tied but otherwise unharmed. The tension in his muscles eased a little. Jackson spun back to the van, but he could no longer see Gorlock in the driver's seat. Had he been hit? Was he dead? The engine shut down, with the van straddling the driveway and the street.

Gorlock yelled something but Jackson couldn't hear it.

Men in blue rushed the vehicle. "Throw your weapon out and surrender!"

No movement from the van.

"Throw your weapon out. Come out with your hands in the air."

After a moment, the driver's door opened halfway and a handgun clattered to the asphalt. It looked like a police-issue Sig Sauer. Gorlock wasn't visible, and Jackson figured he had to be on his hands and knees.

"Throw out your other weapon! Do it now!" The SWAT officer's voice could be heard for three blocks.

A second handgun clattered to the ground.

"Come out the other side with your hands in the air!"

From his vantage point, Jackson couldn't see the passenger door, but the hasty team rushed toward it. He let out his breath again. Whitstone was safe and Tyler Gorlock would be taken into custody, where Jackson would have an opportunity to interrogate him. Maybe he would finally get some answers about what had happened to the Walkers.

CHAPTER 21

Sheila had refused medical treatment, so Jackson drove her downtown, where she would be debriefed by whichever detective Sergeant Lammers assigned to the home-invasion case. This was his opportunity to get the information he needed.

"What's your son's name?" The boy was asleep in her lap.

"John Junior. We call him JJ."

"I'm working a homicide that might be connected to what happened today, and I'd like to ask a few questions."

"Okay." Sheila's voice still quivered.

"Did the two men talk about another home invasion?"

"They didn't talk much at all. They just wanted the guns. If the cop hadn't shown up, I think they would have taken them and left."

Jackson doubted it. The men had not worn masks to protect their identities. "How did the police officer end up as a hostage?"

"I'm not sure. They saw her pull up, so they knew it was a cop ringing the bell." Sheila began to rock a little in the seat beside him. "When no one answered the door, the cop went around the side of the house. The blond guy stayed inside and kept his gun on me. Rico, the short, dark one, went into the backyard to wait for the cop. When they came in, she was a hostage. They tied her hands together, but they let me hold JJ."

"Had you ever seen the men before?"

Sheila shook her head.

Jackson looked over and couldn't catch her eye. What was she keeping from him? "Does your husband know these men?"

"I think a friend of his once mentioned the name Rico."

"Who's the friend?"

"Roy Engall."

A little shiver ran up Jackson's spine. "How does your husband know Roy?"

"I think they've done business together. John is manager at Emerald Construction Supply."

"The blond perpetrator is Tyler Gorlock, Roy Engall's stepson."

"Oh god. That must be how they knew about John's guns." Sheila started to cry. "I hate the damn guns. I begged John to get rid of them when our baby was born, but he wouldn't do it."

Jackson didn't know how to comfort her. Every marriage had its sticking points. This one might break hers apart. As they neared city hall, Sheila called her mother and asked if she could stay with her for a while. Jackson was glad Sheila had parents in town to comfort her and give her a safe place. He suspected she might not go back to John and his guns. Jackson thought about Lori Walker. She didn't have parents waiting to make her feel safe after her ordeal. She had a couple of aunts though, and a home to go to when she left the hospital.

* * *

Lori opened her eyes and sat up slowly, testing to see how she felt. Yesterday, sitting up had made her want to vomit. She'd asked the nurse to cut back the pain medication in her IV line and didn't know what to expect. Was that only yesterday?

She gazed out the window. Bright daylight filled her view but she had no idea what time of day it was. She didn't really care either. Her whole family was dead. At least that's what the cop had told her. Lori chose not to believe it. Sometimes she imagined this was all a bad dream. The hospital, the ugly throbbing gash in her belly, the story about Mom and Dad and Nick being killed by some crazy person. It was too bizarre, too devastating to accept. Because if it were true, what then? What was she supposed to do? Move to Hawaii and lie in the warm sand like nothing had happened? The thought filled her with guilt.

Lori gently slid her feet to the floor. Now that she was less nauseated, she decided to sit in the chair by the window. She thought her brain might work better if she pretended to be normal for a few minutes. Lying in the bed gave her horrible thoughts and terrifying dreams. Sometimes she couldn't tell the difference.

Every small step tugged at her wounds. The pain made her wince, yet it was strangely comforting. At first she didn't understand this feeling, then the term *survivor's guilt* surfaced in her foggy brain. Lori thought she might have heard it from a counselor who'd come to her hospital room, but she wasn't sure. The comings and goings of the last few days were a blur and she'd lost all sense of time. The guilt stayed. She was alive and her family was dead. Why couldn't she have died too? It would be better than this fog of anguish and fear. Better than trying to have some kind of life, knowing the people she loved most were gone forever.

Lori positioned her IV stand near the chair and eased into it. Outside, the sky was brilliant blue, the kind of day she always longed for after a cold winter. The kind of day she had planned to have every day after she moved to Maui.

No! Her family was not gone forever. She couldn't think that or she would be lost. She told herself they had been hustled off to a new location in a witness-protection program. For now, and maybe years to come, they couldn't contact her, but someday she would see them again. Lori stared at the tree outside her window, thinking of nothing, then finally started to drift. She blinked her eyes and fought to stay awake, but the darkness pulled her in.

She was back in the restaurant, doing her side work, getting ready to clock out and go home. She went into the walk-in cooler to grab some vanilla ice cream to bring up front to where they made sundaes. When she turned, he was there. Grabby Greg with his probing eyes and fast hands. He reached out and squeezed both of her breasts. Lori couldn't even slap at his hands because she was holding a five-gallon tub of ice cream. She hurried out of the walk-in, with a chill on her skin and a hot rage in her belly.

Then she was in her car, crying and wanting to quit her job. Someone was there with her, but she couldn't see who.

Lori jerked awake and sat upright in the chair. The scene at the restaurant had played like a dream in her mind, but was it a memory? Was that night coming back to her? Lori shivered and reached for a blanket from the shelf. She didn't want to remember. Knowing her family was dead was more than she could handle. The memory of seeing them slaughtered would send her over the edge.

Lori looked over at the open door to her hospital room. Would the killer come after her? She ran her fingers across the bandage on her stomach. He had intended for her to die with the others. Would he come back to finish the job? If he thought she was a witness, he would want her dead more than ever. The image of a guy sneaking into her room with a knife terrified her. She hoped he would be gentle this time. Maybe suffocate her with a pillow while she slept.

Lori tried to put it all out of mind, but grief and fear took turns torturing her. She shuffled over to her bed and pushed the call buzzer. She would ask for a different kind of medication this time, something to ease her mental pain.

* * *

At headquarters, the detectives met in the conference room. The small space buzzed with energy as five adrenaline-wired investigators waited to tell their stories from the day. Jackson had ordered pizza and was ready to get through the meeting. He had interrogations waiting. To Evans, he said, "How did the arrest go?"

"It would have been uneventful if Noni Engall hadn't come home. Roy was totally cooperative, despite being drunk, then his wife came in and started screeching and crying and begging me not to take him." Evans pulled her eyes open in mock horror. "Noni started going off about Tyler, her baby, and something happening with him. It was ugly."

"What time did you bring Roy in?"

"He's been in the main interrogation room since four thirty this afternoon. I imagine he's ready to talk."

"I've got his stepson, Tyler Gorlock, in the hole right next to him."

"Gorlock is Engall's kid?" Evans put down her coffee. "That's rich. I started hearing the buzz about the hostage situation late this afternoon, but I didn't make the connection. Was that why Noni Engall was hysterical?"

"I called her from the scene and asked her to describe Tyler," Jackson said. "It probably shook her up."

"Poor woman." Evans was the only one to express sympathy. The others had known too many criminals whose wives and mothers were often no better than the lowlifes they spawned and protected.

Jackson looked at McCray, who'd been out chasing a lead and missed the hostage situation, and recapped the afternoon's events. The desk officer came in with pizza while he was talking and Schak stood to take the box. Jackson grabbed a slice as it went around. "Eventually the home invaders released the civilian and her child, then attempted to exit with Whitstone as a hostage. Alvarez was killed by a sniper, and Gorlock was taken into custody. Whitstone was unharmed, although her patrol days are likely over."

"You think these are the same guys who did the killing at the Walkers'?" Evans chewed as she talked.

"It seems likely. They probably knew about Jared's guns from Engall as well."

"Why didn't they take Jared's guns?" Evans asked.

"They were in a locked safe. Maybe Jared wouldn't give up the key. Maybe they were high on meth and went a little crazy. Maybe something interrupted them." Jackson hadn't made sense of it all yet. "This is what we hope to find out from Engall and Gorlock." Jackson set aside his pizza slice, leaving most of the crust. He was too wired to eat right now. "We'll tag-team the suspects. Two detectives in each room. After, we'll confer and switch rooms. We'll play them off each other. We'll do whatever it takes."

McCray spoke up. "I went back out to the Walkers' neighborhood today and questioned everyone again. The woman across the street, Rose Linley, said she made a mistake about when she saw the van. She first told us it was around ten because *Desperate Housewives* had just gotten over, but she realized afterward she had recorded the show and watched it later. Now she says she saw the van around eleven."

"The same time frame the woman next door heard the shouting. That makes more sense." Jackson looked around. "Anything else we need to share before we start?"

"Does this mean Shane Compton is no longer a suspect?" Evans looked concerned. "He's still in jail, right?"

"Shane Compton knows Tyler Gorlock. They both painted houses for Roy Engall last summer. Everyone is suspect until we have a confession. Or two."

Jackson paired up with Evans, who had the least experience, and they started with Engall, who they thought was more likely to crack. Once inside the small room, Jackson realized his pain level had become unbearable. "Excuse me for a moment. Evans, please take care of the legalities."

While Evans made all the formal statements, Jackson hurried back to his desk for naproxen. He located some in his shoulder bag. He also found the Vicodin his doctor had prescribed. He carried it just in case, and for a moment, considered taking one. He put the container back. Opiates sometimes made him nauseated and droopy, and he needed to be fully alert. The anti-inflammatory would take the edge off the pain and that's all he needed.

Back in the gray closetlike room he sat next to Evans, their shoulders almost touching. Across the table, Engall sported a two-day stubble and bloodshot eyes. Alcohol and nicotine seeped from his skin, making the room smell like a tavern. Nice, Jackson thought. Next, Engall would piss himself.

"Will you take these cuffs off, please?" The suspect sounded more sober than he looked.

"Not until you tell us something. Did you participate in the killings at the Walker house? Or were you just there for backup?" Jackson's strategy was to give him an out, a way he could testify against the others and buy himself some leniency.

"I didn't kill anybody."

"You were there. The shoe prints in the front hallway match the shoes you hid in the trash. And the blood on the shoes? We'll soon have a DNA match to the Walkers. It looks very bad. The DA will pin the whole thing on you." Jackson realized he hadn't called Slonecker about this new development. *Crap.* The DA would not be pleased. He would call him right after this.

"Lots of people have Adidas just like mine. My s—" Engall stopped midword.

"Your *what*? Your stepson has some too?"

"I was going to say 'My shoes are very common.'"

"Why did you wrap them in plastic and toss them?" Evans jumped in.

"I threw them away because they were paint stained and worn out."

Jackson made a scoffing noise. "No jury will buy it. The prosecutor will convince them your shoes made the print in the blood, then you hid them from the police. Throw in the blackmail letter from Jared, and we have a guilty verdict."

Engall closed his eyes and his lips moved a little.

Was he praying? Bargaining with God? "We have your stepson in the next room. Tyler is likely to blame the whole thing on you. You're the father, the leader, and the bad influence. He's just a kid along for the ride."

Engall's eyes flew open. "Why do you have Tyler?"

"Don't pretend you don't know. He was driving your van."

"So? He's been driving it for months. I wanted the van back, but Noni said to let him use it." Engall feigned innocence about Gorlock's criminal activities.

Jackson didn't buy it. "Tyler was with you the night you killed Jared Walker. You brought him along to help kill everyone. You wanted it to look like a home invasion. Two birds with one stone.

Kill the man who was blackmailing you and steal his guns at the same time."

"No!" Engall shouted and shook his head. "I did not kill Jared. Neither did Tyler. My stepson's an asshole at times but he would never kill anyone."

"He participated in a home invasion today and took a police officer hostage. I think we've established he's capable of anything."

"Oh shit." Engall's face went slack. He was surprised, but not shocked. "Noni will be devastated."

"But not you?"

"He's not my kid. By the time I met Noni, Tyler was already headed for trouble. She never listened to me about how to handle him."

This was not going the way Jackson had envisioned. He needed to get back to the Walker murders. "Roy, you're not paying attention. We found your bloody footprints at the scene of a triple homicide. We found a blackmail note from the dead man in your van. If a single piece of your DNA comes back from the lab, you'll get the death penalty."

A long silence while Roy stared at his hands.

Evans spoke softly. "If you weren't the only one at the Walker house, Roy, tell us about the others. The first one to confess gets the deal."

Roy closed his eyes again, lips moving.

Evans kept up the good-cop routine. "I don't think you actually killed anyone, Roy. I think you went there to confront Jared about the blackmail." Evans leaned closer and lowered her voice like a conspirator. "You brought your stepson with you. Tyler had other plans. He was after the guns. When Jared wouldn't give him the key, Tyler went crazy and started killing everyone. You wanted to stop him but you couldn't."

Smart play by Evans. Jackson was proud of her.

"It's not your fault, Roy," she soothed. "Tell us what happened and we can help you. We'll get the DA in here for a plea bargain."

"May I have some time alone, please? I have a lot to think about."

Jackson hesitated. He'd had some bad experiences with suspects in this room lately. Evans gave him a subtle nudge. Finally, he stood. "Take the deal, Roy. Your stepson is not worth protecting."

He and Evans headed for the conference room, where a small closed-circuit TV was set up to monitor interrogations. It was wired to cameras in both little rooms. They checked on Engall first. His head tipped forward and he seemed to be praying again.

"Do you think God cares about Roy Engall's little predicament?" Evans said, with more amusement than sarcasm.

"Roy thinks he does. Nice job in there, by the way." Jackson touched her shoulder. Not a man clap, but not a squeeze either.

Evans broke into a smile. "Thanks."

Jackson noticed, and not for the first time, that she was really quite attractive when she smiled. At moments like this, when she was a good detective *and* a pretty woman, he wondered what it would be like to date her. To really get to know her.

He pushed the thought out of his mind and eased away from Evans. "Let's check the other room and see how Schak and Quince are doing." He clicked the TV to the other circuit, but they had no sound. He shut the unit off and turned it back on. Still no sound.

"This has been a piece of crap since day one." Evans smacked the side of the TV to no effect.

They watched without sound for a few minutes. Schak slapped the table and jumped up, while McCray looked casual, leaning back with his arms crossed. Tyler Gorlock seemed unaffected. He shook his blond, shaggy head a few times, but his mouth was set in a firm line, not moving. Jackson itched to get in there. He wouldn't interrupt the other detectives though.

"I'm going for a soda." Evans headed for the door. "Do you want one?"

"Sure. Diet whatever."

Schak and McCray joined them in the conference room ten minutes later.

"The shithead says he's never been to the Walker house." Schak's face was flushed on his cheeks but pale everywhere else.

"Are you feeling okay?" Jackson kept it casual.

"I'm fine." Schak scowled and peeled off his jacket. "Why?"

"You look a little flushed."

"It's hot as hell in that room."

Jackson had never noticed the heat, but the proximity of the walls definitely got to him. "Did Gorlock tell you anything useful?"

"Not a damn thing." McCray glanced at the clock. Jackson looked too: 8:35.

"Go home, McCray. There's no need for all of us to be here. You too, Schak."

"I think I will," McCray said. "I'm meeting with Detectives Bohnert and Rios in the morning. Lammers assigned me the home-invasion case, and she hopes to connect it to the carjackings."

"I'm staying," Schak said with a grin. "I want to get in Gorlock's face for while."

"Let's go." Jackson downed his soda and tossed the can in the trash on the way out. In his head, he heard Kera and Katie both nag him about recycling. At the moment, he didn't have time for it.

The second interrogation room was even smaller than the first. From the chair, if he leaned hard, Jackson could touch the walls on either side. He realized the claustrophobia he was now experiencing elsewhere stemmed from too much time in these damn windowless rooms. How bad would it get? he wondered.

Jackson plopped down and grinned at Tyler Gorlock. Next month was Jackson's twenty-year mark with the department. He hadn't let himself think about it much, but right now it pleased him to know he didn't *have* to do this much longer. He could retire and collect his pension if they didn't lay him off first.

"What are you smiling about?" Gorlock was hard to look at. His face was too narrow, his eyes were too close together, and he had a plethora of scars and sores. Acne as a teenager and meth use as an adult had ruined his skin and made him creepy.

"I'm smiling because you and your father are both going to prison for a long time. The town I love is already a better place."

"My father is dead."

"Your stepfather, on the other hand, is sitting in the next room talking about how you killed Jared Walker and his family."

"Bullshit."

"About how you decided to steal Jared's guns and when he wouldn't open the safe you took a bat to his head."

"I wasn't there." Gorlock popped out of his chair. With his hands cuffed behind him, he was relatively powerless, but Jackson and Schak leapt to their feet.

"Sit down!" they shouted in unison.

Gorlock hesitated long enough to show defiance, then eased back into his chair.

Jackson kept it up. "When Carla tried to defend her husband, you killed her too. You took the knife to the kids, just to take out the witnesses."

"That is such bullshit. I don't hurt people." Gorlock must have remembered his actions earlier that day, because for a moment he looked chagrined. Then the defiance was back. "Today was fucked up. I never intended for anyone to become a hostage.

It was supposed to be a smash and grab, but the cop came to the door and Rico went a little nuts."

"You fired on a police officer."

"That was Rico. He was high. I don't have a death wish."

"Yet you're likely to get the death penalty," Schak said, smiling.

Jackson added, "Based on your stepfather's testimony about last Sunday night, you'll be convicted of three counts of premeditated murder."

Tyler looked confused, then stunned. "You're saying Roy was at the Walkers' house when they were killed?"

"And you were with him."

"This is unbelievable." Gorlock shook his head. "He's blaming it on me?"

"He says you killed everyone and he tried to stop you." Jackson sometimes felt a little guilty about lying to suspects, but not this one. Hostage takers were less than human.

Gorlock coughed up a strange laugh. "The bastard. I can't believe he hates me that much."

"All criminals turn on each other eventually."

Gorlock scooted forward on his seat and tried to look earnest. "Listen, I did not go to the Walkers' house with Roy or anyone. I did not kill Jared and his family. I was not there."

Tyler was a skilled liar. No blinking, good eye contact, and earnest expression. Jackson was tempted to uncuff him to see what Tyler would do with his hands, but he couldn't take the risk.

"Do you know five upstanding citizens who are willing to swear you were somewhere else Sunday night?"

The suspect licked his lips. "No, but I will take a lie-detector test. I wasn't there. I didn't kill the Walkers."

Jackson sat back, surprised. Could this shithead be telling the truth?

Schak spoke up and Jackson could feel his frustration. "Even if you beat the lie detector, we can't use it in court. It will still be Roy Engall's word against yours."

Gorlock had a glimmer of hope. "Roy will never testify against me. My mother won't let him. Hell, she'll leave him the minute she finds out he tried to frame me for murder."

"We already have Roy's testimony," Jackson reminded him. "The jury will believe the video. The only thing you can do to help yourself is tell us what really happened."

"This is fucked up." Gorlock slumped in his chair. "If Roy says he was there, he must have killed them. The fucker must have been drunk out of his mind." He looked up at Jackson. "I heard Lori was still alive. I hope it's true."

"Do you have a special interest in Lori?" Jackson worried that even from jail, Gorlock would find someone to silence Lori as a witness.

"What do you mean? She's a friend."

"How do you know Lori?"

Gorlock seemed surprised by the question. "I worked with her dad. Shane brought her over to the trailer a few times."

"Why would Shane bring Lori to your trailer?"

Another puzzled look. "She's Shane's girlfriend. They needed a place to screw."

Jackson tried to hide his surprise. "Were their families okay with it?"

"Her parents didn't know because Lori didn't want them to." Gorlock shrugged. "I don't know what the big deal is. They're not really cousins. Jared and Tracy are stepbrother and sister."

Jackson thought about Lori saying Shane's name in the hospital. Had she been crying out for her boyfriend instead of naming the killer?

Schak jumped in. "Is that how you knew about the rifles? From Lori?"

"Everybody knows Jared has a Remington 700. He brags about it when he's drinking."

"What's it worth?" Schak pressed.

"I don't know and I don't care." Gorlock brought his cuffed hands up to scratch his chin, and Jackson knew he'd just lied.

"Like hell you don't." Schak pushed to his feet and shot around to Gorlock's side of the table. "Those guns represented cash. Just like John Northrup's guns would have been sold for cash. Detectives are searching your house and your car right now. They'll find any stolen items you haven't sold."

"Good luck to them."

"You cocky bastard." Schak grabbed Gorlock's face and squeezed. If not for the camera, Jackson thought his partner might have struck him. "You took a cop hostage, you sorry son of a bitch. You'll never get out of jail."

Jackson waited for Schak to step away from the suspect. When he did, Jackson said, "Tell us your side of the story, Tyler. Don't let your stepfather pin the Walker killings on you." Jackson tried to sound empathetic but it was a struggle. "Roy is the one who was being blackmailed. He's the one who was drunk and started the assault. Maybe you were just trying to defend yourself." All Jackson needed was for Gorlock to admit he was there. "A life sentence is better than the death penalty. People with life sentences walk out of prison all the time."

"I was never in the house." Gorlock leaned back. "I want a lawyer and a lie-detector test. Until then I'm done talking."

CHAPTER 22

"He thinks he can beat a lie detector? Cocky little bastard." Schak opened the door to the conference room and they found it empty. McCray had gone home and Evans was probably at her desk.

"Maybe he's telling the truth." Jackson was anxious to pressure Engall again, but he couldn't go back into the interrogation closet just yet. "Walk around the block with me? We'll take on Engall again when we get back. One of those lowlifes was in the Walker house."

"Maybe both." Schak pulled on his jacket. "The little rooms getting to you?"

"A little."

The sun had set, but the air was gloriously warm, the first real summer evening of the season. The kind of night where people sat out on their decks and drank beer and made plans to go camping or hiking. Jackson yearned for that life. He wanted real weekends that didn't get interrupted with calls to look at dead bodies.

"I haven't been fishing in a long time," Schak said, echoing his sentiments.

"Or camping."

"Maybe we should all go. You, me, Quince, Rios, and Bohnert. McCray doesn't camp and we're not taking Evans."

"Sounds great. Let's make it happen." Their pace picked up just thinking about it.

Evans called before they made it back. "Where the hell are you? Engall is pounding on the door and demanding to make a statement."

"Schak and I went out for some fresh air. We'll be there in three minutes."

Engall started talking the moment Jackson and Evans sat down. Evans had argued for the right to finish up with Engall because he was her collar. Schak had grudgingly gone to watch on the TV unit. "I got drunk Sunday night, I told you already. I started drinking during the game and by eight o'clock I was out of it." Engall rushed his words, as if he wanted to get it over with.

"What bar?"

"The Time Out Tavern. I was with some of my crew and somebody mentioned Jared. I started thinking about him. After the guys went home, I had another beer or two, then decided to go see Jared."

Engall paused and licked his lips. "When I first got the black-mail note I was pissed off, but I never took it seriously. Jared's not really like that. He was a good guy. He just was feeling desperate about his situation. I felt awful about letting him go. I decided to go over there and tell him to come back to work. Tyler hadn't shown up for damn near a week and I was done with him."

"Do you mean Tyler Gorlock? Your stepson?" They were recording and Jackson wanted everything to be perfectly clear.

"Yes. He's worked for me off and on for years. I can hardly stand him but Noni pressures me to keep him employed. When he didn't show up for a week, I figured he was using again. I decided to ask Jared to work a job I was starting the next week."

Roy was silent for a long time. Jackson prompted, "So you went to the Walkers' to tell him."

"Yes. Only, I don't remember driving or knocking on the door. I was shitfaced by then."

"What happened when you got there?"

Engall seemed to be a little short of breath. Evans offered to get him some water.

"No thanks. I'm just scared to tell you this."

"Just tell the truth, Roy," Jackson coached. "You'll feel better if you do."

"I'll feel better if you take these cuffs off me."

Evans looked at Jackson for approval and he nodded. She uncuffed Engall and he rubbed his wrists for a moment. Finally he said, "After leaving the bar I have only one real memory of that night, and it's not exactly clear."

"Just tell us, Roy."

He pulled in a quick breath. "I walked into the kitchen and saw the bodies. They were already dead. It was horrifying, and for a moment I thought I was hallucinating." Roy squirmed in his chair. "It happens sometimes when I drink too much, but this was too real. I could smell the blood. It was everywhere." Roy gulped for air. "I freaked out and ran from the house."

Jackson weighed this new development. Roy seemed to believe what he was saying. Yet if he was that drunk, he probably did the killings, then blacked them out.

Evans spoke up. "Describe where the bodies were positioned."

Roy closed his eyes, then opened them again. "It's a hazy memory."

"Do your best," Evans prompted.

"Carla and Lori were lying in the middle of the kitchen with Lori on top, as if she'd been trying to save her mother. Jared was on the floor near the sink, and I don't think I even saw Nick. I just ran."

"Why didn't you call 911?" Jackson thought Engall was working on an insanity plea. A jury would never buy it.

"I was drunk out of my mind. I wasn't even sure it was real. I remember thinking I needed to go home and sleep. The next thing I remember is waking up in the back of the van the next day."

"A neighbor saw your van at the Walkers' at eleven o'clock, but you didn't start swinging the ax until midnight," Jackson lied. "What were you doing during that time?" Jackson hoped Roy was dumb or scared enough to correct him.

Roy blanched. "They were killed with an ax?"

"Did it belong to the Walkers, or did you bring it with you?"

The room turned sour with the smell of sweat. "I don't own one. We have a gas fireplace."

"A neighbor says your van was at the Walkers' for a long time. What were you doing?"

"I don't remember anything but seeing the bodies." Roy's face was moist and slack, and his left eye started to twitch. "You said they were killed with an ax. Did you fingerprint it?"

"Of course."

"My prints aren't on it, are they?"

"So you were wearing gloves."

"You questioned me the next day. I was still wearing the same clothes from Sunday morning." Roy got louder as panic set in. "There was no blood on me. That's how I know I didn't do it."

"Listen, Roy." Jackson used his come-to-Jesus voice. "Juries are more sympathetic if you give them a full confession and express regret. Later down the road, the parole board will be more sympathetic if you take full responsibility for your crimes. Consider it an investment in your future."

"I didn't do it." Roy shook his head. "I've done some regrettable things when I was drunk but I've never hurt anyone. Not physically." He let out a weird laugh. "I was just a very drunk man who stumbled into the wrong place at the wrong time. You have to believe me."

"Actually, we don't. You'd better hope a jury does."

They decided to let him sit for another hour, then try again. While they waited, Schak went home, Evans took a nap, and Jackson called Kera to tell her he planned to crash at his place again. Her words were supportive, but her tone signaled disappointment.

Engall's story perplexed him. The suspect seemed to believe what he was saying, and the evidence didn't exactly contradict him. Still, Engall could have thrown his bloody clothes away anytime during the twelve hours he claimed to be blacked out. He also could have been wearing gloves. Would a drunk think to wear gloves? Jackson needed the damn DNA analysis. It had only been three days, though, and the lab was processing dozens of blood samples. He'd be lucky to have anything by tomorrow. What would the DNA prove? Engall already admitted to being there. They might have to charge him with the crime and see if a jury would convict him based on a blackmail scheme and some bloody shoe prints.

Jackson called Slonecker. It was nearly ten, but he needed to get the district attorney in the loop and see if he was ready to file charges. It took a while for the DA to pick up his cell phone. "Victor, it's Jackson. I have a break in the Walker murders."

"Excellent."

"It's a little messy though. We photographed bloody footprints in the foyer and matched them to Roy Engall. We found the shoes in his trash and a blackmail note from Jared Walker in his van. Tonight Engall admitted to being at the scene. He says he was drunk, walked in and saw the bodies, then panicked and left."

"Arrest him for murder, and I'll file the paperwork in the morning. You need to keep building a case against him, but the blackmail note will convince a jury."

"He has no defense wounds and his prints aren't on either weapon."

"We've seen it before. Anything else I need to know right now? My wife is holding a movie for me."

"That's it. Good night."

Jackson felt a measure of relief. He was about to make an arrest in the worst homicide Eugene had ever experienced. The department's public-relations officer would make a statement tomorrow, and for a moment the public would think the police were doing their job.

He started down the hall to the interrogation room and his phone rang. He noticed he'd already missed two calls from Katie. "Hey, sweetie, what's going on?"

"Mom's drunk and going a little crazy."

CHAPTER 23

Jackson woke Evans and told her to book Engall into jail on murder charges. He left before she could ask questions and ran for the exit. His gut hurt as he bounded down the stairs but he couldn't slow down. His daughter was sitting in a park, at night, waiting for him. Located between the river and the base of Skinner's Butte, the park was bordered by a bike/pedestrian path connected to downtown Eugene in one direction and the River Road neighborhoods in another. The park was also the site of two recent murders of homeless men, and it served as the sleeping grounds for many others.

Jackson's heart hammered from more than exertion as he ran across the underground parking lot. He told himself nothing would happen to his daughter in the next five minutes while he drove over. Still, he gunned the cruiser and was relieved to see no traffic. He went through a red light and sped down High Street toward the park.

Renee lived in an upscale apartment near the park's downtown side, a whole different neighborhood than the area adjacent to the other end, where transients wandered in from their pan-handling gigs along busy Sixth and Seventh Avenues. Katie had been spending time with her mother, as she did every Wednesday, then things had gotten ugly. His daughter hadn't wanted to talk about it on the phone. "Just come and get me" was all she would say. This was not the first time he'd responded to such a call, but he hoped like hell it would be the last.

Jackson pulled into the parking lot near the playground equipment and visually scanned the area. One other car was there, a light-colored sedan he noted out of habit, but in the dark he didn't see any people. In the distance, a cyclist's headlight zoomed along the river bike path. As he climbed from the car he heard Renee's voice, the all-too-familiar sound of her drunken belligerence. He ran toward the commotion coming from behind the public restrooms.

Katie sat on the end of a picnic table and Renee stood nearby, pleading her case. "Call your dad and tell him everything is fine." Her voice had the loose control of someone trying not to slur. "Please, Katie. He'll overreact to this, like he always does."

"Katie, I'm here." Jackson jogged up to his daughter, avoiding eye contact with Renee. He'd learned a few things over the years.

Katie hopped off the picnic table and started for the parking lot without saying a word. She'd learned a few lessons too.

"I'm not drunk, goddammit," Renee called after them as they quickened their steps. "I just took too much Xanax."

Jackson prayed his ex-wife would stay where she was and accept what was happening. He didn't get that lucky.

"Damn it, Jackson. You can't just take her. This is my night with my daughter."

He heard Renee stumbling along, so he started to jog. Katie did too.

"You can't bully me anymore, Jackson. I'll take you to court."

They crossed the perimeter sidewalk and headed for his car. Behind them Renee tripped and landed with a thud on the asphalt. She cried out in pain.

"Crap." He and Katie said it at the same time and stopped nearly in unison.

"We should make sure she gets home okay," Katie said, as they turned back. It was the last thing on earth Jackson wanted to do. Yet it was the right thing to do.

Renee was crying softly as they approached. "I think I twisted my ankle."

Jackson wanted to shoot her. "Would you like a ride home?"

"I don't need your holier-than-thou help."

Jackson bit his tongue so hard his eyes watered. The idea of hauling his drunk ex-wife into the back of his car and driving six blocks was right up there with the nonsedated stent removal he'd gone through recently. If Katie hadn't been present, he would have walked away, but for his daughter's sake, he would escort this miserable woman home and provide an example of compassion.

His reward was a kick in the shins.

When they were finally alone in the car, Jackson kept quiet and let Katie process her emotions. He didn't have to tell his daughter her visitations with her mother were suspended for now. In fact, he suspected Katie was feeling so betrayed, once again, that she would punish Renee by not even taking her calls. He drove south across a quiet downtown and finally said, "I'm sorry your mother disappointed you again. Try not to hate her."

"Don't *you* hate her?"

Jackson laughed. "Sometimes, for a moment or two. Then I remind myself she's an addict and life must be hard for her."

"Alcohol is disgusting. I don't understand the attraction."

"People want to feel better, and they reach for something they think will soften the edges. Then they can't stop."

"What about her promises to me?" Katie raised her voice and he heard the tears coming. "What about making me feel better?"

"Addicts get focused on themselves. It's part of the disease."

"I'm done with her." Katie waved a dismissive hand. "Can I file some paperwork with the court saying she's not my mother anymore?"

Jackson reached over and held his daughter's hand. "We can revoke her visitation, but she'll always be your mother. Sorry, but you're stuck with your parents."

Until they die. Jackson had been thinking about his own dead parents more and more lately. They had been murdered ten years ago. The man who'd committed the crime would come up for a parole hearing soon. Jackson thought he might attend.

Katie said, "I want to go home. To our house. I want it to be just you and me for a while."

Jackson turned left and headed for their bungalow. Kera would understand.

CHAPTER 24

Thirteen days earlier

Carla checked her face in the mirror, grabbed her small briefcase, and got out of the car. She pulled her shoulders back and marched into the insurance office. She wanted to project confidence, to seem like a person you couldn't say no to, a salesperson you wanted on your team. This was a cold call; the business had not advertised for an open position. There were so few listings in the classifieds, her strategy was to target successful businesses and try to get a foot in the door.

Stomach fluttering, Carla walked up to the receptionist and smiled. "May I speak with the manager?" She reached in her briefcase.

"Is that a résumé?" The receptionist was her age, but thinner and prettier and better dressed.

Carla suddenly felt like an aging stewardess in her navy-blue skirt and jacket. "Yes. I'd like to give it to the manager."

"I'll take it, but don't get your hopes up. We're not hiring." The receptionist held out her hand with a grim smile.

Carla did not want to let this woman take her perfectly crafted list of qualifications and toss it in the recycling bin. What else could she do? Stand there and be obnoxious about it? She handed over her résumé. "I would like to speak to someone about a part-time internship."

The receptionist raised an eyebrow. "You mean like a college student who works for free just for the experience?"

"Something like that, yes." Carla smiled and stood straighter, trying to look thinner. This was humiliating.

"I don't think we do that kind of thing here. Thanks for stopping in." The woman went back to her computer work.

Carla fled the building. Back in the car she took long, deep breaths. She didn't want to sell insurance anyway. In fact, she didn't want to sell anything. She was sick of sales, sick of the pressure. Yet that was the experience on her résumé, except for the recent jewelry-design position. It had been a miracle to get that job. The one thing that kept her going now was the hope that Silver Moon would hire her back when the economy turned around. She told herself she wouldn't have to work in sales forever.

Carla pulled out of the parking lot and headed for the Planned Parenthood clinic in West Eugene. Her procedure was scheduled for nine fifteen. Anxiety flooded her stomach every time she thought about having the abortion. She pushed it out of her mind. She had no choice but to go through with it.

On the drive to the clinic her legs began to shake. She decided she would ask for a sedative as soon as she got there. The nurse who had counseled her yesterday had offered to send her home with one, but Carla had turned it down. She regretted that now.

The nearly new clinic was located at the back of a cul-de-sac, with Court Sports on one side and the Target shopping center on the other. In case she wanted to play handball or go shopping afterward, Carla thought, feeling bitter. In reality, she had been instructed to take it easy for several days after the abortion, which was why she had visited the insurance company this morning.

The group of protesters on the sidewalk in front of the clinic made her heart nearly stop. She eased past them into the driveway, glancing back at their signs. Carla parked the Subaru, shut it off, and willed herself to get out of the car. She had to do this. They had no jobs and no money and soon they would have no place to live. She couldn't bring a baby into such a life. Babies were expensive and needy. A baby would make her life way more stressful than it already was. When Lori had been born, they'd lived with her parents for years because they couldn't afford anything else. She couldn't do that again. Not at thirty-six. She and Jared were the parents now, the ones who were supposed to be stable and provide for their kids. Lori was eighteen, the same age Carla was when she had Lori. What if Lori got pregnant? Who would give her a place to live and help her with her baby?

Carla leaned back against the seat and let the warm tears roll down her face. She was ashamed and disgusted with herself. Getting pregnant, losing her job, stealing the baseball card to pay for an abortion. How had she gotten to this point? Part of her blamed Jared for his lack of ambition and refusal to get a real job, but it was her fault too. She had taken the jewelry job to make herself happy, even though it paid less and was less secure than the sales position she'd been offered. Now her whole family was paying for it.

With a burst of resolve, Carla jumped from the car and hurried across the parking lot. *Don't look at their signs. Don't think about the baby. It's not a person yet.* Considering her age, the baby probably had Down's syndrome, she told herself. She was doing the right thing for everyone involved. Carla entered the clinic and waited in the four-foot-square glass foyer. From yesterday's visit, she knew the interior door was locked for security purposes. A receptionist at the counter ten feet away asked her to state her name and business.

"Carla Walker. I have a nine fifteen appointment." Her hand went to her stomach. This was Jared's baby too, and she hadn't even told him. The lock on the door buzzed, letting her know she could proceed through. Carla didn't move. She heard Jared's voice in her head saying, *It'll be okay, sweetheart. As long as we have each other, we'll be happy. We'll find a way to make it work.*

Carla turned around and walked out, fresh tears rolling down her face.

CHAPTER 25

Thursday, June 4, 5:30 a.m.

Jackson got up early out of habit, but he had no need to rush in to the department. Engall was in jail and would be charged with the Walker murders. His team still had to examine all the DNA reports and blood analyses from the victims, but the urgency was over. Building a case against the accused was a long, tedious job.

He went for a slow one-mile jog, the first since his surgery, then took a leisurely hot shower. He and Katie had breakfast together, scrambled eggs and cantaloupe, before he dropped her off for her last day of middle school. He was back in his routine and it felt great.

On his way into the department, Jackson called the task-force members and scheduled a wrap-up meeting at nine. When he walked into the violent-crimes area, Lammers was sitting at his desk.

"Jackson, I hear we've made an arrest. Great work on this case."

He waited for the real reason she was in his space.

"I want you to meet with the press and announce we have the Walkers' killer in custody. You can tell them we've caught the carjackers too. Bohnert brought one of the victims in last night, and she identified Gorlock and Alvarez as the men who assaulted her and took her car."

Jackson hated talking to the media. "Why me?"

"The public likes you. You look good on camera and you solve murder cases. The press conference is scheduled for two this afternoon. Do not blow it off."

Jackson resisted the urge to give her a mock salute. "Right out front by the fountain?"

"Be there." Lammers got up from his desk and strode out.

Jackson went across the plaza to Full City and bought a tall coffee and a pastry, figuring he'd earned it. By the time he got back to headquarters, the other detectives had gathered in the conference room. The aroma of McCray's fruity tea filled the air again.

"Thanks for coming on short notice. This meeting will be brief. It's a chance to get everyone caught up before we move on. I'll do most of the legwork getting this case ready for court and you guys can start taking other assignments."

"I've already got the home invasion assigned to me and I'm meeting with Bruckner this afternoon," McCray said.

"Do you have anything new to add to our body of information?" Jackson gestured at the board where the Walker family and its connections had been mapped out.

"I don't think Engall did it," Evans announced. She looked fresh and perky as usual, but also troubled.

Schak stared, openmouthed. "You're flip-flopping. You backed Engall as a suspect even when we all thought it was Shane."

"I know." Evans gulped some coffee. "But I participated in the interrogations and I talked to Engall as I drove him to jail last night. I think he's telling the truth. He didn't take Jared's black-mail letter seriously and he has no history of violence."

The room was silent. Jackson had been having the same thoughts and pushing them away. "The physical evidence doesn't implicate him."

"We still don't have the DNA analysis?" Evans looked at Jackson.

He made a note to call the lab. They had to have some results by now. He remembered something he hadn't shared with the group yet. "When we questioned Tyler Gorlock, he told us Lori was Shane's girlfriend. It surprised me."

"I thought they were cousins," McCray said, scowling.

"Not biologically," Jackson explained. "The parents, Jared and Tracy, are stepbrother and sister. It's a little weird, but does it change anything?"

"Sure it does." Evans jumped up and hustled over to the board. "If Shane is in love with Lori, it gives him motive to hurt anyone who comes between him and his girlfriend."

"Gorlock says her parents didn't know."

"Maybe they found out."

"He knifed Lori too," Schak reminded them.

"Maybe she tried to protect her family," Evans countered.

Jackson cut in. "I'll go see Shane at the jail today and use the information as leverage when I talk to him." His phone rang and he checked the ID: *Jasmine Parker.*

"Hey, Parker. I'm in a task-force meeting, but if you have information about this case I'll put you on speaker."

"I finally do. I've got the two suspects' DNA comparisons with the trace evidence we sent over." Parker's voice was soft and scratchy coming from the phone's tiny speaker. "A hair found on Carla Walker's shirt matches Shane Compton's DNA sample."

A mix of emotions washed over him. Surprise, relief, excitement.

"There's the physical evidence placing Shane at the scene," Evans said.

"Do you have anything else?" Jackson asked the lab tech. "What about the analysis of the victims' blood?"

They heard paper shuffling, then Parker said, "Carla Walker showed hormones consistent with pregnancy but nothing else unusual. Jared's blood had an alcohol content of point zero four, which is also not significant. And Nick Walker's had a trace of marijuana."

"What about Lori Walker?"

"We don't have her blood because we didn't do an autopsy."

He'd forgotten to ask the hospital to send a vial of Lori's blood for analysis. Jackson wondered if the hospital had done a tox screen. He made himself a note to call them. At this point, though, it seemed like a waste of time. "What about the hundreds of fingerprints you processed? Any hits on CODIS?"

"Shane Compton's prints were on the front door and on one of the kitchen cabinets. We also got a match on a print we took from the door leading to the garage. Roger Acker, convicted twice of check fraud, but he's been dead for two years. The print has been there for a while."

"Thanks, Parker." Jackson hung up and looked around at his team. "Any thoughts?"

McCray spoke up. "What if Shane Compton is part of Gorlock's smash-and-grab campaign? They know each other. They could have busted into the Walker home looking for the guns and killed everyone in a rage when they didn't find them."

"Without Gorlock or Alvarez leaving a single print or hair?" Jackson might have bought the theory before Parker's report.

"You know it happens sometimes."

"We'll never convict either of them even if they were there. Alvarez is dead and Gorlock is going away for a long time on the other home invasion. He has no reason to confess or plea-bargain in this case."

A silence followed.

"We have to focus on Compton again." Jackson stood. "I'm heading over to the jail now."

"I'd like to go with you." Evans stood too. "Maybe he'll respond better to a woman."

"Can't hurt to try."

CHAPTER 26

They took Jackson's car and drove the five blocks to the county jail. Yesterday's summerlike weather was gone and the sky was dark with rain clouds, a more typical June day in Oregon. On the way, Evans said, "How are you doing? I mean, with your recovery?"

"I'm fine."

"I noticed you're not staying with Kera. Is everything okay with you two?"

"How do you know I'm not staying with Kera?"

"You brought in your black coffee container the last couple days. When you were staying at Kera's, you carried a silver container."

"Your powers of observation are improving, Detective Evans, but you're still too nosy." Jackson turned left on Fifth Avenue and looked for a place to park.

"I don't let it get in my way." She grinned, unabashed. "So tell me, are you still seeing her?"

"Yes." He decided to be polite and ask about her personal life. "What about you? Still dating the painter?"

"No. He's too soft, too liberal. How can I date someone who doesn't think cops should carry stun guns?"

Jackson laughed. "I told you. You need to start going out with law-enforcement guys."

"I'm thinking about it." As he parked, she caught his eyes. "The good ones are all married or taken. I'm feeling a little SOL."

"Be patient. It'll happen." Jackson was ready to change the subject. "Good cop, bad cop again? It got Engall to finally talk."

"That's the plan."

The two-story redbrick building sat at the base of Skinner's Butte less than a mile from the park where he'd picked up Katie the night before. The jail was also within shouting distance of the Hult Center, Eugene's performing-arts venue, and the Fifth Street Public Market, where upscale shoppers spent their money. It seemed like an odd spot to house criminals, but at least the county-run facility was close to the city-run police department.

A crowd of newly released inmates hung out in front of the jail, some waiting for rides or to catch a bus, others simply socializing with their peers before they wandered downtown to look for more trouble. A disheveled women looked him over, but no one else paid any attention to their arrival. Jackson's jaws tightened as they strode through the group. Criminals were arrested and released faster than you could throw back an undersize fish. One whole wing of the jail had been shut down for years because of lack of funding, and the morale of uniformed cops was plummeting as a result. What was the point of making arrests if the criminals didn't suffer any consequences?

Evans jogged up the stairs to the admitting desk and Jackson pushed through his pain to keep up with her. He was paying for his jog that morning. They waited while a haggard-looking woman tried to convince the deputy on the other side of the plexiglass that her inmate son needed a certain prescription. The deputy noticed their presence and asked the woman to step aside. She glanced at the two of them in their dark jackets with gun bulges, rolled her eyes, and lumbered out of the way.

"Detectives Jackson and Evans. We're here to see Shane Compton. We need an hour with him in the interrogation room."

"I'll see where he's at this morning." The deputy, who looked ready to pop out of her beige uniform, keyed the name into the computer system. After a moment she read from the digital file. "Shane Compton was transferred to North McKenzie yesterday. He developed a fever and our staff doctor thought he needed IV antibiotics." She looked up. "I'm sorry. Would you like me to call the hospital and check on him?"

"Did you send a deputy with him?" Jackson knew better than to hope.

The deputy gave him a quizzical look. "Compton was officially released after he left the facility."

Jackson tried to keep his irritation in check. "Why was he released? He's a suspect in a murder investigation."

"He was booked in on possession of a controlled substance. He has no history of violence." The deputy didn't even sound apologetic. She dealt with annoyed and angry people all day and Jackson was just one more. "There was no reason to keep him in jail except your request for a twenty-four-hour hold, which expired last night. Our staff doctor sent Compton to the hospital because he was too sick to turn out on the street. I'm sure he's still there."

Jackson started to say something sarcastic and caught himself. He turned to walk away, then spun back. "Please make a note that the detective who brought him in would like to have been notified about Compton's transfer and release."

"I will, sir."

* * *

Lori wished her Aunt Rita would go home. She knew Rita was missing work, and it made her feel guilty. There was nothing anyone could say to make her feel better and nothing Lori wanted to talk about either. They were trapped in this room together, Rita quietly reading her book and Lori wishing she could be alone.

The nurse who'd said she could probably go home tomorrow had meant well too, but Lori had no home. The house was still there but she would never set foot in it again.

How was she supposed to keep on living when her family was dead and Shane no longer wanted to be with her? Thoughts of suicide came and went. The act would require planning and follow through, and she wasn't capable yet.

Her cell phone rang on the sliding tray next to her bed. The familiar ringtone made her smile. When they'd heard she could leave soon, Rita had rounded up her cell phone and backpack from the police, and these small pieces of her old life gave her some comfort. She picked up the phone, looked at the ID, and her heart quickened. "Shane. I'm glad you called. Why haven't you been in to see me?"

"I was in jail. Now I'm in the hospital."

"Oh my god. What happened?" Lori got out of bed and padded toward the window where her aunt couldn't hear.

"They questioned me about the—" Shane paused. "About what happened to your family. They think I did it."

"No. That's crazy! Why?" Lori didn't understand. Rita tapped her shoulder and signaled she was going out for coffee.

"They found my fingerprints on the bat."

"We play softball together. Did you tell them that?"

"It doesn't matter; they don't believe me. They see me as a drug addict. To them I'm a criminal just like rapists and murderers."

"Why are you in the hospital?"

"My tooth is abscessed and the infection made me feverish. I took advantage of that and got myself transferred."

"I want to see you. I mean, we're still friends, right?"

"Lori, I love you. I think we should get the hell out of here. Go to Maui like we planned."

Shane wanted to be with her! A surge of pleasure found its way through her wounded soul. "I would like that. I'm getting released tomorrow."

"We can't wait. The police will eventually realize I'm not in jail. We have to go now."

Lori was frightened and excited at the same time. Why not? She had nothing to live for here in Eugene anymore. "What about money? I have five hundred saved but it's not enough."

"I'll find the money. Just be ready when I get there. What room are you in?"

She told him, then added, "The nurse is here. Gotta go."

Lori's blood pulsed with life. She had something to look forward to.

* * *

Rain battered Jackson's car on the quick drive to the hospital, but it had cleared by the time they walked out of the parking garage. Jackson had no idea where Shane would be in the building. They started with the information desk in the lobby. The volunteer smiled brightly as they walked up. After a quick look in the computer, she told them Shane was on the third floor, in the ICU. He and Evans headed for the elevator.

"IV antibiotics sounds serious," Evans commented.

"It could be. Drug users are prone to nasty infections because their immune systems are ruined." Jackson pressed the button. "They can die from an infected fleabite."

"Let's hope not. I'd hate to see Engall get the death penalty because the real perps are all dead."

"Don't feel too sorry for Engall. He's an irresponsible cheat and a worthless drunk, at best, and a possible killer, at worst. He'll probably plead out when Slonecker gets hold of him."

They hurried off the elevator and turned right as instructed. Daylight filled the wide hallway between the wings, then disappeared as they rounded the corner into the ICU. Jackson noticed a young couple and a middle-aged woman in the waiting area, but no patrol officer. *Damn!* Someone was supposed to be protecting Lori. How hard was it to stay in the area and screen visitors?

They followed a guy in scrubs through the double swinging doors. Jackson glanced in the rooms as they passed but didn't see his suspect. An older man was behind the counter at the nurses' station. He finished his task on the computer before looking up.

"We're here to see Shane Compton."

"Are you family members?"

"Detectives Jackson and Evans with the Eugene Police Department."

The nurse looked at his monitor, then said, "Room 413." He gestured for them to keep heading down the hall. "It's on the left toward the end."

They found the room, and its sliding pleated door was closed. Jackson pushed it open and rushed in. The bed was empty.

The door to the bathroom stood open, and it was empty too. Behind him Evans said, "This is not good."

They hustled back to the center station and this time Jackson didn't wait for the nurse's attention. "Alert security to watch for a missing patient. He's about six feet tall, broad shouldered but skinny, with blond hair and green eyes."

"What do you mean, *missing*?"

"He's not in his room."

"He could have gone to the lounge." The nurse scowled. "He's probably too weak to want to leave the hospital. Is he a criminal?"

"He's a suspect in a homicide." Jackson lost his patience. "Alert security now." He turned to Evans. "Call in an attempt-to-locate, then search this entire wing. I'm going to check with Lori." Jackson hustled down the hall, going around a kitchen worker with a food cart. He had half a hope Shane would be visiting his girlfriend.

The room was empty. No Shane. No Lori. No Aunt Rita. He checked the bathroom just to be thorough.

At the nurses' station he said, "Lori Walker is missing too."

A nurse in yellow scrubs said, "Lori was transferred to another room yesterday. She's recovering nicely and may go home soon."

"Where?"

"Second floor. Room 112."

"Tell Detective Evans I'm headed there." He walked quickly through the ICU, then broke into a jog as he exited the swinging doors.

Jackson took the stairs to save time. He pounded down the cement steps and his still-healing incision felt every thud. He slowed a little when he entered the busy ward below. A young, stocky patrol officer was seated in the waiting area, but his eyes were closed. They popped open as Jackson walked up.

"How's Lori Walker?"

The officer jumped to his feet. "She's fine, sir. Her aunt is in with her now." He held out his hand. "Officer Ray Garrick. I took your crime-scene workshop last year."

"I remember you." Jackson shook his hand. "Have you seen a young male patient go through here this morning? Blond, six feet tall, broad shouldered, and skinny?"

Garrick blinked, then cleared his throat. "He came through about twenty minutes ago. He was wearing a hospital gown, so I thought he belonged on the ward."

"He's a suspect in the Walker murders."

"I'm sorry, sir."

"If you see him again, stop him." Jackson started for the open ward. His heart pounded with fear of what he would discover.

The bed in room 112 was empty and Rita Altman was on the phone, talking excitedly. She looked up, said, "Gotta go," then clicked her phone shut. "I'm glad you're here. Lori is missing and I'm worried sick."

"When did you see her last?" Jackson already knew the answer.

"Maybe around nine thirty. She asked me to go out and get her a copy of *Entertainment Weekly* and a Snickers bar. When I got back, she was gone." Rita's voice bordered on hysteria. "Do you think the killer came back for her? Why would he take her?"

"I think she's with her cousin Shane. Do you know where they might go?"

"What do you mean, *go*?" The aunt registered more confusion. "Why would Lori leave with Shane? She was supposed to come home with me tomorrow."

Rita apparently didn't know the cousins were romantically involved. Jackson repeated his question. "Where would they go together?"

"I don't know. Maybe to Shane's parents' house." Her lips trembled and a tear rolled down her cheek. "Please tell me what's going on."

"I'm not sure, but I have to find them. Lori might be in danger."

Evans burst into the room. "Lori's gone too? What the hell?"

Jackson eased away from Rita, not wanting her to hear his theories. "Best-case scenario, Shane is scared about being charged with murder so he's on the run and taking his girlfriend." He and Evans strode into the hall. "Worst-case scenario, Shane is the killer and plans to silence Lori as a witness."

"If Lori doesn't remember that night, maybe she's safe for now." Evans looked around at the layout. "How did they get out past the patrol officer?"

"I'm not sure it matters right now."

The nurse at the computer in the hallway offered, "They could have gone out through the surgical area, then crossed over on the physicians' skywalk."

"Let's go," Jackson said. "We're only fifteen minutes behind. They could still be in the facility." He handed the nurse several business cards. "This has my cell phone. Give one to Officer Garrick and one to the head of security. I want to be updated on the search of the hospital. First, take us to the surgery area and show us the way out."

As they started off, Evans said, "Should we call the other team members?"

"Let's search the building and parking garage first. Shane is sick and Lori is wounded. They may not get far."

The nurse led them through another set of double doors, into an area where the lights were brighter and the temperature cooler. The hospital personnel wore blue scrubs, mouth masks, and hair coverings. Jackson stopped once to ask a doctor if he had seen the patients, but after getting only a peculiar look he decided to skip the effort.

Even following this route was likely a waste of time, except they would end up in the garage where his cruiser was parked. They might also get lucky and find the couple still in the parking structure. Would they leave on foot, or would Compton steal a car? Shane hadn't been arrested in more than a year, but if he was using again and running from the law, anything was possible.

As they hurried through the sky bridge over Hilyard Street, Jackson called headquarters. "Have you had any reports of a stolen car near the hospital?"

"Let me check." After a moment, the desk officer said, "No. Do you want me to call you if one comes in?"

"Please. Would you also find out if Shane Compton has a vehicle registered to him?"

The sky bridge connected to a medical building across the street where outpatient surgeries were conducted. Doctors, nurses, and nursing assistants hustled in and out of rooms, yanking open curtains and chatting with patients in white-and-blue-print hospital gowns. Many looked up as Jackson and Evans strode through, but no one tried to question or stop them.

As they passed the admitting desk, Evans trotted over and said, "We're looking for two young patients, a male and a female, eighteen and twenty. They came through here ten or fifteen minutes ago. Did you see them?

The administrative aide looked confused. "What do you mean, *came through*? They didn't check in with me, if that's what you're asking."

"They would have just passed by, probably in a hurry."

The aide shook her head.

"Any reports of anything stolen? Like a jacket or car keys?"

"No."

They hurried forward, glancing into rooms and opening doors. They searched the public bathrooms and found no sign the couple had been there. Beyond the elevators were automatic doors leading to daylight and the top level of the adjacent parking garage. Jackson and Evans went in separate directions to scan the perimeter, then they each took two rows and jogged from vehicle to vehicle, glancing in to see if Lori and Shane were hiding. Even though it had to be done, Jackson instinctively knew it was a waste of time. The couple had most likely boarded the elevators and quickly traveled to street level. From there, Shane probably called a friend or they walked a few blocks to the university area where he probably knew people.

Still moving along and peeking into cars, Jackson called McCray, who didn't pick up. He left a message: "Shane Compton and Lori Walker have both left the hospital. We assume they're together and Lori could be in danger. Evans and I are headed to Zor's, the dealer on Eighth where we picked up Shane. Call me when you get this message."

Next he called Schak, who picked up and said, "What's going on? I heard the attempt-to-locate for Shane and Lori."

"They're both missing from the hospital, and we think Lori is in danger."

"Oh shit. Poor girl. What are the assignments?"

Jackson checked the last car in the row and turned back. "Evans is still with me, and we'll question Shane's mother and his dealer. Will you check the Walker house? Lori may go home to get clothes or one of the family cars. Is Quince at his desk?"

"No, but he's around here somewhere."

"After you check the Walker house, head out to the airport. When you see Quince, tell him to call me."

"Will do." After a pause, Schak said, "I thought Compton was in jail."

"He developed an infection and they transferred him to the hospital. The sheriffs released him because it was the easiest thing to do."

"Ah shit."

"If you see any sign they've been to the Walker house, let me know."

Jackson clicked off as Evans jogged up, looking pink-cheeked and excited.

"What did you find?"

"A sleeping toddler in the back of a car. Idiot parents. I've got the plate number. Let's notify security and get a patrol unit out here."

Ten minutes later they were in his cruiser, headed west toward Almaden. Jackson mentally looked back over the investigation and wondered what he'd missed, because he hadn't seen this coming at all. After the home invasion on Stratmore and the connection to Roy Engall, he'd put Shane on the back burner as a viable suspect. That had been a mistake. What could he have done differently? Trump up phony charges against Shane to keep him in jail? Jackson had still not accepted the reality of only violent offenders staying incarcerated until their court dates.

"Stop blaming yourself," Evans said. "Engall was in the Walker house the night of the murders, and he was connected to the home-invasion perps. We all thought he was going to confess."

"How do you know what I'm thinking?" Jackson was both irritated and amused.

"One, you're shaking your head. Two, you always think you could have conducted a better investigation."

"It's always true. For every investigation, not just mine. That's how we get better at this, by examining mistakes." They passed

Garfield Street, then West Eleventh changed to two-way congested traffic. Jackson wanted to pop out the siren and get everyone the hell out of his way, but he didn't.

"What are we supposed to do?" Evans lamented. "We can't hold suspects for more than a day without charging them. Booking them into jail is a waste of time; they could walk out three hours later. And we don't have the resources to put a tail on every suspect in every investigation. It's fucked up."

Jackson agreed but kept quiet. Doing police work in Eugene had gotten harder and harder over the years. Left-leaning citizens complained about everything. They were outraged when officers shot and killed an emotionally unstable young woman with a knife. The department responded by buying tasers and starting a trial program to test their effectiveness. When officers used the tasers, citizens complained and filed lawsuits. It *was* fucked up.

The ring of his cell phone cut into his thoughts. "Jackson here."

"It's the front desk at headquarters. Shane Compton has a '92 Toyota Nissan pickup registered to him. Color, white. His registration expired two months ago and he hasn't renewed it."

"Thanks. Call the vehicle in to the state police. Give them Shane Compton's and Lori Walker's descriptions. Read the stats from the attempt-to-locate I called in earlier." He clicked off the phone, wondering if he had covered all the possibilities.

"Do you think Shane's parents will protect him?"

"I believe they already are. Neither Tracy nor Kevin has called me back."

"It's a triple homicide." Evans' voice was excited again.

"They don't believe their son could have done it. It's parental blindness. All parents suffer from it."

"Another reason not to have children."

Jackson turned left on City View and raced up the empty street. His cell phone rang, and he was glad his earbud was already in place. It was now illegal in the state to drive and talk on anything but a hands-free unit. And it had always been reckless, even when he did it.

"This is Kevin Compton returning your call." Kevin spoke slowly, his brain dysfunction obvious even over the phone.

"Have you seen or heard from Shane today?"

"No. I thought he was in jail." Voices buzzed in the background, meaning Kevin was likely at his business.

"Shane was transferred to the hospital, then he and Lori—"

"Shane was in the hospital?" Despite his flat tone, Kevin sounded worried.

If their suspect was not keeping in touch with his parents, it was a sign he was deep into drug use again. "Shane developed an infection while he was in jail. They transferred him to the hospital, then released him. If he's on the move now, he's probably doing okay."

"Not necessarily. He could die if he doesn't take all the antibiotics."

Jackson thought Kevin was probably overreacting. Meanwhile, he had bigger concerns. "We think Lori Walker is with him. Do you know where they might go?"

There was a long silence. Finally Kevin said, "I think Shane and Lori have feelings for each other."

"Do you know where they might go?"

"Lori has her heart set on moving to Maui."

"Do they have money for plane tickets?"

Kevin wasn't listening. Jackson could hear someone talking to him in the background. After a moment, Kevin said, "I have to go," and hung up.

"Any ideas?" Evans asked.

Jackson turned up Brittany Street and braked to miss a cat. "Kevin says Lori wants to move to Maui."

"I don't see them coming up with the money for tickets, but I'll call the airport anyway."

"Might as well alert the train and bus stations too, in case it's not Maui."

The Compton house came into view on the right and Jackson slowed, then parked on the street out of its line of sight. He didn't want to spook Shane and have them bolt out the back. If they were even here.

"If no one answers, can we justify going in?" Excitement flared in Evans' voice.

She's still such a rookie, Jackson thought. "We are going in. A woman's life is in danger." He shut off the engine and they climbed out. The neighborhood was quiet, except for the sound of young kids playing somewhere in the distance.

He and Evans trotted up the sidewalk toward the big brown house. No cars were in the driveway and they didn't see any activity, but that didn't mean Shane and Lori weren't hiding in the house.

Jackson cut across the lawn at a diagonal, not wanting to be seen from the front window. Images from yesterday's hostage situation flashed in his mind and he instinctively brought his hand up to his weapon. He had no reason to think Shane was armed, but that kind of thinking had almost cost Officer Whitstone her life yesterday. Behind him Evans said softly, "Should I go around back?"

He thought about Whitstone going into the backyard of the Stratmore house by herself. "No." At the front door Jackson quietly turned the handle. It didn't budge. Jackson whispered, "I'll go to the back door. Give me two minutes, then pound and call out Shane's name." His thinking was, the couple would hear Evans' voice in front and run out the back, and he would be there to stop them.

Cutting across the grass, he hurried past the bedroom windows, their blinds closed, and rounded the corner of the house. A tall gate latched from the inside, but he was able to reach over and let himself in. Jackson paused, listening for a dog, then jogged along the side of the house to the backyard. A giant hot tub blocked his path and he scooted around it, keeping an eye on the sliding-glass door. No one seemed to be moving around inside the house. He hugged up against the back wall for protection and waited for Evans to call out. The sickly scent of flowers in bloom tickled his nose.

He heard pounding and brought up his gun. Evans called, "Shane Compton? It's Detective Evans. I need to talk to you."

No response.

She called out again, but the house was silent and the back door didn't budge. Jackson counted to five, then rushed to the sliding door. It had been installed decades ago and the lock mechanism soon gave from upward pressure. As he opened the door, a black cat rushed out. Jackson stepped into the dining room where he had questioned Tracy and Kevin just days ago and knew instinctively the home was empty.

CHAPTER 27

Thursday, June 4, 12:12 p.m.

Lori stared at the house where her family had lived and died, and started to shiver. "Shane, I can't go in. Just grab some jeans and a few of my favorite shirts."

"What about the car keys?"

"There's an extra key to the Subaru under the pink pig on the kitchen counter." Lori pulled the ugly black coat tighter, but her bare legs still felt the cool wind. "Don't forget to bring my pink Keens."

She leaned against the car and looked around at her neighborhood, probably for the last time. She wondered if the old woman, Rose, was peeking through her curtains, watching Lori in the stolen black coat over the hospital gown and wondering what the hell she was up to.

What am I doing? Lori asked herself again. Getting the hell away from Eugene and starting a new life with the man she loved. What other choice did she have? Stay here with the ghosts of her dead family and be reminded of her grief at every turn? Watch Shane be wrongly convicted of killing them? No, this town held nothing for her now. Their future was in Maui, where it was warm and sunny and beautiful. She already had an apartment and roommate waiting for her. All they had to do was get there.

Lori glanced back at the pale-green house and heard her mother say, *You're a housepainter, Jared, and we live in the only place on the street that needs to be painted.* Her mother had laughed when she said it. She had never been able to stay pissed at Dad for very long, no matter how he screwed up. Tears rolled down Lori's cheeks. How could she survive without her mother?

Shane came out of the house wearing some of her father's clothes. Another wave of grief hit her like a blow to the stomach. Lori doubled over.

"Babe, you okay?"

She pulled in a deep breath. "No, but that's the way it will be for a while."

Shane threw a pillowcase stuffed with clothes in the backseat. "Let's go then. They'll be looking for us soon."

Lori climbed in the car, reminded again of the newly stitched gash in her stomach. Shane started the engine and she reached over the seat for the pillowcase. The pocket of Shane's zip-up sweatshirt bulged with a familiar shape.

"Why did you bring the .38?" Lori said, pointing at the handgun.

"We'll sell it for cash." Shane gave her a wistful look. "I know your dad loved it, but it was the only gun left in the house and we need the money."

Panic made her voice squeaky. "You're not feeling suicidal again, are you?"

"No, babe. We're starting a new life. I'm optimistic."

Lori wished she hadn't shown him where her father stashed his guns. This one, a Walther P-38, was Dad's favorite. It had belonged to Grandpa and her dad had cherished it. He kept it under a false drawer bottom in the nightstand by his bed where it would be handy to protect his family. Somehow that plan hadn't worked out.

"You should put it back. It could cause us trouble." They were already backing out of the driveway.

"I'll only have it for an hour before I sell it." Shane grabbed her head and pulled her in for an intense kiss. "Stop worrying. As long as we're together, everything will turn out okay."

"You won't change your mind again, about being with me?"

"Never. That was a mistake. I love you."

Lori hoped it would be enough. She leaned back and closed her eyes. When had he broken up with her? She had the knowledge of it but not the memory. A quick scene came to her. The breakup had happened in this car, only she had been in the driver's seat. They had been parked outside the restaurant where she worked and she was crying.

It was only a brief memory and it didn't matter now. They were back together.

"What is it?" Shane asked. "Something's on your mind."

He knew her so well. "My memory of that night is starting to come back in little pieces."

"What do you remember? Do you know the killer?"

"No, and I hope I never do."

Their next stop was the jail. Lori had argued against it, but Shane was adamant about getting his backpack, wallet, cell phone, and whatever else had been in his pockets when he was arrested.

"I don't have to go inside," Shane explained. "There's a little window in the front, and they'll just hand me a plastic bag with all my stuff. It'll take two minutes."

"If the cops are looking for you, won't someone come out and stop you?"

He gave her a quick kiss. "These are sheriffs, not city cops, and this is the last place they'll look for me."

Lori watched Shane stride up to the redbrick building, amazed by his confidence and optimism. This was what she loved about him. His gorgeous face was just a bonus.

Shane was back in no time, grinning at his own audacity. "Told you." He tossed the bag in her lap and started the car.

Ten minutes later they pulled into the parking area behind the building where his mother worked as a bookkeeper. Lori knew they did some kind of publishing here, but she wasn't sure what. Textbooks, maybe.

Shane pressed speed dial and waited only a few seconds. "Mom, it's Shane. I'm in the parking lot with Lori. Can you come out?"

Lori couldn't hear Tracy's response but she could imagine it. Did his mother know he'd been arrested? Or that the cops might be looking for him?

Shane pleaded, "This is the most important favor I've ever asked you, Mom. If they pin these murders on me, I'll get the death penalty."

Another long silence.

"Thank you. I love you."

Five minutes later, Tracy hurried out of the building. She looked tiny in her dark work suit, her face pinched with worry. Lori rolled down her window because Tracy was headed for her side of the car.

Shane's mother leaned in and stroked Lori's face. The gesture almost made her cry. "You don't have to go with Shane. You're not in trouble. You can stay with Kevin and I until we get this sorted out."

"I want to get out of here. Eugene will always be the place where my family was murdered."

"You'll miss their funerals." Tracy's eyes locked on hers.

"They would be too painful anyway."

Tracy looked past her at Shane. "Meet me at the bank. It's about five blocks down."

"I know where it is, Mom."

"Of course." She gave them a worried smile and trotted to her own car.

At the bank Tracy went inside for cash. Lori realized Shane had asked for more money than his mother could get out of the ATM. "Is she giving us enough for plane tickets to Hawaii?"

"She's giving us a thousand. That's all she has. I'll get the rest from Zor. He owes me."

"Have you called your dad?"

"I can't yet. He won't lie to the cops."

"Is he getting any better?"

"Not yet." Shane's mouth pulled into a thin line.

Lori felt bad for bringing it up. "I'm glad you came for me in the hospital." His broad shoulder offered comfort and she leaned against him. "For a while there, I couldn't see my future. I had nobody."

"I couldn't stay away. I love you too much."

For a moment the smell and feel of Shane enveloped her and Lori felt content.

Tracy's heels clicked outside the car and reality was back. "Call me when you get there," she said, handing Shane an envelope with cash.

Shane got out and hugged his mother with the intensity of someone who believed he might not see her again. "I love you. Tell Dad I love him too."

Tracy came around the car, so Lori climbed out and hugged her too. "Thanks, Aunt Tracy."

Tears streaming down her face, Tracy pulled away and ran for the building.

"We have to make one more stop," Shane announced.

* * *

The Compton home was as empty as it felt, and Jackson saw no signs that Lori and Shane had been there. Of the two smaller bedrooms, one was used as an office and held mostly computers and their peripherals, and the other seemed to be a guest bedroom: no art on the walls, nothing personal on top of the dresser. Yet the Comptons had said Shane stayed with them sometimes. Jackson assumed the clothes in the closet belonged to their son. Jackson hunted through them, finding a package of rolling papers in the pocket of some jeans. If the young couple had come here recently, wouldn't Shane have taken his clothes?

As a sofa surfer, Shane probably didn't own much and carried his few possessions around in a backpack. If he had left the hospital in a patient gown, where was his backpack? Still at the jail? *Oh crap.* Jackson hurried up the hallway, calling the jail's admission desk on the way.

"Detective Jackson here. Yesterday when Shane Compton was transferred to the hospital and released, what happened to his belongings?"

"Let me check. Most likely they stayed right here, waiting for him to pick them up."

"Are they still there?"

"I'll have to transfer you downstairs."

Jackson was on hold for three long minutes, only to find out Shane had picked up his stuff forty minutes earlier. He let loose with every curse word he could think of.

Evans rushed in from searching the garage. "What's wrong?"

"Shane Compton waltzed up to the jail this morning and picked up his possessions, and nobody stopped him."

Evans grimaced. "At least we know he's still in town."

"*Was* in town. That was forty minutes ago."

"What next?"

"Tracy's work place. If Shane has contacted anyone, it's his mother. I think Tracy might lie to protect her son, but it will be harder for her to do it in person."

In the car, Jackson flipped through his notes, looking for Tracy's employer.

"Did it ever come up at our meetings?" Evans asked.

"I'll bet the other aunt would know. I'll call Rita." Her number was right there on his list.

"I'll call the front desk and have them run her in the database."

Rita proved to be a faster source. Tracy Compton worked as a bookkeeper at Emerald Publishing on the corner of Oak and Fifteenth. As they drove over, Quince called in. "Schak updated me on the Shane Compton development. What can I do?"

"Check the bus station and the train depot, then get back to me."

"Yes, sir."

Jackson had never heard of Emerald Publishing and he'd lived in Eugene all his life. It still happened frequently though. Sometimes he'd pass by an old building and really see the business for the first time, even though it had been there for decades.

The structure had once been an oversize home, and it still looked like one, with no sign out front announcing the company name. The two stories had small old-fashioned windows, but the wide wraparound porch and wooden front steps were welcoming.

A headset-wearing receptionist looked startled to see them. "Can I help you?"

"Detectives Jackson and Evans. We're here to see Tracy Compton."

"I'll let her know you're here." The young woman pressed a button on her phone, turned away, and spoke softly into her mouthpiece. She pivoted back and said, "Tracy will be right down."

Nobody wanted to have police officers visit them in their work space, where all their peers could witness the spectacle and gossip about it. While they waited, the receptionist asked Evans if she could have one of her business cards. "I might need to call you someday," she said, cheeks turning pink.

A few minutes later, Tracy came down the stairs. "Let's go out on the porch." She brushed past them without making eye contact. Outside, she walked toward the padded bench, but remained standing. "How's your investigation coming?" She sounded casual but her eyes were worried.

"Have you seen Shane today?"

"Are you still trying to blame him?"

"Answer the question!"

Tracy hesitated for a half second. "No."

"Did he call you?"

"I thought he was in jail."

Jackson had no patience for her cover-up. "Lying to an investigator is obstruction of justice. If that charge doesn't bother you, think about this. We believe Lori Walker is with Shane and that she is likely in danger. If Shane kills her, you will blame yourself for not helping us."

Tracy pulled back, eyes wide. "You're wrong. Shane would never hurt Lori. Why would she go with Shane if he had killed her family and tried to kill her?" Tracy twisted the top button on her jacket as she talked.

Evans took a turn, using her good-cop voice. "Lori doesn't remember the event, but she will eventually. When she does, Shane could kill her to keep her from going to the police." Evans forced Tracy to meet her eyes. "Can you image how Lori is going to feel when she realizes she's involved with the person who murdered her family? You need to spare her. Tell us where Shane and Lori are."

A long silence passed while Tracy weighed her instinct to protect her son against the ramifications if she was wrong. Her face a mask of control, she pleaded, "Stop hounding Shane and find the real killer." She brushed past them again and marched into the building.

"Talk about a protective mother," Evans commented. "My mom had a much more hands-off approach." They were headed back to Jackson's cruiser.

"That's why you're a police officer and Shane is a drug addict turned killer."

"It can't be that simple," Evans argued. "My brother is a slacker and he was raised by the same people I was."

"Does your mother help him out?"

"Hell no." Evans laughed. They reached the cruiser and Evans said, "Can I drive for a while?"

"Hell no." This time they both laughed.

Back in the car, Evans' phone rang. She listened for a moment, thanked the caller, and hung up. Jackson could tell by the spark in her eyes it was important.

"That was the receptionist." Evans gestured at the building they'd just left. "She says Tracy Compton met Shane in the parking lot twenty minutes ago. They both drove off, then Tracy came back ten minutes later."

"I knew she lied to us." Jackson shoved the car door open and climbed out. "They went to a bank for cash is my guess." He trotted for the door with Evans right behind him.

"Are we going to arrest her for obstruction?"

Jackson tried to calm down, to put himself in Tracy's shoes. How far would he go to protect Katie? Especially if he believed in her innocence? "As much as I'd like to, probably not. We'll see."

"Where is she?" he said, as they rushed through the old-style door.

"Upstairs, second door on the right."

Tracy was on the phone when they burst into her office. She terminated her conversation and stared at them with a blank face.

"You lied to us." Jackson raised his voice, not caring if her coworkers heard. "You're coming in to the department. Either you walk downstairs with us willingly, or I will cuff you and haul you out in front of everyone."

Tracy's lips quivered. Silently she reached for her purse and stood, ready to go. Jackson gestured for her to lead the way, and they followed her outside.

As they stood by his cruiser, in full view of the upstairs windows, Tracy finally started to cry.

Jackson spoke softly. "Just tell us where Shane and Lori are or where they plan to go. If Shane is innocent, as you believe, then the evidence won't hold up and a jury won't convict him." Jackson would do everything he could to make sure that wasn't the outcome, but it was always possible.

"Shane didn't say where he was going because he didn't want to put me in this position."

"Give me your best guess."

"South. Maybe Mexico."

"How much money did you give him?"

Tracy blinked. "A thousand."

"Did he mention buying a plane ticket?"

"Not exactly."

"Are they headed to the Portland airport? For a flight to Maui?"

"I don't know."

"You're willing to go to jail to protect him?"

"I love my son more than I can put into words." Tracy's eyes glimmered with unshed tears. "But I haven't been able to protect him since he was sixteen. I can only do what I believe is right."

Jackson had a flash of sympathy for her. His own daughter was nearing the age of independence, and he didn't look forward to the feeling of helplessness that would accompany it. "If you have contact with Shane, please tell him to turn himself in. He'll end up in custody sooner or later, and sooner will be better for him. And Lori."

Jackson got back in the car, and Evans, seeming disappointed, hustled around to the passenger side. He backed out, leaving Tracy standing there with her head down.

"Why did you let her off the hook?"

"She's not going to help us and we gain nothing by making her more miserable. I can't imagine what it's like to be the parent of a heroin addict." He shuddered at the thought.

"Where now?"

"A quick stop at Shane's dealer."

CHAPTER 28

Thursday, June 4, 2:07 p.m.

They drove west and turned on Almaden. As they neared Eighth Avenue, Lori's muscles tensed and her pulse quickened. "Where are we going?"

"To Zor's. He owes me money."

"I don't think we should stop there."

Shane snapped his head to stare at her. "Why? Are you worried I'll get high while I'm in there?"

"I just have a bad feeling."

Shane stroked her hair. "I told you. I'm clean except for methadone, and I take it like medicine. You have to have faith in me or this won't work."

"Are you going to buy methadone from Zor?"

"If he has some."

Lori understood how important the methadone was to Shane's recovery, but she hated the connection to the drug world.

It had been much safer when he was dosing at the clinic. "Do they have methadone clinics in Maui?"

"Of course. Stop worrying." Shane gave her one of his hundred-watt smiles.

It didn't make her happy. A darkness hovered and crept into her bones, making her feel a little ill. Was the dread coming from Shane? Was he using heroin again? Lori didn't see the signs, but it was still early. He'd only been kicked out of the clinic a month ago. She felt guilty for doubting him. This feeling had to be grief; she'd lost her whole family.

As they neared Zor's crappy little house, her stomach began to churn. "I feel kind of sick," Lori said, touching Shane's shoulder for comfort. "I think I'll stay in the car."

"What kind of sick?"

"A little nauseated and a little shaky."

"You probably need to eat something. They don't feed you much in the hospital."

Shane parked two houses away, per Zor's standing instructions, and shut off the engine. "You should come in with me and eat a sandwich or something. Zor probably has some Vicodin for your pain too."

Lori didn't want to go inside the dark, crowded house, but she didn't want to be alone either. They both got out of the car and started up the walkway. A sense of déjà vu came over her. She had done this before; she'd walked up this path with the grass growing wild around the crumbling redbrick steps. Lori turned to Shane. "Have I been here with you before?"

He gave her a look she couldn't read. "No, babe. I quit coming here after I enrolled in the clinic."

As Shane knocked on the door, a vague memory slipped into her conscious. She had stopped here that night on her way home from work, but why? The scene in her brain expanded and Lori remembered being in the car with Shane at one point. Yet he'd just said they hadn't come here together.

Zor answered the door and looked surprised to see Lori. "Shane, good to see you're okay. Hey, Lori."

Zor rolled back in his wheelchair and let them in. As they passed him, Lori saw Shane give Zor some kind of hand signal. What was that about? She stared at Shane, hoping he would explain, but he flashed her a smile and scooted toward the kitchen. "Have you got some bread? Lori needs to put something in her stomach."

Lori's legs shook and she couldn't think straight. The dark dread gripped her entire body. She wanted to bolt from the house but there was no point. The dread would stay with her. The bad thing had not happened here. It had happened at home, of course. Someone had brutally murdered her family and tried to kill her too. The memory was coming back in vivid little chunks and she couldn't stop it. *Oh god. Why now?* She didn't want to relive that night.

Lori plopped on the ratty green couch and closed her eyes against the cluttered space and its permanently closed drapes. The pain medication they'd given her in the hospital must have kept the memory at bay. It had been hours since she'd taken any pills, and now that horrible night was coming back. Lori called out to Zor, who had followed Shane into the kitchen. "Do you have any Vicodin?"

Zor turned back. "Sure." He rolled toward the hallway, stopped, and looked at her with pity. "Oh yeah. You were stabbed. You must be in a lot of pain."

"I am." Her knife wound was a constant source of physical discomfort, but Lori barely noticed anymore. This time her brain needed quieting. Shane came into the living room and handed her a piece of bread folded in half with peanut butter and brown sugar in the middle. Her favorite. "Thanks." She reached for the snack but couldn't stomach the idea of eating it. "I'll get a baggie and save it for later."

"Okay, babe." Shane followed Zor down the hall. Lori noticed the gun still in his pocket. Was Zor the buyer he had in mind? She shivered again and lay down on the couch. She tried to imagine Maui, blue sky, white beaches, and a warm breeze blowing against her skin and making her feel good inside. For a moment she could feel paradise, then the dread pushed it away.

Lori saw a quick flash of the last time she'd been here. She was upset when she arrived, shaking and crying. Zor had been kind to her. He'd brought her a blanket and given her a beer. She remembered Zor offering her something else to make her feel better. What had she taken?

CHAPTER 29

Thursday, June 4, 2:47 p.m.

Jackson and Evans arrived at Zor's house moments after McCray did. They parked behind him, and the three detectives pounded up the sidewalk. Jackson gave one loud rap on the door, waited for a count of three, and grabbed the handle. It was locked.

"Police! Open up or we're taking the door down."

"Hang on. I'll be right there." The voice came from deep inside the house and Jackson thought it was Zor's. Dealers often had company though. Jackson stepped away from the direct line of fire and the other detectives followed.

After a lengthy wait, the door came open a few inches with the security chain still in place. "What do you want?"

"We're looking for Shane Compton."

"He's not here."

"Prove it. Let us in."

"Why do you want Shane?"

"We think he's going to kill his girlfriend."

A short hesitation, then, "One of you can come in."

The security chain flopped down and the door opened. Zor rolled back and Jackson pushed in. "Have you seen Shane?"

"He and Lori were here about twenty minutes ago."

"Mind if I check the house to see if they're still here?"

"Don't touch anything! Don't open any drawers."

Jackson conducted a fast check of the two small bedrooms and their closets. The house had no garage or storage unit to hide in. Back in the living room, he asked, "What happened when Shane and Lori were here?"

"They made a purchase."

"Tell me what drug you sold them."

"You can't make me incriminate myself." Zor sounded a little less confident.

Jackson didn't give a shit about this small-time dealer and he didn't have time for bullshit either. "Tell me everything about Shane's visit and we'll be on our way. Dick around for another minute and I'll personally drag your ass to jail for obstruction, then send vice out here on a raid."

Zor weighed his options. Finally he said, "Shane came here looking for methadone. After a few minutes, Lori started freaking out and they went out to the car." Zor lit a cigarette, stalling. "They sat out there for ten minutes. When they came back in, they were both freaked out. They'd been crying. They wanted to score more methadone."

"Did you sell it to them?"

"I'm doing my best to tell you what happened without incriminating myself."

"Try harder."

"They were both on their way to getting high when they left the house."

"Did they say where they were going?"

"No, and I didn't ask."

"Do you know where they might go?

Zor shook his head. "Shane had a gun in his pocket. It's the only reason I'm telling you this."

Oh crap. Where in the hell had Shane acquired a gun? "Did he say anything about it?"

"When I asked him about it, he said he planned to sell it. I made him take it out to the car. I don't allow weapons in here."

"Good for you." Jackson resisted rolling his eyes. He was frustrated and anxious to get out of there. "Lori's life is in danger. Is there anything else you can tell me?"

"No. Sorry."

Jackson squatted next to Zor's wheelchair, where he could look him in the eye. "Your dealing days are over. Vice detectives will be on you and everyone who comes and goes from this house. You might as well find an honest way to make a living or get the hell out of Eugene."

Outside, Jackson took a deep breath of lukewarm June air. He would have felt even better if the sky had been clear, but at least he was in the open.

"What's the story?" Evans asked. She and McCray were standing on the lawn, making the neighborhood nervous.

"Shane and Lori left twenty minutes ago and they were both high on methadone."

"Lori's a doper?" McCray looked surprised, an expression Jackson didn't often see on the seasoned detective.

"Apparently she is now."

"I didn't think you could get really high on methadone," Evans said. "It's supposed to have a slow, steady effect."

"If you crush the tablets you can."

Evans scowled. "Did we ever get Lori's tox screen?"

"Not yet. Parker said she would call as soon as she has it." Jackson was not surprised Lori had turned to drugs. She was grieving, physically wounded, and her boyfriend was an addict. It seemed inevitable. "We need to call everyone connected to this couple and ask where they would go. Evans, call Lori's friends you've been talking to." He turned to McCray. "Go see Kevin Compton at his business. I'll call Shane's sister."

Jackson headed for his vehicle and the others followed. "Schak is out at the airport in case the couple tries to get on a plane." Now that Shane and Lori were loaded, it seemed less likely. Jackson didn't know what their plan was and it worried him. At the sidewalk he said, "Zor told me that Lori and Shane were freaking out about something. I don't know what it means, but let's assume Shane is dangerous and Lori is unpredictable."

Jackson drove toward headquarters, thinking it made sense to be in a central location until they had a real lead about where to find the couple. Next to him, Evans was on the phone with one of Lori's friends. Jackson waited to make his call to Shane's sister, Lisa.

Evans clicked her phone shut. "Ashley hasn't heard from Lori today and I left a message with Jenna."

On impulse Jackson turned on Monroe. The bakery where Shane's sister worked was two blocks away. This time he hoped to get the truth in a face-to-face conversation.

When he and Evans rushed into the commercial kitchen, Lisa looked up from the table where she was frosting brownies and scowled. Another woman watched as they crossed the room.

"What do you want now?" Lisa was even less friendly this time.

"I'm looking for Shane."

She looked down at the brownies. "I still haven't heard from him."

"Don't lie to me. Lives are at stake."

Lisa shook her head. "You don't know Shane."

"Maybe *you* don't know Shane. Your brother took Lori out of the hospital and now he has a gun. We think Lori's in danger."

Lisa's eyes widened and her mouth dropped open. "A gun? I don't believe it."

"Have you seen him or heard from him?"

"He called an hour ago and asked to borrow money. I told him I didn't have it."

"Did he say what his plans were?"

"He said he wanted to get out of town before he got blamed for murders he didn't commit."

"Anything else?"

"No." Lisa looked troubled.

"What are you holding back?"

"I'm just confused by all of this. And depressed. Will you please stop bothering me at work? I can't afford to lose my job."

On the way out, the comforting smell of brownies baking made Jackson's stomach growl. He'd missed lunch again.

"I couldn't work there," Evans said as they left the bakery. "I'd get fat."

"I'm sure you get used to it."

Jackson and Evans stood in the conference room and studied the board.

"Tyler Gorlock." The name jumped out at Jackson. "Shane has stayed with Gorlock. Maybe he can tell us something." He started for the door. "I'm going over to the jail to talk to him. You should run out to Gorlock's place and see if anyone's around. Have a patrol unit meet you there for backup."

"I'm on it."

They charged out of headquarters ten minutes after arriving. Gorlock could be a waste of time, but Jackson had to keep moving, to keep asking and searching. Sitting around would make him crazy. They had been only twenty minutes behind Shane and Lori all day, but without knowing where they were headed next, twenty minutes was the same as an hour...or a day.

Having committed the crime of holding a police officer hostage, Gorlock had not been matrixed out and was still incarcerated when Jackson arrived. It gave him little comfort to know that's what it took to be retained for trial.

He still had to wait fifteen minutes while a sheriff located the inmate and brought him to the interrogation room. Jackson paced in the hall, mentally reviewing everything. This case perplexed him. Engall's story was a fluke, yet seemed plausible. A drunk stumbling into something so shocking he wasn't sure it was real until he saw it on the news. Shane's hair on Carla's clothes placed him at the crime scene, but why had he wiped his prints off the knife and not the bat? How had he come and gone with none of the neighbors seeing him? Shane hadn't driven there, Jackson reasoned. The cousin also spent enough time at the house that no one would think twice about seeing him.

What had sent him into a murderous rage? Shane was bitter about his father's brain damage and blamed Jared Walker for it, but was it enough? Or as Evans had pointed out, if Lori's parents had tried to keep their daughter from seeing Shane, that may have been the catalyst, especially if Shane was high at the time. If Lori and Nick had tried to protect their parents, they could have been caught up in Shane's drug-induced onslaught.

A middle-aged deputy reeking of tobacco led Gorlock to where Jackson waited. "Do you want him cuffed?" the deputy asked.

"Yes." Gorlock had taken a police officer hostage, and Jackson suspected he was reckless enough to try it again. The sheriff clicked the wrist locks, leaving Gorlock's hands in front of his body, and led the prisoner into a sickly green room about the size of a walk-in closet.

Jackson sat at the scarred wooden table and decided he wouldn't waste more than ten minutes here. "I need to find Shane Compton. Where would he hide out with his girlfriend?"

Gorlock quickly calculated the situation. "What are you offering in exchange?"

"I'll tell the jury you helped track down a killer."

Gorlock let out a scoffing sound. "I want a decent plea bargain."

"That's up to the district attorney."

"Get him in here."

"If you help us find Shane, I'll work with the DA to reduce your charges." *Not a chance in hell*, he thought.

"I want a promise I won't be charged with crimes against a police officer." Gorlock's voice held little hope.

Jackson shook his head. "Lori Walker's life is in danger, you prick. If you don't help me, I'll make a point of testifying about what a cold bastard you are at every parole-board hearing for the rest of your life." Jackson stood to leave.

Gorlock was silent. Jackson opened the door and motioned for the guard. As the sheriff led the inmate out, Gorlock tossed out, "Try Alton Baker Park. Shane likes to feed the ducks. Back when he was really strung out, he would sleep in the bushes near the concert stage if he couldn't find anywhere else to crash."

CHAPTER 30

Four days earlier

Lori walked away from her customers, shaking. They were so rude. Every nerve in her body wanted to run screaming out the door. You can do this, she coached herself. The coaching had become a mantra. Sometimes her head was so filled with self-talk that she forgot what she was supposed to be doing and didn't bring the extra napkins or the side of ranch dressing. That only made things worse. She looked at the clock: 7:38. Her shift was almost over. She would make it through one more day in this hellhole. This morning, when she missed the old guy with the little dog and failed to give him his dollar, she'd known this day would be a nightmare. Lori prayed they would not seat her station with another customer in the next twelve minutes. After 7:45, the closing servers had to take all the tables.

Lori took another round of sodas to the rude family in the corner, then started her side work. With a sense of urgency, she hustled around cleaning and filling and praying to not be seated and to not encounter Greg. At 7:42, Lori watched in horror as the hostess sat five college boys in the corner booth. *Oh fuck.* Lori went in search of Jaylene, one of the closers.

"Will you take the guys they just seated? I really need to get out of here."

Jaylene kept making salads and didn't even look at her. "I can't. I'm too busy."

"It's five cute guys. You know it will be a good tip."

"You take 'em. I'm slammed."

"If I get them started, will you take the ticket?"

"No." Jaylene gave her a bitchy look. "Just do your job."

Lori started to ask the other closer, but Jason saw her coming and shook his head. She clamped her teeth together, grabbed her tray, and marched out there.

The guys were half-drunk and it took six minutes just to get a drink and appetizer order. During the process, one said he liked the way her uniform fit and another asked if she was of the "age of consent." Lori finally walked away. The pricks. She was just trying to earn a little money. They had no right to make her feel like a pole dancer.

Lori took their ticket to the hostess. "I'm not feeling well. I have to go home." Her jaw tensed and she could barely squeeze out the words. She hurried away to avoid a discussion, then finished her side work. She couldn't quit or let herself get fired. She had to keep this job until she had enough money to move to Maui. The apartment and roommate were already lined up and she had enough for a ticket, but she still needed money to live on after she got there.

A few minutes later the manager called her into the office. Oh great, she thought. This would be the frosting on the shit cake of her day.

Greg closed the door behind her. "I keep hearing you won't take late tables," he said, standing between her and the door.

"Just tonight. I have a migraine, I've been here for eight hours, and I need to go home."

He slid close and laid one hand on each shoulder. "I can make your job here a lot easier." His fingers stroked her collarbones.

"I need to go home," she repeated, not knowing what else to say. Grabby Greg stood directly in front of the exit. What was she supposed to do? Push him out of the way? Lori could feel an outburst coming. All the control and self-talk would not get her past this.

"In just a moment, you can." Greg ran his hands over her breasts, giving each a gentle squeeze.

Lori exploded. Both hands came up and slammed into his chest, shoving him back. Greg staggered, but caught himself before he bounced into the wall. Too stunned to speak, he stared, openmouthed.

"Get out of my way!" Lori screamed.

The manager shuffled to the side, straightening his glasses. "You don't work here anymore."

"No shit."

Lori grabbed her backpack and sweatshirt from the cabinet and ran from the restaurant. Her coworkers glanced over as she hurried past, but only Jason said good-bye. *Fuck 'em*, she thought. *It was a crap job anyway.*

Outside, the sun was low on the mountain, the sky was pink, and the air was warm. Another blue-sky day spent inside. Wasted. Lori ran to the Subaru. Thank god it was Sunday and her mother had let her take the car to work. Behind the wheel, she burst into tears. It was so unfair. Why couldn't she have found a fun job? Like working at a camp? Now she had no job and her parents would be mad as hell.

Lori couldn't go home and face them yet. She hated what was happening to her parents. Her sweet, fun-loving father never made jokes anymore, and they hadn't played softball together in weeks. Dad was either at the computer looking on Craigslist for jobs or at the tavern drinking. Her mother had become a stranger—a quiet, worried imitation of herself. Lori just wanted to grab Shane and take off. They both needed to get away from Eugene and start fresh somewhere else.

Tears still rolling down her cheeks, she started the car, then called Shane. He didn't pick up and she left him a message. Where was he? He was supposed to meet her after work. With Shane, it was hard to know. Once he lost his job and gave up his apartment, he was all over. Sometimes he was at his parents' place, but he also stayed with Damon and sometimes at Tyler's. Shane didn't stay long enough in one place for people to get tired of him. That way he could always come back.

When Lori looked up, Shane was there in the twilight, sauntering across the parking lot. Some of the tension left her shoulders. Shane put his face to the windshield and grinned, dimples popping, and her heart lightened. If he would only come with her to Maui. He had to.

"Hey, babe." He climbed into the passenger seat, kissed her gently, then pulled away.

Lori's anxiety flooded back. "What's wrong?" She peered into his eyes, but saw no glassiness.

"How come you're so perceptive?" Another gentle smile.

"Tell me what's going on." Dread filled her stomach.

"Let's get going. I'll tell you on the way."

Lori started the car. "Where are we going?"

"I need to stop at Zor's and pick up some medicine."

"I wish you could find another source." She pulled onto the street. When they were in Maui, they could bike everywhere and she wouldn't have to feel like a chauffeur any more.

After a few minutes on the road, Shane said, "I'm not going to Maui with you. I'm sorry, babe." He stroked her hair.

She took her eyes off the road to stare at him. "Why not?"

"I can't. I'm too vulnerable right now. It's all I can do every day just to find and pay for methadone."

"There's methadone in Maui."

"But can I find it? Or afford it? I'm not going to let myself relapse." Shane's jaw muscles contracted.

Lori glanced up at the heavy traffic, then over at Shane again. "What are you keeping from me?" She was in full panic now.

"It's my dad. His head injury isn't getting any better. Mom wants me to stay here and learn the business."

"Are you kidding? After all these years of refusing to give you a job, now he wants you to work for him?"

"Mom wants me to train with him. As an intern."

"For no money?" Lori didn't understand.

"I owe them for a year's worth of methadone. I owe them a year's worth of rent." Shane squeezed her leg. If she hadn't been driving, he would have grabbed her hands. He always made contact when he was trying to be persuasive. "I owe them everything. They saved me."

Lori loved his loyalty to his mother. She also hated his loyalty to his mother. "What about our life together?"

Shane seemed to brace himself. "I can't be with you."

"What are you saying?" Lori's heart hammered. Her body shook and she considered pulling off the street.

"My parents are unhappy about us being together. Especially Dad. He's still pissed at Uncle Jared about the fight and at Nick for taking his Lou Gehrig card. After Dad saw us together he stopped speaking to me."

"None of that has anything to do with us." Lori knew it wasn't true, even as she said it.

"Of course it does. I hope our families can work everything out, but Dad may never forgive Jared or Nick."

"How many times do I have to tell you? Nick didn't take the damn baseball card." Lori thought she knew who did, but this wasn't the time to say it.

"Don't cry, babe. I feel bad enough as it is."

"Don't call me *babe*. Not if you're breaking up with me." She turned on Almaden, grateful to get away from the traffic.

"Your parents would have found out eventually. Your father, cool as he is, would never accept us."

Lori was crying too hard to respond. Shane was dumping her at the worst point in her life. She drove the last five blocks in silence, then pulled up in front of the shabby blue house.

"I love you, Lori. This breaks my heart too."

"Just get out."

Shane started to say something else, then decided against it. Lori watched him walk up the path. After he disappeared inside, she rested her head on the steering wheel, while silent tears rolled down her cheeks. How had everything gotten screwed up so fast?

Her parents had lost their jobs, that's how. After that everything turned to shit. Now she had to go home and tell them she'd lost hers too. Lori started the car and drove away. She practiced what she would say and how they would respond. She couldn't even make it go smoothly in her imagination. Her pulse raced, pumping stress into her nerves and muscles, making her feel poisoned. She pulled into a Safeway parking lot and called Jenna, but her best friend didn't answer. "I'm totally stressed and I need to talk," she said to the machine. "Call me."

Lori heard Jenna's voice in her head telling her to score some pot and bring it over. If there was ever a time to get high, this was it, Lori decided. It was unhealthy to feel this stressed. Shane took methadone to keep himself on track. Why couldn't she? It was a legal prescription, not some street drug. She turned the car around and headed back to Zor's.

The dealer opened the door and said, "Shane already left."

"I'm not looking for him."

"What do you want?"

"Methadone."

"Seriously?" Zor rolled his wheelchair back and let her in.

"Of course I'm serious." Lori hated when people patronized her for looking young. She was a legal adult.

"This is for you? Not Shane?"

"I'm stressed to the max." Lori held out her hands where he could see them shaking. Why did she need to justify this to him? He was a drug dealer.

"Let me get you a blanket and a beer to start with." Lori waited by the door in the dark room. It creeped her out to be here, but she desperately needed to soothe her soul. A constant dull anger had been eating away at her and turning her into someone she didn't like. She needed to take the edge off before telling her parents she'd lost her job, followed by the information she was planning to take her small savings and move across the ocean.

Zor came back with a lightweight blanket. Lori wrapped it around her shoulders and took the beer he offered.

"I don't have any methadone," Zor said, "but that's not what you need anyway. It's slow acting and addictive." He rolled toward the hallway. "Come with me."

They went into a back bedroom with blankets over the windows. Zor gave her a sly smile. "Have you ever been high before? I mean really high?"

Lori shook her head. She'd smoked pot a couple of times with Jenna but it mostly made her sleepy.

"You'll never understand Shane unless you understand what it's like to get loaded. You should try it once, just to know what his world is like."

"Shane just broke up with me."

"Then you should get high just for the fun it. You've had a crappy day."

Lori felt entitled. If there was ever a day for taking a mental break, this was it. If she looked older, she would have gone into a bar and had a drink. Since that wasn't an option, she'd try whatever Zor was offering and escape her own ugly head for a while.

"I have some great ecstasy," Zor said, unlocking a large black case. Jenna had taken ecstasy once, so Lori figured it was safe. Part of her didn't really care. Dying of an overdose and not having to face her current reality didn't seem that bad. Or ending up in the hospital with people hovering over her, worried, could be okay too. Would Shane take her back if he thought she'd overdosed because of him?

Lori swallowed the little pink tab and washed it down with a slug of beer. Zor wanted her to hang out for a while to make sure she was okay. She drank half her beer and tried to make small talk. Her body started to hum with energy and the walls of the little house started closing in. She was suddenly aware of the stink radiating from the carpet, every spilled beer, every cat hair, every molecule of mold growing in it now. Suddenly, she had to get out.

She paid Zor twenty bucks, a third of her tip money, and bolted from the house. The cool night air felt delicious on her skin and the scent of fresh mowed grass hung in the air. Crickets chirped and the moon shimmered. She loved summer and all its sensory richness.

Lori drove to her favorite riverside park and lay down in the middle of a wide field of grass. Staring up at the stars, she listened to the river gurgle by and wondered what it would be like to live on the water. Maybe on a houseboat in Maui. She had to find a way to get there. In this precious moment, she felt gloriously alive and amazingly free. Free of her job, free of high school, and free of her worries.

The stars changed colors, flashing bright blue, red, and gold. At first the fireworks were pretty, but soon they sent daggers of light hurtling across the sky at each other. Worried about being hit by burning debris, Lori hurried to her car. She wanted to be at home, in her room, listening to music with her eyes closed.

The drive took forever. She kept pulling off the road, thinking other cars were aiming straight for her, trying to crash into her. Finally she pulled into the driveway and stared at the house. This was her home, wasn't it? Something didn't seem right. As she stumbled out of the car, Lori realized her bladder was about to burst. She squatted between the garage and front of the car and relieved herself.

Lori rushed across the short walkway and into the house. Her skin heated up as she moved and her throat dried out. Water! She needed to consume liquid before she burst into flames. Lori rushed to the kitchen and downed half a glass of water from the faucet. She spotted tiny things floating in the glass and slammed it down on the counter. Had the little floaties gotten inside her? Should she vomit them up?

She strode into her bedroom, dropped her backpack, and kicked off her shoes. The walls seemed to close in and the orange of her bedspread was putrid and overwhelming. Still feeling incredibly thirsty, she rushed back to the kitchen for more water.

"Lori, are you okay?" Her mother stared as if she'd grown a third eye.

"I'm fine."

"Was work okay? You look upset."

"Work was the usual shithole of degradation."

"I wish you wouldn't swear." Her mother's green eyes blazed with anger.

People told her she looked like her mother, but Lori didn't see it. This woman was completely different from her. She was artsy and simplistic and complacent. "I wish you would leave me the fuck alone."

"I don't appreciate your tone. Have you been drinking?" A red fire flared in her mother's eyes and she looked possessed. Her hand snaked toward Lori and her face was a mask of hatred.

The anger building inside Lori burst like a giant pus-filled pimple. She jerked free. "I don't answer to you anymore! You failed me! Dad failed me!"

"What's going on?" The man she used to think of as her father came into the kitchen. He too had blazing red eyes and a mask of hatred.

What the hell was happening? Had these people been taken over by demons? Lori felt trapped against the counter. "I quit my job. So what?"

"Oh shit, Lori. That was pretty selfish." Jared pulled at his own hair.

"You're the one who's selfish. You're the one who's supposed to have a job."

His red eyes flashed and his body tensed, ready to lunge.

The mother-demon touched his arm. "I think she's been drinking. This is not a good time to talk about it."

"Let me smell your breath." The father-demon lurched at her.

Lori dodged, putting herself farther into the corner. "Get out of my way. I want to leave."

"You're not driving my car." The mother-demon spun out of the room. "I'm taking your keys."

Lori didn't care. She would rather run than drive anyway. Energy kept building in her muscles and she thought she would burst.

The father-demon spoke, his voice bouncing around the kitchen. "Your pupils are dilated. Did you take a drug?"

"Get out of my way. I want to leave."

"You're not going anywhere."

"Are you going to assault me the way you assaulted Uncle Kevin?"

His eyes flared in a bright-red burst. "That was an accident!" He lurched toward her. Lori made her move and tried to run past him toward the garage door. The father-demon grabbed her, his fingers digging into her burning skin. He barked like a madman, but the words were only sounds and made no sense.

Lori easily pulled free, surprised by her strength. She spotted the baseball bat leaning against the counter. Why was it there? Did he plan to assault her? Lori grabbed the bat and spun back around. She held it like a weapon. "Don't come near me." She hated the father-demon for his weakness. His failures. He'd started this family's descent into hell, then made it worse. It was his fault Shane had broken up with her.

The father-demon's eyes burned bright and his face morphed into a gargoyle's. It raised its hands and spoke again, but the words were a garbled echo. Suddenly, the thing was coming at her, shouting in an alien language. Heat filled her chest and adrenaline surged though her brain.

"I'll kill you," Lori warned.

It kept coming. Lori swung the bat with all her might.

Smack! The red fire went out of his eyes. Smack! The father-demon dropped to his knees. Lori swung the bat again. Smack! He fell against the counter.

Shrieking filled the air. Lori spun around and saw the mother-demon rush at her, eyes blazing. Lori charged forward and took her down with a single blow. The mother-demon landed on her back, momentarily weakened. Lori hated her too.

The mother-demon had stolen the baseball card and let Nick take the blame.

Lori's chest burned white-hot and she expected her heart to burst into flames. She was going to die and she didn't want to do it here.

She rushed to the cabinets and leaned the bat against the counter. Out of the corner of her eye, she watched the father-demon struggle to get up. He would come after her again if she gave him the chance. The knife holder was in her line of sight. Lori grabbed the biggest knife and spun around. In three strides, she stood over him and plunged the knife into his heart. Sounds kept coming from his mouth. She drove the knife in again. And again, shredding his treacherous heart.

The mother-demon sat up and made a heinous sound. Lori ran to the middle of the floor. She knelt, raised the knife, and slammed it down on the mother-demon's wrist. Blood pooled on the floor, but the hand was still attached. Lori slammed the knife one more time and the hand separated. It would not steal again.

As she rose from the floor, more screaming filled the room, then something rushed at her. It looked like her brother Nick, but its eyes flashed like a demon. Lori was stunned by the betrayal. Not Nick too! Her hesitation worked against her, and the Nick-demon took the knife and threatened her. Lori lunged for him and felt the knife enter her body. She felt no pain, only a slight cooling sensation. She glanced down, fascinated by the blood flowing from her abdomen. The Nick-demon was trying to kill her. Lori encircled his wrist with her right hand and squeezed with all her might. He cried out, and as his grip gave away she grabbed the knife handle. He turned away to prepare for another attack. Lori stopped him with a final plunge into his back. The Nick-demon took two steps and collapsed.

Lori glanced around, still in the grip of paranoia. They were all on the floor, dead or dying. Their attack on her was finally over. Her pulse began to slow, no longer racing like a jet boat engine. Her heart still beat loudly in her ears, but it no longer felt like it would explode in her chest. She stared at the knife in her hand, revolted by the blood. Using the bottom of her shirt, Lori wiped the knife from one end to the other. She started for the counter, intending to put it back in its slot, but her legs felt weak and she stopped. The knife fell from her hand.

The heat in her chest died and power oozed out of her. Lori felt cold and sluggish. She needed to rest a bit before she started packing for her trip. She kneeled next to her mother, thinking she would say good-bye, but she couldn't form the words. Her brain was shutting down. Lori laid her head on her mother's chest and listened for the familiar beat of her heart.

It was gone.

CHAPTER 31

As he jogged down the stairs, pain stabbed Jackson's lower abdomen. In his car, he tossed back two naproxen and chased them with cold coffee from his thermos.

His cell phone rang and he glanced at the caller ID. Opening it, he said, "Parker, tell me you have good news."

"I have news, but I don't know how to rate it. The hospital sent over Lori Walker's tox screen. She had MDMA and phencyclidine in her system."

"Ecstasy and PCP?" Jackson was stunned.

"I wish we had a hair sample the lab could test for long-term use of all recreational drugs."

"I'll see what I can do. Thanks, Parker." Jackson sat in the underground lot for a full five minutes, his body unmoving while his mind raced. What the hell did this mean? If Lori was high on PCP at the time of the murders, it changed everything. Phencyclidine was the most dangerous drug on the street. It could give people superhuman strength and sometimes trigger horrendous violence. Three uniformed cops had once tried to subdue a man near campus who was pulling traffic signs out of the ground with his bare hands. They had used repeated baton strikes on his legs to make him go down. After the first few blows, he'd laughed and said, "Ouch."

A dark suspicion overwhelmed Jackson. Had Lori committed this heinous attack on her family? *Oh, dear god.* Jackson felt like the wind had been knocked out him. He had never suspected Lori because she had almost died. Because the medical examiner and the pathologist had both said the assailant was incredibly strong. Because it was unthinkable.

He understood why her brain had blocked the horrific memory. Maybe she and Shane had gotten loaded together and both participated. Shane, with his upper-body strength wielding the bat, and Lori going after her parents with the knife. If that were the case, how had Lori taken a stab to the stomach? It must have come from Nick, fighting for his life. Jackson felt ill. The pain medication and coffee in his empty stomach churned into a toxic brew that wouldn't stay down. He opened the car door and heaved up the partially intact pills.

He had failed this case but it wasn't over. Jackson put in his earpiece and started the car. Zor had said Lori "started freaking out." Had her memory come back? If so, what would she do next? Jackson headed for Alton Baker Park, just over Ferry Street Bridge, about a five-minute drive. His first call was to a vice detective, requesting he pick up Zor. The drug-dealing bastard would pay for his part in this tragedy.

Next he called Evans. "Where are you?"

"Gorlock's trailer was empty. I'm on my way to Alton Baker Park. Lori's friend Jenna called back and said it was Lori's favorite place."

"I'm headed over too. When you get there, wait in your cruiser for me. We have a new development." Jackson clicked off before Evans could ask questions. He had two more calls to make and didn't want to have to repeat himself.

He pressed speed dial #5 as he raced up the ramp to the bridge.

"Schak, are you at the airport?"

"Yep, but our little lovers are not. Do you want me to stay and keep scouting?"

"No. If airport security is watching for them, that's all we need. I don't think they're getting on a plane this afternoon."

"Do we have any idea where they are?"

"Evans and I are heading to Alton Baker Park on a tip. You might as well meet us there." Jackson had planned to tell the task force all at the same time, but he realized Schak would arrive late and they would already be searching the massive area. Schak needed the information now. "We have a new development."

"I'm listening."

"Lori had PCP in her blood when she was admitted to the hospital." Jackson waited to see if his partner would go in the same direction he had. Schak had been one of the officers trying to take down the PCP-crazed man.

It took him a full second. "Oh fuck. She killed them, didn't she?"

"I'm starting to think so."

"Jesus christ. Did you see the dent in her father's head? It looked like it was made by an enraged giant."

"What about her mother's hand?" Jackson still felt shell-shocked. "I've never seen anything like it." He slammed his brakes as the traffic slowed. Rush hour was over and the sun was dropping in the sky. The traffic surprised him. "Will you call McCray and update him? Tell him to meet us at Alton Baker. Lori and

Shane bought methadone tablets this afternoon and may have crushed them to get high. I don't know what to expect."

"I'll get there as fast as I can."

Jackson was soon on the circular exit to the city park that stretched for acres along the river. Named after the man who founded the city's newspaper, Alton Baker was connected by bike paths to other parks along the south bank of the river, and to the Valley River Center mall on the north bank. Its four hundred acres contained a duck pond, covered picnic areas, a slough for canoeing, and an outdoor amphitheater.

The parking area was surprisingly full. It was early June and all the high school and college students had just started summer break. The day had been overcast, but the young people playing disk golf wore shorts and sandals anyway. Jackson had one of those moments where he resented his long-sleeved sports jacket. It wasn't required, but it was necessary to be taken seriously.

He locked his car, then jogged the length of the parking lot looking for the Walkers' green Subaru. He didn't see it, but there was another parking area closer to the amphitheater. On the return search, he saw Evans pull in. Jackson picked up his pace.

She hustled over, vibrant with energy. "What's the new development?"

Jackson suddenly felt tired and wounded. "Parker called with Lori's tox screen. She had PCP in her system when she was admitted to the hospital."

"Holy shit."

"It changes everything."

A moment of silence. "You think she might have killed her family."

"We have to consider it." Jackson mentally kicked himself again. "We should have already considered it."

"She has such a baby-girl face and she's so scrawny. I can't see her doing it." Evans wasn't arguing with his theory; she was going through the same process of rationalization he had.

"She was critically wounded too," Jackson added.

"Do you think Nick stabbed her? Defending his parents?"

"Probably. He wasn't knocked down with the bat, so he had a fighting chance."

"Oh god. Poor girl. No wonder she blacked it all out." Evans scanned the area as they talked, checking everyone who passed. "So Lori's probably not in danger from Shane."

"We can't assume anything. Shane has a gun, and he may have participated in the murders."

A flash of understanding registered on Evans' face. "I don't think so. The only bloody prints leaving the house were Roy Engall's. The killer never left the scene."

She had nailed it. The thing that had been bothering him since Engall confessed to being there. "I think you're right."

"If her memory comes back, she could be suicidal. I would be."

"Let's put on our Kevlar vests and go find her."

As they covered the main grassy area between the parking lot and the duck pond, Jackson noticed the frolickers thinning out. The sun was dropping fast, the wind had picked up, and it was past dinnertime. It would have been more efficient to split up, but Jackson didn't want Evans finding the suspects and confronting them on her own. Seeing Whitstone as a hostage yesterday made him feel protective. They needed Schak and McCray to help them cover the park thoroughly and safely.

"Let's check out the area by the theater," Jackson said after they searched the park's bathrooms. "Gorlock said Shane has been known to sleep there."

"Wouldn't their car be here somewhere if they were in the park?" Evans asked.

She had a point, but two people had given them the same tip. They had to be thorough. "They could have ditched the car, knowing we're looking for it," Jackson answered. "Or parked on the other side of the river and come over on the footbridge."

The outdoor concert stage was in the east end of the park, closest to Autzen Stadium, where the university's football team played. They jogged along the curved road leading to the theater. Cuthbert's seating area was empty and they saw no sign of activity. Jackson and Evans did a quick search of the brush anyway, finding plenty of trash, empty beer bottles, and a rain-weathered sleeping bag. They were wasting their time.

* * *

The river flowed by, singing its song, and the sky turned a glorious pink as the sun dropped toward the horizon. To sit on the bank, mesmerized by the current and the songbirds was a gift, Shane thought. He stayed in the moment for as long as he could. This was the last time he would ever be this high, he promised himself. Today was an exception. He was struggling with the most unbelievable fucked-up thing he'd ever faced. Even at the peak of his euphoria, the horrible thing Lori had done lurked underneath, waiting for him to acknowledge it.

The buzz from the crushed methadone was already wearing off, and he felt the hard coolness of the rock under his ass. He glanced at Lori. Eyes closed, with worry lines puckering her forehead. Very soon, they had decisions to make. Lori had to consider her future and decide how to live with it. Or not. He hoped she would turn herself in.

"Shane?"

"Yes?" He lifted her hand and kissed the back of it, his lips gentle on her cool freckled skin.

"Do you love me?"

"Of course." *Did he?* When he looked at her, she was still his lovely Lori. When he thought about her, she was someone else.

"I want you to kill me."

"Don't even say it." When Lori's memory of that tragic night had come flooding back, she'd become hysterical, and her first coherent thought was that she wanted to kill herself. Shane had tried to soothe her but his clumsy efforts had been wasted. He couldn't even bring himself to tell her it would be okay. This was not something she would ever get over. He didn't know if he still loved her but he couldn't take her life. "I can't do it, Lori. It's too weird."

Her eyes pleaded for understanding. "I can't live with this. I killed my whole family. I'm a monster and I want to die." Because of the methadone, her voice was soft and melodic. As she came down, her self-hatred would only intensify.

Shane had wanted her to experience a few hours of peace before she turned herself in and went to jail. "You're not a monster. Zor gave you a drug you didn't ask for. A drug that made you hallucinate and act violently." He kissed her forehead. "A jury will understand. You won't be in jail long." He didn't believe it but he wanted to give her some hope.

"This is not about a jury or going to jail. I can't live with *myself*. Would you want to go on living if you had done this?"

Shane wanted to be encouraging but he couldn't. "No, I wouldn't." Thinking about her dreadful situation shredded the last of his peaceful bliss. His heart ached for her and he wanted to help, but he didn't know how.

"Thanks for giving me these few hours. And thanks for not hating me." Lori rose slowly, still moving in a haze. "Let's go up on the pedestrian bridge and look at the river from up there."

"Okay." She had so little time left. If she didn't turn herself in soon, the police would find them. Shane almost hoped they would.

They strolled down the cement path toward the newly built footbridge. Feeling guilty, Shane said, "We could still go to Maui. You were willing to go on the run with me, so I should be willing to go on the run for you." He prayed she would say no. It was one thing to be a fugitive when you knew you were innocent. It was another to hide out with a wanted killer.

"I can't run from this," Lori said. "It's inside me. Thanks for being sweet."

They took the pedestrian steps connecting to the bridge. From their vantage point, Shane could see the park had mostly emptied. A couple of cars were in the parking lot, but he didn't see anyone in the grass below. A breeze tickled his skin, but it gave him no pleasure.

They ambled up to the peak of the arch.

"If I jumped from the bridge, would it kill me?" Lori peered over the railing at the cold, green river below.

"Maybe." Shane thought about what jumping from the bridge would be like. "The drop isn't that far but the impact would stun your body, then the cold water would send you into hypothermia. Especially if you weren't strong enough to swim to shore against the current."

"That's what I thought."

"I think you should turn yourself in."

She gave him a sad smile. "Hold me for a while, please."

CHAPTER 32

Jackson and Evans hurried along the asphalt to the parking area. He started to regret listening to a lowlife like Tyler Gorlock. Yet Evans had heard the same tip about the park. Maybe they hadn't looked in the right places yet. Or maybe Shane and Lori were in the Subaru headed south on Interstate 5. What did people do when they were high on drugs? He honestly didn't know. Violence was not usually in a junkie's bag of tricks, but the thought gave him little comfort. Jackson was now more worried that Lori would kill herself and take Shane with her.

Jackson would not underestimate Shane when and if they encountered him, but he had serious doubts Shane had been involved in the killings. His hair found on Carla could have been transferred from Lori as she lay on her mother. Shane belonged in jail, or maybe inpatient rehab, but he wasn't a throwaway yet.

"What if they're not at the park?" Evans said, breathing easy as they ran. "What next?"

"We put Lori's picture on the news and hope someone turns her in." Jackson's abdomen burned in a steady pain he tried to ignore. He wished he'd been able to keep the pain tablets down. He wished he'd had a decent meal today too. Was he getting too old for these round-the-clock cases?

In the fading daylight, McCray stood next to his cruiser, waiting for them. The three city-issued Impalas, plus one old VW bug, were the only vehicles in the area.

"Hey, McCray. You must have heard from Schak."

"He's still on the way. I don't want to believe that girl is a killer, but I've seen what PCP does to people." McCray shook his head. "This is why I can't work narcotics."

"Ready for a search party?"

McCray glanced at the VW parked in the far corner. "I don't see the Subaru. Is this a dead end?"

"We haven't searched along the riverbank yet." Jackson hadn't coordinated this kind of search in years. "Let's work in teams. Evans and I will search this whole bank to the left." He gestured in the direction of the electric plant across the river. "McCray, start on the area past the footbridge. Let's make short work of this. We don't have much daylight left."

They started off in different directions, then McCray called out softly, "On the footbridge."

A couple stood near the railing at the peak of the bridge, arms around each other. In the fading light and distance, Jackson couldn't identify either person, but their sizes matched Shane and Lori.

The three detectives herded back together and Jackson laid out a plan. "McCray, I want you on the other side of the footbridge. We'll wait until you have the exit covered. Evans and I will approach from this side. Shane and Lori may still be high, and they could be unpredictable. Go." McCray took off running, his lean body covering the forty yards to his car in a few seconds. Jackson hoped to be that fast and agile when he was in his fifties.

The two bridges formed a tight V, with the pedestrian path curving down into the park, while the vehicle bridge went straight across the river and connected to Coburg Road. To reach the other side of the footbridge, McCray had to drive in a 180-degree semicircle, then cut across the viaduct and park near the utility company. The late hour and lack of traffic would work in his favor. Jackson called dispatch and quietly asked for backup. "Possibly armed and dangerous," he added.

He and Evans crept along, hoping they would not attract the attention of the couple on the bridge. Long tree shadows loomed across the grass, the daylight nearly gone. When they reached the last point where they could still see the other end of the raised footbridge, Jackson stopped to wait. The couple stayed in their clinch, arms wrapped tightly around each other. The woman had her head on the man's shoulder while he watched the river.

While they waited, Jackson and Evans stood close, facing each other like a couple and trying not to look like cops. He didn't want Lori and Shane to get spooked and escape off the other side before McCray was in place.

It was a long five minutes. Finally Jackson spotted a figure at the bridge's other entrance. It was impossible to know for sure if it was McCray, but the person waited, unmoving. "Let's go."

They ran to the short stairway leading up to the bridge path. Behind them in the distance, Jackson heard a car pull into the parking lot. He hoped it was Schak. At the top of the steps he drew his Sig Sauer and paused, waiting for Evans to come up beside him. Together they approached the intertwined couple. At the other end of the bridge, the dark figure slipped closer too.

The couple suddenly broke apart and the woman said, "Oh shit. The cops are here."

"Lori Walker. Put your hands in the air and step away from Shane." Jackson pitched his voice loud enough to carry authority, but without aggression. "Shane Compton, put your gun on the ground. Very slowly."

Neither person moved. In the quiet, the river rushed by forty feet below.

Jackson took three steps forward. Evans stayed with him, her weapon held out front with both hands. He could smell her sweat and hear her shallow breathing. Evans had the right training, but did she have the right instincts?

"Shane, put down your weapon. Do it now. Do it slowly." Jackson gave his voice more volume, more authority. "Lori, put your hands in the air and move away from Shane."

They were close enough now to recognize their two suspects, but the twilight worked against them. Jackson's heart hammered as possible scenarios flashed in his mind. The bridge had a low railing and widely spaced support cables. Going over would be too easy.

"I'm getting it from my pocket now." Shane's voice sounded gravelly and scared. "Don't shoot me. I only meant to sell the gun." They heard the zip of his pocket, then he pulled something out, bent his knees, and placed it on the cement.

Jackson let out his breath. "Both of you, take three steps away from the gun."

As Shane started to move, Lori lunged for the gun. A second later it was pointed directly at Jackson.

Oh fuck.

"Stay back!" Lori shouted, her voice filled with panic. "Just let me kill myself." She scooted to the middle of the bridge, out of Shane's reach.

"Put it down, Lori. You don't want to do this," Evans called out. Jackson flinched, then thought Lori might listen to a woman.

Lori jerked the gun and pointed it at Evans. "I want to die. You understand, don't you? I killed my family." Her voice broke with grief and she put the gun to her temple.

Jackson inched forward. "You took the wrong drug. It's not your fault. Killing yourself won't make it better." He knew he lacked conviction. For some people, death was better.

Lori jerked the gun away from her temple and pointed it in his direction again. "Stay back or I'll shoot you!"

Jackson held his position. Without pulling his eyes off Lori, he watched McCray moving in behind her, still twenty feet away. Shane inched toward the railing. Again Jackson yelled, "Drop the gun!"

In a quick moment, Shane leapt up on the railing and grabbed the closest cable for support. "Put the gun down, Lori, or I'll jump."

Jackson's teeth clamped together. This could not turn out well.

Lori shouted, "Get down, Shane! Just let me do this." She jerked the gun back up to her temple.

For a moment, the five were locked in their positions; the only thing moving was the river below. Lori started to sob. She pulled the gun away from her head, chest heaving.

Jackson inched forward.

Lori brought the weapon up and aimed it at Jackson's chest. "Just kill me, please!"

Jackson's teeth ground together. She wanted suicide by cop. "No, Lori. I won't do it for you. Put the gun down." He wondered if the gun was even loaded.

He whispered out the side of his mouth. "McCray."

Evans gave a slight nod.

Lori jerked her arm and a loud boom shattered the night. Jackson instinctively returned fire, putting two shots into her chest, his eyes not leaving the shooter until she went down. Her weapon clattered to the cement.

All was still.

Then a cry came from the water below. Shane was no longer on the railing. *Oh fuck.* Jackson looked past Lori's prone body. McCray was also on the ground.

"McCray!" Jackson rushed forward and scooped up the gun. The shooter didn't move. Evans flew past him, reaching McCray first.

Pulse pounding, Jackson knelt next to McCray and dialed 911. His partner's eyes were closed and blood seeped into his brown corduroy jacket from the top of his shoulder. He wasn't wearing a protective vest. Evans peeled off her own jacket and pressed it into the wound. "It doesn't look that bad." Evans' voice caught in her throat.

"It's not," McCray responded, eyes fluttering open.

Jackson waited for a dispatcher to answer. On the fourth ring, a young woman said, "What is your emergency?"

"Jackson here. Officer down on the Peter DeFazio footbridge." He glanced back at the shooter. Lori was still. "A second person has been shot and is probably dead, and a young man went into the river off the bridge. We need a rescue team to look for him downstream."

He closed his cell and gulped for air. His heart raced like an engine about to throw a rod. He had just shot and killed an eighteen-year-old girl, her boyfriend was in the river, probably drowning, and his good friend Ed McCray had a bullet in his shoulder. Jackson looked at the wound again. The bullet couldn't have come from him. He had fired two rounds and he was certain they had both hit Lori. McCray's bullet hole seemed to be in the top of his shoulder.

"I didn't fire my weapon," Evans said, meeting Jackson's eyes. "When you said 'McCray,' I thought you meant for me to hold my fire."

"The bullet came from above." McCray's voice was weak but he was coherent.

Jackson looked up. "I think it came from Lori's gun and ricocheted off that giant metal support."

"She wasn't aiming at you," Evans said. "She just wanted one of us to shoot her."

Jackson couldn't respond. He rose from his squat and breathed in the cool night air. He heard patrol units pull into the parking lot, and in the distance the faint sound of a siren.

CHAPTER 33

Jackson followed the ambulance to the hospital, alternating between worry about McCray and worry about Schak. His partner's car was in the parking lot at Alton Baker, but Schak seemed to have disappeared. Jackson had dialed his cell phone and was routed into voice mail.

Evans had wanted to come with him to the hospital, but Sergeant Lammers had demanded someone stay and answer questions. Jackson was expected back at headquarters soon to make a statement as well, but he wasn't ready. He needed to know McCray would recover. He needed to know where the hell Schak was. He needed to figure out what had gone wrong up there on the bridge. One dead, one wounded, and one in the river, not likely to survive. *Jesus!* Jackson shook his head, still stunned by the outcome.

He found a place in the hospital parking lot and sat for a moment. Images of Lori, blood gushing from her chest, wedged their way into his frantic thoughts. What could he have done differently? He replayed the scene, step-by-step. When he told Shane to put the gun on the ground, should he have told him to kick it away? That would have posed a risk of accidental fire, and Lori still could have reached the weapon first. The ricochet that hit McCray was a fluke, beyond his control. Shane getting up on the railing had caught him off guard. He'd been dealing with two people high on drugs, one an idiot and the other holding a gun with nothing left to lose. Jackson told himself it was not his fault. He hoped the internal review board would see it his way too.

Once inside the hospital, there was nothing to do but wait. McCray was taken into surgery, but the ER nurse assured him his partner was stable and the wound was not life threatening.

Jackson called Kera, needing to hear her comforting voice.

"Hey, sorry to call this late." He looked at the clock on his cell phone: 10:16. "It's been a long, crazy day."

"What happened? You sound stressed."

"I shot and killed an eighteen-year-old girl." Hot tears pooled in his eyes. Jackson dug fingers into his leg for distraction. He blamed the prednisone for making him emotional.

"Oh, Jackson. I'm so sorry. Where are you?"

"At the hospital. McCray was shot too, but not by me."

"I'm coming down." Clicking noises in the background told him Kera was on the move.

"Don't come here. I have to go back to headquarters and make a statement. I could be there for hours."

"Tell me what happened."

"We found our two suspects at Alton Baker Park." Jackson moved to a corner in the waiting room. "They had a gun. Lori Walker threatened to shoot me, then fired the weapon."

"What? I thought Lori was in the hospital. Why would she threaten you?"

He sympathized with her confusion. "It's a long story, but the short version is Lori took PCP, went crazy, and killed her family. When we tried to arrest her, she committed suicide by aiming a gun at two cops and pulling the trigger."

"She shot at you?"

"Yes, but she pulled her shot into the air. That's how McCray got hit. The doctors say he'll be okay though."

After a stunned silence, Kera said, "That is the most tragic thing I've ever heard. The poor girl. Jackson, you can't blame yourself. You did what you had to do."

"I still feel horrible."

"If she really wanted to die, she would have found a way to kill herself in prison anyway." Kera's voice was soft and soothing. "Lori used you. Maybe you should get mad at her instead."

Jackson smiled. This was why he loved Kera. She cut to the heart of a situation and always knew how to make him feel better. "Thanks. I'll call you again tomorrow."

"You're staying at the Harris Street house again?" Kera tried to sound neutral, but he could hear her disappointment.

"For now. Katie needs the security. She's taking Renee's relapse pretty hard and needs my full attention."

"I understand. Fifteen is a critical age for girls." A short silence, then, "Don't be a stranger."

"We're not breaking up. I'm just moving back into my house for a while."

Kera laughed, amused and wounded at the same time. "My house, with Danette and the baby, is too crazy for you, isn't it?"

"A little, but this is really about Katie."

"Okay. I'll talk to you tomorrow." She hung up and Jackson felt crushed with guilt. Who else could he hurt today?

He wandered into the hallway and paced for a while, then headed for the vending machines near the kitchen. He wolfed down a bland beef sandwich and hurried back to the ER waiting room, thinking he would write up some notes about the day.

The rumble of an ambulance caught his attention. Jackson jumped to his feet and rushed outside to where they would unload. As the medics pushed past him with a gurney, he glanced at the bundled body. Shane Compton. His skin was a little blue but he was breathing. Jackson said a little thank-you to God. Maybe Shane's dip in the river would be a wake-up call and he would get his life together. Jackson liked to think it was possible.

Another pair of medics pushed a second gurney up to the doors. This one carried Schak, who was awake and complaining. "I told you, I'm fine. I don't want to be admitted. I just need some hot coffee." His partner was pale and wet.

"Wait." Jackson put up his hand and the paramedics stopped. "Hey, Schak. Where the hell have you been?"

His partner grinned. "I thought I'd take a little dip in the river. I found some lowlife in the water and pulled him out so I could arrest his sorry ass."

"I didn't know you could swim."

"I can dance too," Schak called back as the gurney passed into the treatment area.

Jackson had his doubts, but it made him smile.

The next morning he stopped in the hospital and was surprised to find McCray sitting up and looking rather perky. His wife, Julie, was working a crossword puzzle in a chair next to his bed.

"Hey, Jackson," McCray called out. "Haven't you had enough of this place yet?"

"Apparently not."

"Hello, Wade," Julie said. "How are you holding up?"

"I've got a lot on my mind, but I'm okay." Jackson turned to his partner. "What's the word? Is this going to ruin your golf game?"

"Hell no. I'll be out on the green next weekend."

"And every weekend," Julie added.

Something in her tone made Jackson pause and pull up a chair. "What's going on?"

"I'm retiring," McCray said, his tone neutral.

Jackson tried to read him. Was this Julie's idea?

"It's time," McCray said, smiling now. "I've been on the job twenty-eight years. I've seen enough shit. I've taken enough shit. After this week, I'm done."

Jackson scowled. "If Mrs. McCray wasn't here, I'd give you a little more shit. I think you should take some time, wait until you feel better to make a final decision."

"I've already called Lammers. She intended to lay off two people today. My retiring will keep someone else from losing their job."

For a second Jackson wondered if his own position had been spared, then decided it didn't matter. "That's very noble, pal."

"It works out for me too."

"The department won't be the same without you."

"I'll be around. I'll probably join the cold-case volunteers, work a couple days a week just to get out of the house."

Julie cleared her throat. "We'll see."

They joked for a few minutes about Schak going into the river to save Shane, then McCray said, "You ran a good case, Jackson. That scene on the bridge was volatile. You did everything right."

"It doesn't feel like it, but thanks." Jackson rose to leave. "Lammers wants to see me in her office in a few minutes, so I've got to go. She's probably going to ask for my resignation."

"Tell her to fire her own bossy ass."

"I'd have to be wearing my vest."

McCray rolled his eyes. "Yeah, I know. I should have had it on."

"See you around."

As he left the hospital, Jackson saw Shane Compton get into a car with his parents. Considering how protective and loyal Shane's mother was, Jackson assumed they would take the young man home, fatten him up a little, and send him back to the methadone clinic. Shane was too young for anyone to give up on him yet.

On the drive to headquarters, Jackson once again mulled over his options. If he stayed in the department he'd either have to sell his house or take out a loan to pay off his ex-wife's equity. If he retired next month, he could collect a pension and work another job. He would be able to stay in the house until Katie was older and still afford to make payments to Renee. He would never have to look at another dead body. He would never again be forced to shoot a troubled young person.

It was tempting, and Jackson was torn. He'd see what Sergeant Lammers had to say and then make his decision.

ABOUT THE AUTHOR

L.J. Sellers is a native of Eugene, Oregon, the setting of her thrillers. She's an award-winning journalist and bestselling novelist, as well as a cyclist, social networker, and thrill-seeking fanatic. A long-standing fan of police procedurals, she counts John Sandford, Michael Connelly, Ridley Pearson, and Lawrence Sanders among her favorites. Her own novels, featuring Detective Jackson, include *The Sex Club*, *Secrets to Die For*, *Thrilled to Death*, *Passions of the Dead*, *Dying for Justice*, *Liars, Cheaters & Thieves,* and *Rules of Crime*. In addition, she's penned three standalone thrillers: *The Baby Thief*, *The Gauntlet Assassin*, and *The Lethal Effect*. When not plotting crime, she's also been known to perform standup comedy and occasionally jump out of airplanes.

Printed in Germany
by Amazon Distribution
GmbH, Leipzig